MW01688751

Table of Contents

Dedication

This is dedicated to my family.
Thank you for your patience and support

When that unexpected chance comes, take it.
Don't let it pass you by.
You never know what you could be missing.

This is My Chance

Chapter 1

I FOUND ENOUGH AIR TO barely speak one word: Alex.

"Yes," he said.

I couldn't believe this. I stood there trying to sort things out in my mind, which was currently on overload.

"Aubrey? Please say something. Talk to me. Let me know you understand." Alex sounded worried.

I tilted my head, trying to comprehend the situation. "It's you? You're Chance? You've been with me all this time?" I didn't understand what was happening. I tried to move, but I couldn't. My feet felt as though they were in cement. I couldn't breathe. I pictured an airplane oxygen mask falling from the ceiling, but I couldn't reach it. I'd come to Chance's apartment for dinner, but instead I found out that Chance was my ex-boyfriend Alex. How did I miss that? Not to mention all the time we'd spent together while I'd been in Paris. I felt as if I was having an out of body experience.

He took my shaking hand, and I didn't pull it away. I was stunned and confused. He pulled me close, and I felt his breath on my ear. My heart raced. Alex was so close. I felt his five o'clock shadow on my cheek and his hand in my hair, making my skin prickle.

He whispered, "Baby, it's me. It has always been me. I'm sorry. Please don't be upset. I needed to be with you."

His scent was different: no orchids. I knew the smell of his skin, the taste of his pores, the essence of Alex. Memories flooded my brain like a movie of our past, played out with an unknown ending. I moved back, praying I wouldn't stumble. I was unfamiliar with my surroundings, so I didn't move far. I squeezed my eyelids closed and prayed that when I opened them, I'd see what the hell was happening. But I opened them to darkness. *Damn it!*

I heard him breathing. Was the music still playing? I felt as if I was in a tunnel. I heard my pulse beating in my ears.

"Please say something, Aubrey."

I felt his hand on my arm. My hairs stood up, and a chill ran through me. I stood there motionless. How could I not have known? Tears ran down my cheeks, but I didn't bother swiping them away. I knew more would follow, and I let them fall.

"Your accent and voice . . . They were so different." I shook my head, trying to make sense of it all. "You misled me. You sent me text messages when I was with Chance! Why would you do that? You knew I couldn't see, and you tricked me!" The more I thought about it, the more pissed off I got.

"I told you why. I needed to be with you, to make sure you were okay. I didn't intend to come up with a different name, but when I saw you in the café, I panicked. I sent you the texts to see your reaction to me; not Chance, but me. The way you looked when you talked about me. I'm sorry. I didn't know what else to do."

"You could've told me the truth instead of deceiving me."

He exhaled in a huff. "Really? I could've? What would you have done? Would you have run away, hit me, told me to go to hell?"

I shook my head, and more tears fell. "I don't know." I rubbed my temples.

He moved his hands up and down my arms, caressing them. "When I saw you, your face was peaceful. I couldn't bring myself to tell you it was me. I was afraid you'd get upset and leave. I needed to make you want me again. Do you know how nervous I was when you talked about me? I saw it in your eyes; you still love me. I was scared of killing that."

He was scared? Well, I was petrified. Without him, I felt as if a piece of me was missing. I closed my eyes, took deep breaths, and tried to relax. I opened my eyes, and his shadow came into view. I extended my arm until my hand rested on his chest. I needed to touch him, to know that he was really Alex. My mind went through my time with Chance like a film, frame by frame, shot by shot. I waited for something to click. Nothing, nothing hinted that he was Alex. I'd touched Chance, kissed Chance, and I didn't know.

His chest rose and fell as though he was taking deep breaths. I brought both my hands to his face, and he lowered his head to give me better access. I ran my thumbs over his eyebrows, and my fingers traced his forehead. I ran my hands down his strong jawline to his collarbone. That was how I saw things, by touching.

My hands were my eyes. I ran my palms down his pecs to his abs, which I felt through his soft knit shirt. I traced the muscles to his magnificent hips and found the V that I loved so much. He was definitely Alex. My hands roamed all over him, and he never moved.

I stopped. I couldn't go any further. I returned my hands to my sides.

"Talk to me. Please, say anything. Just say something." He sounded hurt, or maybe that was fear in his voice.

I barely whispered, "I want to see you, but I can't. I want to extinguish this pain in my heart, but I can't. I want you, I want us. But I can't." My chest hurt, and I tried to control my breathing.

I dropped my head. All of the shadows were gone. I felt his hands in my hair. He tilted up my head.

"I love you so much. Please try to forgive me," he said. "I'm not asking you to forget, although I wish you would. I wish I could. Just be with me. Please, Aubrey, come back to me . . . to us. I'd follow you to the end of the earth. Please be mine again. I need you; I need us."

His lips were so close. I felt them brush mine like a feather. His nose grazed mine. His words still affected me. I wanted him so badly I couldn't breathe. I missed him. Maybe I could be with him one more time and then say good-bye. I needed to feel him inside me.

I hadn't been the same since I left New York, as if a part of me was still there. That was probably why I couldn't let myself be with Chance. I shook my head. Alex was Chance. He'd talked to me about the clouds, described people to me, and read to me. I needed him, just one more time.

My head spun, but one thing was certain: I wanted Alex. Maybe not forever, but for the moment. It was more a "need" than a "want."

My hands rested on his trim waist. I felt for his belt buckle and opened it. I moved my fingers under his waistband, and I felt him. He was ready. I unfastened the button on his pants and felt for the bottom of his shirt. I was thankful the shirt didn't have buttons. I pulled his shirt up and off of him and brought my lips to his chest. I kissed him, slipping my tongue out to taste his skin. He didn't help me with his pants or shirt; I did it on my own. I loved him for that. He was letting me be independent.

His hands went to my hips. "You're so beautiful. I've dreamt of this moment ever since I lost you. For weeks, I've prayed for this moment. Every day, I wanted to touch you"—his hands moved to my face—"to kiss you"—his lips grazed mine—"to love you again. Let me love you. I need us. Do you know how hard it was when we were together? Every time I saw you, I wanted you. Every damn time."

His voice penetrated my soul. But even if we had only one night, it was my night on my terms. "I want you too. I need to feel you inside me. I want your arms wrapped around me."

I slid my hands to his back and followed them. I raised my hand to his left shoulder blade and kissed his tattoo. He turned around and grabbed me so tightly I thought my ribs would crack. The next thing I knew, my dress was off, and my legs were wrapped around his waist. He walked with me in his arms as he kissed my cheeks, my lips, my chest, and back to my lips.

He set me down on what must have been his bed,

and I felt the mattress dip. He lay beside me and trailed his fingers up and down my stomach. I flinched. I'd heard about having sex while blindfolded, but I'd never thought of doing it. I had no choice anymore.

He kissed my cheek. "I love you, Aubrey. I never stopped; I never will. You're my one and only; no one or anything else. I'd give up my life for you."

I couldn't speak. I didn't want to encourage him or reciprocate his feelings. It killed me, but I kept silent. He pulled down my thong, and I reached for his boxers. All I felt was skin and his great ass. He must have shed his boxers already. His hands traced my thigh, and my legs instinctively parted, giving him access.

His fingers rubbed me. I missed that feeling, I missed feeling him. He slid in one finger and then two. He circled them, stimulating parts that had missed him. I didn't realize how much until I felt my body come to life. I felt myself clenching around him, pulsing, and becoming damper.

He kissed me hard. Our need was evident. His tongue mirrored his fingers' movement. He trailed kisses down my neck, and I heard him sigh.

"Still sensitive. I love that." He nibbled and sucked my earlobe. His tongue traced the back of my ear and down my neck.

I beamed. He made me feel so good. My back arched, and I couldn't speak. I was afraid that "I love you" would fly out of my mouth. I didn't want to say that. I felt it, but I couldn't say it. Just one night . . . our last night.

He pulled his fingers out of me, and I felt the loss until he settled between my legs and ran his tip in my wetness. He felt amazing, like silk and velvet wrapped around the best man I'd ever known. He gently entered me on a groan. He felt beyond good inside of me. I grabbed his hair, and I noticed it was longer. I tugged as he thrust in and out.

"Aubrey, I want to make this last." Thrust. "I don't want this to end." Thrust. "I need to keep you with me." Thrust. "I want you." Thrust. "Forever."

Then he stopped talking, but he kept moving in and out of me. I tried to memorize everything about that moment: the way he felt, what he said, his spirit, and how I felt. I didn't want to forget one moment. I loved him more than life, and losing him tore at my soul.

My release was imminent. I wrapped my legs around his hips, forcing him deeper. That was all he needed. He picked up his pace, and my breathing altered. I bucked my hips to meet his as we yelled each other's names.

He kissed me, and I felt emotion pour out of him. I felt a drop of liquid on my cheek; I prayed it wasn't a tear. I felt my heart shatter, and my chest shook as I tried to contain my sobs.

He ran his fingers along my forehead, moved the damp strands of my hair, and tucked them behind my ear. "Please don't cry. I don't want you to be sad. I know you probably still don't forgive me completely, but I'm hoping you will. I want to show you the world, for us have kids. I love you. I want to spend the rest of my life with you. I want to take care of you and make you happy. I'm nothing without you."

I heard his sadness. A part of me wanted to forgive and forget everything, but it wasn't easy. Every time I thought about the way we were in New York, I thought about the way we'd ended: the kiss, the lie, the lack of trust . . . the hurt. My heart ached at his words.

I couldn't be with him like that again, especially while I was blind. I didn't want his life to be reduced to taking care of me because of guilt or obligation. Then it hit me. Was that what his words were? Did he feel obligated to love me? Then I heard it over and over in my head . . . *to take care of me. . . . take care of me . . . care . . . of . . . me.* Did he feel responsible? I panicked, shifted, and pushed him off me. I felt around for the edge of the bed and moved my legs until my feet found the carpet.

I stood. "No. I'm sorry, but I can't. I can't do this. I can't be that woman anymore; I'm not that woman anymore." I wiped the tears off my cheeks.

His hands found my face. He kissed me. "Don't say that. Please don't say that." He rested his forehead against mine. "I can't lose you, not again. I need you more than I have ever needed anyone."

I knew what those words meant to him. The last person he had truly needed was his mom. I willed myself not to shed more tears, not to get upset. My feelings were all over the place. My head told me to walk away, but my heart told me the exact opposite. I lowered my chin to my chest and threw my hands into my hair. I felt like pulling it out at the roots to take the pain away from my heart.

I raised my head and sighed. "I don't want to be a burden. I don't want your pity or your guilt. I can't be everything you need me to be. What if the operation my doctor suggested doesn't work? What if I'm blind for the rest of my life?" I burst into tears. "I'd never be able to see the world with you. I'd never see our kids' faces or to see you with them. I can't do those things. I th-think I should g-go. I need to leave."

I felt around for my clothes. "Shit! Where's my stuff? I can't find my things!" I dropped to the floor, my knees hitting the carpeting hard. "Where are my clothes? Alex . . ." I dropped my head into my hands. "Why? Why did this happen? Why didn't you trust me? Why didn't you trust my love for you? Why did you believe those bitches? Why did you kiss her? You fucking kissed her in front of me! Do you know how humiliated I was? All I see is her smug face! She loved every minute of it, and so did you! If I hadn't come in, would you have slept with her?" My voice softened, but my breath kept hitching. I felt lightheaded. "Why did you hurt me? Why did you let the shoe drop?"

I felt his hands on my wrists. My bracelet pushed into my skin, another reminder of what was. I jerked my hands away. "I need to go."

"Please don't leave. Let's talk."

"No, I can't."

"You threw out a lot of questions. Very different from the first set you asked me."

He must have been talking about my bullshit speed dating questions. That seemed so long ago. I couldn't even smile at the memory.

"Yeah, they are different. I don't even know if I want answers to them. I don't know if I could believe your answers. I don't know if I can ever believe you again!"

"That hurts, Aubrey, but I want to answer them, so I will." His voice was even. "You can choose whether or not you want to believe me, but you're going to listen. I don't know why this happened to you. I'd give anything for me to be blind instead. I wish I could take that burden from you. But just because you can't see doesn't mean that we can't be together. I thought Chance proved that to you. I don't think—I mean, I wouldn't have slept with her. I only want you."

I wiped away a tear before it fell. I didn't want to cry anymore. "You don't think you would have slept with her? Oh my God, Alex, you might have?" I walked away.

He grabbed my hand. "I don't know why I didn't trust you. I guess I was shocked and felt let down. I told you that I haven't felt love since my mom passed away. You lied to me too. That's why I did what I did. Why didn't you tell me that your initial reason for being with me was to use me? Every woman I've ever been with has used me for one reason or another: my money, my dad's connections, for fun." He exhaled. "I got hurt, and then I got pissed off. That kiss, that mother-fucking stupid kiss . . . It was a stupid reaction, that's all. I felt betrayed, and I wanted you to feel it too. If I'd known what would happen after that, I never would I have done it. God, I'm so sorry."

"The difference is I didn't mean to hurt you. My journal. . . ." I shook my head. "If you'd read the whole thing, you would have realized that I loved you with all my heart. It was just a diary. My diary! I wrote about all of your wonderfully romantic gestures, how happy you made me. It's pretty ironic, right? I thought writing about romance would make me happy, and it has made me the unhappiest I've ever been."

He dropped my hand, and it landed on my thigh. "Loved? You don't still love me? We just made love. I thought—"

"I don't know."

He let out a long breath. "I wish you did know." He must have walked away from me because I heard the refrigerator door and then the sound of a bottle opening.

"I think I'll always love you, just like I told you, or 'Chance.'" I made sure to use air quotes when mentioning his alias. "What would you have done if I'd told Chance I loved him? Would you have come clean? What if I had wanted to sleep with him before I knew he was you?"

"I don't know what I would have done." He sounded frustrated. "I think I would have been a little sad that you fell for another guy, even if it was me. Did you fall for him?"

"Did I fall for him?" I lowered my head and remembered the time I'd spent with Alex as Chance. I raised my head. "I did a little, yes. But I felt guilty about it. He reminded me of you, and now I know why. Your accent threw me off. I didn't know you spoke such fluent French. I mean, I heard you speak it when we were here before, but it was different. You tricked me. I'm tired. I want to go home."

"Fine, if that's what you want, then go. I assume Frank is downstairs. I'll walk you down." He sounded defeated and slightly angry.

"No! I can do it." I didn't know what else to say except good-bye, and I couldn't say that. So I walked out the door and heard it close.

I didn't move right away. I felt for the wall and leaned my back against it. I slid down until I was squatting. I tried to regain some form of composure. I didn't want Frank to see me like that.

I got up, took my walking stick out of my bag, and headed downstairs. Frank called to me, and I gave him the best smile I could, which I'm sure was hardly one at all. Occasionally, Frank cleared his throat, but otherwise we drove in silence. I'm sure my eyes were puffy and red when he met me at the curb outside my house.

Chapter 2

I WALKED INTO MY ROOM and laid on my bed, thinking of everything that had transpired. I'd gone to my friend's apartment only to find out that he was the man I loved. I missed Chance. I wanted my friend back. I had to keep reminding myself that I had been with Chance. My head still had a hard time wrapping around what had happened.

I couldn't sleep, so I grabbed my tablet. I needed to talk to Julie. I felt for the phone button, but I noticed that I had missed a text message. I opened it and listened.

> ***Alex 11:55 p.m.****—I'm going back home tomorrow. I'm sorry for everything. Maybe someday you can find it in yourself to forgive me, like I forgave you. Good luck with your surgery. I'll be thinking of you.*

He was leaving . . . I cried . . . again. I don't know if I'd ever stopped. I needed to stop. I didn't respond to his text. I stayed on course and dialed Julie's number, praying she'd answer.

She sounded out of breath. "Hi, *chica!*" She giggled.

I could tell she wasn't alone. "Are you busy?" I sniffled.

"No, not at all. Are you okay?"

"No, I'm not. I'm so confused, Jules. I need my best friend."

"Hold on a minute, I'm going into the living room."

"I knew it; you're busy. I don't want to interrupt you and Brett." I could only assume they were in bed. It was evening in New York.

"Don't be silly. We weren't doing anything. Now talk to me. What's up?"

I took a deep breath. "Well, the good news is I'm coming home."

Julie squealed. "Yay! Okay. Sorry, go on."

"The confusing news is . . . Are you ready?"

"Yeah. You're freaking me out. Talk already."

"I told you about my new friend, Chance. Well, I went to his apartment for dinner tonight, and to tell him that I was going to go to New York . . ."

"Oh my God, what did he do to you? Did he hurt you? I'll kick his ass."

"No, it turns out that Chance is Alex. He has been here the entire time."

Julie didn't miss a beat. "Get the fuck out! Holy shit! What did you do?"

"I slept with him."

Silence . . . followed by . . . more silence.

"Jules?"

"You slept with him? So you guys are good? That's great. I mean, if you can forgive him, I can. This is great; the four of us can hang again. Is he coming back with you? Brett's going to be psyched."

"No, it's not great. We aren't together, and he isn't coming back with me. I slept with him, he told me he loved me, and I didn't reciprocate. We had words, and I left him thinking that I don't love him." I needed to breathe. "He texted me and told me he's leaving tomorrow. I've lost him, Julie. I don't know why I let this happen. I had him back, and then I thought about that skank, and I lost it. I thought he was just being nice out of obligation."

"Okay, um . . . well . . . shit. Let's think about this. Why did you sleep with him?"

"Because I needed to. I love him. I just don't know . . . I can't be with him if I'm blind."

"Seriously? Like he gives a shit about that. God, Aubrey! He left everything for you: his home, his club, and his life. Don't you get that? All.For.You." Julie sounded annoyed. "I'll have your back no matter what, and I guess I sort of understand how you feel, but damn! What are you going to do?"

"That's the thing. I have no idea. I'm going to come home and hope to get good news about my eyes, but other than that, I don't know. I think he feels guilty and that's why he came here. I asked him if he would have slept with Leah. He started to say he didn't think he would've and then stopped himself. I think he would have."

"That is total bullshit, and you know it. He loves you. Yes, he screwed up, but you're it for him. Even Brett said so. He said he's never seen Alex the way he was with you. I think you're scared, which is understandable, but take a chance."

"Ha! Chance. This whole thing started with me taking a chance. So you think I should text him back?"

"I can't tell you what to do, and you know that. What do you want to do? How did you feel when you got that text? Take that feeling and make your decision. Deep down, do you love him?"

I nodded. Not that Julie could see that. "I've got to go. I'll let you know my flight info when I have it."

"For once, follow your heart, okay? I love you."

"I'll try. Thanks. I love you too."

I ended the call and thought about her advice. *Follow my heart . . . my heart . . . my heart.*

12:50 a.m. Aubrey—*What time?*

12:51 a.m. Alex—*What?*

12:51 a.m. Aubrey—*What time are you leaving?*

My heart was breaking . . . literally breaking. I felt it. I didn't even know why I was asking.

12:52 a.m. Alex—*At 4:45 p.m. Why?*

12:52 a.m. Aubrey—*Can you call me? I don't want to text.*

I really wanted to hear his voice. He called; I answered.

"Hey."

"What do you need, Aubrey?" He sounded cold and distant, not like the man I'd just left.

"Um . . . I need more time to—"

"You can have all the time that you want to do

whatever it is you want or need to do. But I can't sit on the sidelines anymore. I can't be around you without being with you."

"So we can't even be friends?" I asked. "We were friends. You've been here as my friend. My only friend . . . my best friend. I don't want to lose you. Please . . . I can't lose you. You're my missing piece. Please, can't you just do this for me?"

"For you? Everything I've done has been for you. After tonight, I don't have a shot at being your friend or anything else. Maybe I'm the one who needs time now. I have a business to run. I don't give a shit about it, but it's all I have and I need to get back to it. I don't know what more I can do here. I gave you everything I had, and you still don't know if you can forgive me. Are you asking me to wait around for you to decide whether or not you can love me again? I told you I didn't want to lose you. I didn't want to lose us, but I did. We're broken. I was hoping Chance could fix us, but he couldn't, and I sure as hell can't. So we'll do this your way and stay apart."

"Alex . . ." I covered my mouth with my hand to stifle my sobs. "Please, Alex, please. Don't you care that I need a friend? That I need you?" *I love you.* Naturally, because I'm an idiot, I didn't say that out loud.

"Are you seriously asking me if I care? I care about you, but you did a mind fuck on me tonight. I just don't know, Aubrey. I poured out my heart to you. I made love to you and declared my love for you. I practically proposed, and you left. You don't trust me. You don't even know if you love me. This is different for me too, you know. I told you in the beginning that

I'd fuck up, and it looks like I did and you can't get past that. So . . . yeah . . . that's it." He exhaled as if he had just spent his last breath. He was done.

He was telling me he wouldn't be my friend. He'd practically proposed? My hand rubbed my chest. I wanted the pain in my heart to leave, and it wouldn't. I opened my mouth and could barely speak. "O-o-okay. Maybe . . . I guess . . . I'll see you around." See him around? That didn't even make sense. I couldn't *see* anything.

"Yeah, maybe. Good luck with everything. Bye, Aubrey." He hung up.

I threw my tablet and slammed my head into the pillow. I shook. I was mad and devastated. I'd thrown away the love of my life. I did it. I hurt him. I hurt myself. I didn't only drop the shoe; I'd demolished it. And my heart.

I woke up in my clothes. My dress smelled like Alex. I ripped it off and threw it. I didn't want to get up. I didn't want to face my parents. I didn't want anything or anyone near me. I hated my life, and I hated myself. I rubbed my eyes. "Damn it! Why, God? Why?" I slammed my fist into the mattress.

I didn't know how much time went by. I didn't even want to know what time it was because then I'd wonder where Alex was. I felt sick. I heard a knock on my door.

My mom called, "Can I come in?"

No. "Yes."

"Honey, why are you still in bed? It's almost noon."

Great. I knew what time it was. "I was tired."

"What's wrong? Have you been crying?"

"I really screwed up, Mom." Well, at least I could admit that.

"What do you mean?"

"At Chance's last night . . . Don't freak out, but Chance wasn't real. I mean, he was real—he wasn't an imaginary friend or anything. He was Alex."

"You lost me."

"Yeah, I was lost too." I took a deep breath. "Alex wanted to be with me to prove that we could be together, that he didn't care that I was blind. He told me he'd show me the world through his eyes. He told me how much he loved me and wanted a life with me. Then I left him."

"Oh, Aubrey." My mom sounded so sad.

"Yeah, I know. I'm stupid, right?"

"Honey, you aren't stupid. I'm sure you were surprised, and to be fair, he wasn't honest. Our hearts are tricky. They want what they want."

"I guess so. I messed up. I love him, and I lost him."

Obviously trying to change the subject, she said, "Well, I have good news. While you were sleeping, the doctor's office in New York called. You're scheduled to have tests on Monday. If all goes well, you'll have surgery on the following Wednesday. We can be on a flight this Wednesday, so you have three days left in Paris. Is there anything you'd like to do?"

I'd arrive a couple days after Alex. What would he do during those days? Would he go to someone else? I panicked. "There's a flight today at four forty-five. Can you get me on that flight?"

"Today? You want to leave today? Why?"

"I need to. Please, can you just check? I'll fly with assistance, and Julie will pick me up. Please, Mom."

"I'll check, but your father and I can't leave today."

"I understand," I said.

"I don't like this. But if it means that much to you, I'll have your father check. This has something to do with him, right?"

"Yeah, he's on that flight." I prayed there was only one flight at four forty-five. "Please, Mom, I need you to help me."

"Okay, I'll call our travel agent. You'd better go shower because if there's room on that flight, we'll have to get to the airport fast. I'll lay out clothes for you on the bed."

My mom kissed my cheek, and I went into the bathroom. I showered as quickly as possible. I toweled off and brushed my hair into a wet pony tail. I stepped off the tile on to the carpet of my bedroom. I felt for the clothes my mom had laid out and got dressed. I couldn't find my tablet on my side table and then remembered I threw it. I felt the carpet with my foot until I kicked it. I picked it up to put it in my bag. I walked to the dresser and found my walking stick.

My parents were in the kitchen when I was ready to go.

"So, what's the plan?" I asked.

"Well, the agent found a ticket," my mom said. "You'll be flying first class. Airport personnel will escort you to your seat. You'll most likely board before everyone else. She knew someone at the airline, and they confirmed Alex was on the flight. Don't tell anyone she did that because she could lose her job."

I was so relieved. "Thank you. I know this wasn't the plan, but I need to do this."

"Then let's get you there," my dad said.

I boarded the plane before any other passengers. According to the flight attendant, I was seated in the last row in the first class cabin. He offered me juice or water, which I declined.

"I'm Steven," he said. "If you need anything, please let me know."

"Hi, Steven. I'm Aubrey. Thank you, but I should be all set." I gave him my best attempt at a smile.

He told me he'd be working in coach, but he'd check on me. I heard the opening and closing of overhead compartments.

I heard a female voice that sounded vaguely familiar. "Hey there, handsome. Long time, no see. Let me see your ticket, and I'll show you to your seat. Oh good, you're in 2C. Right up front with me. Would you like a pillow or blanket?"

Was it Alex? My ears perked up as my body sank into my seat.

"I'm Alex." He sounded surprised but happy. "I've never seen you at my club. You know, you still have VIP access for helping me and my . . . uh . . . ex out."

Oh my God! That's why she sounded familiar. She was the one who'd kept quiet while Alex and I cuddled on our flight to Europe. He called me his ex. My heart plummeted into my stomach. I listened and prayed he didn't say anything more.

"How about you and I get together when we land?"

he asked. "I can show you the club. We'll have some drinks, do a little dancing, get to know each other. I can take you to dinner and . . . who knows. I'm up for anything. I could use the distraction. I never got your name, sweetheart."

Get to know each other? Who knows? Needs a distraction? I held back my tears, but my heart shattered. I felt as though I was going to be sick. Getting on his flight was a bad idea. I wanted to leave.

"I'm Lauren. I'd love to get together. Sounds like a good time, and you look like a good time."

What? *Please don't respond,* I silently pleaded.

"Trust me, sweetheart, we'll have a good time. If you weren't working, I'd give you a good time right now. I don't need a pillow or blanket, unless you plan on joining me. I'm all about the mile-high club."

I pictured him talking to her. I bet he looked as sexy as he had when he first spoke to me all those months ago. She giggled, and I died a little. I didn't have anyone else to blame. I broke us.

I heard more passengers board and the sounds of luggage being stowed. I felt someone sit next to me. She said hello, and I nodded. At least, I think I did. I wished I was somewhere else. He wanted to sleep with her? It hadn't even been twenty-four hours.

I leaned my head against the window, hoping the chill from the Plexiglas would calm me. It didn't. I wished I could get sucked out of the window like a cartoon character. My heart literally hurt. I wanted to disappear. I pulled my cardigan tightly around me and prayed it would camouflage me.

I heard the engines come to life and then the

automated instructions of what to do in an emergency. We moved faster, and then we were in the air. Lauren took dinner orders in first class. As soon as she finished flirting a little more with Alex, she moved on to the rest of us.

There was a tap on my shoulder. "Miss, the flight attendant would like to know what you would like for dinner."

I kept my head down and said, "I'm not hungry, thank you." I didn't have an appetite. I listened to the tray tables lower. I heard Steven talking to Lauren, Miss I'm-Gonna-Get-Some-Later-With-Your-Ex.

Steven's voice was kind. "There's a woman named Aubrey in 6A who's visually impaired. Since we're well staffed in coach, I'd be happy to help if she needs assistance."

I put my hand on my forehead. How embarrassing. I could get around on my own. I didn't want assistance. I hoped Alex didn't hear them. I heard footsteps in the aisle.

"Do you need something, Alex?" Lauren's voice was cotton-candy sweet. It was nauseating.

"What are you doing here, Aubrey?"

His voice startled me. Yup, that's what he'd do: come and find me.

"Aubrey? Did you hear me? Excuse me, ma'am, would you mind switching seats with me? I'm sitting in 2C."

The woman next to me tapped my arm. "Miss, is that okay with you? Do you want to sit with this man?"

I raised my head. "Yes, that's fine." I heard them exchange pleasantries, and then I felt him next to me.

"So what are you doing here?" he asked.

I tried to keep my voice steady. "I'm going home. I needed to talk to you. I didn't want to lose you by waiting days for my parents' flight, but from what I just heard, I guess I've already lost you. I shouldn't have taken this flight. I'm sorry." I put my head and hand on the window. My fingers made my nervous figure eights.

"What are you talking about?"

Great, Alex, play dumb. I kept my head where it was. "I heard you ask that flight attendant out. Or was it more you asking her to your bed? I guess I'm easy for you to get over, just like I was for Garrett. It must be me . . . I'm forgettable."

"Who the hell is Garrett?"

"My ex-boyfriend. I told you about him. I thought you were different. I thought we were different." My heart was shattered, and I was sure he heard it in my voice, but I didn't care. I didn't care about anything anymore. "Garrett and I were friends. Good friends, or so I thought." I shrugged. "Then we slept together, and he dumped me. He moved on just like you just did. Everyone moves on."

"I'm not like that guy. I didn't dump you. I loved you, and you left me." He didn't sound like he did when he'd talked to Lauren. When he spoke to her, his voice was sexy and seductive, not annoyed and irritated.

I turned toward him and kept my voice even. "You love me. You asked someone else out, or was it more of a proposition for sex?"

Did he say "loved"? I closed my eyes and didn't move. If I moved, I'd break. I wanted off the plane. I idly wondered if I could get off. I felt for the latch for my seatbelt. At that point, I'd trade seats with someone in the back of the plane. I lifted the metal plate, and his hand was on mine, stopping me.

"Aubrey, what do you want from me? I don't know what to do here," he said.

Here goes . . . "You. I want you, us. But I'm a day too late. Actually, hours too late. I lost you when I pushed you away. I shouldn't have gotten on this flight. I'm sorry. I'll stay away. I just want you to be happy."

"Wait a minute. What do you mean you want us? Last night you . . . Did you change your mind? Is that what you're telling me?"

"I'm telling you that when I heard your text and then spoke to you last night, I was devastated. I realized I can't . . . I don't want to be without you. I need you. I made a mistake walking out on you. I talked to Julie, and she told me to follow my heart. My mom said pretty much the same thing. I had to try to get you back, so I came here."

"Is that what you're doing? Or are you just afraid?"

"Afraid? I'm terrified of everything: of never being with you again, of being blind forever, of you moving on. But am I following my heart?" I gently shook my head. "Not just my heart. I'm following every part of me. I'm sorry I lied to you last night. I'm sorry that I lied to myself. I'm sorry for everything." I exhaled and felt my breath squeak a little. I didn't want to have a total meltdown. I didn't feel anxious or apprehensive; I just felt empty.

I rested my cheek on the seat. I lifted my right hand and felt for his face. I moved his head so he was facing me. I couldn't see him, but I needed him to see me.

"I love you, Alex. I never stopped. I never will. I want you by my side, and I want to be by yours. I just don't want to be a burden. You deserve better. If you think you'd be happier with someone like Lauren, I don't want to stop you."

"You wouldn't be a burden, I told you that. I don't want to be with her," he said.

"Then why did you ask her out?"

He didn't say anything for a few seconds, but it felt like an eternity. He let out a breath and said, "I don't know. I guess I was trying to forget you."

"You wanted to forget me by sleeping with her? Would you have slept with her if I hadn't been here?"

"Aubrey. I . . . What do you want me to say? I don't want to hurt you and say yes, and I don't want to lie and say no. The truth is, I don't know what I would have done."

I hated that answer, but I'd asked the question. It was the second time I'd asked that question in less than twenty-four hours. "I see." I didn't, but what was I supposed to say? "I have another question."

"Okay." He sounded uncertain.

"Well, you don't have to answer this now, but will you think about taking me back? No more secrets, no games, just me and you. We'll talk about everything. We both made mistakes and we'll make more, but we'll talk this time. No jumping to conclusions, no lies, no hidden truths." *Please say yes. Please say yes. Please say yes.*

I felt his hand brush mine, and he gave my hand a gentle squeeze. Then his lips met mine in a loving kiss. Our lips just stayed pressed against each other's as we were inhaling each other. He pulled back, and I licked my lips, wanting to taste him. I wasn't sure if that would be our last kiss.

"No," he said.

My heart dropped. I felt as if each of my ribs were cracking and going straight into my heart, piercing it. The weight on my chest was excruciating. I lowered my head. "No?"

"That's right. I don't have to think about taking you back because I never let you go. I'll never let you go. You're mine, and if you want me, I'm yours. You own my heart, and you have since I first laid eyes on you." He exhaled, and I felt his lips near my neck. "Don't you get it? It's just you. It will always be just you."

He kissed the corner of my jaw, and my head instinctively went back. He ran kisses down my neck, making me squirm.

"I take it plans changed?" Lauren said.

Neither of us said anything. I had no clue if Alex was making any gestures toward her.

"That's okay, handsome. From the looks of you two, it would have been a waste of my time."

I was pretty impressed by her impassiveness. She must get propositioned a lot. Alex asked for some champagne for us, and he asked her to offer it to the other passengers on the plane.

"You're one lucky lady," Lauren said to me. "Your Alex is very good looking and apparently a romantic." To Alex she said, "I'll need a credit card to charge the drinks to."

I felt Alex shift. I could only imagine the way she was looking at him. She left after saying she'd come back with his card.

When I was satisfied that she was gone, I spoke. "You're a good-looking, romantic man, but you're my man. Got that? Just mine."

"Yes, ma'am, I've got it. Just yours." He kissed me. "Always yours. Forever yours."

I smiled and rested my head on his shoulder until our champagne arrived.

"Here you go," Lauren said.

I felt for the champagne glass with my right hand. "I'd like to propose a toast to the most wonderful man I've ever met."

He clinked his glass against mine. "I'll toast to that. I really do love you with all that I am. I meant what I said in Paris. I want forever with you."

I nodded and swallowed a sip of champagne. He gave me a soft kiss and ran his nose next to mine. I felt his eyelashes against my cheek.

"When we get off this plane, I'm taking you home," Alex said. "I don't ever want to be without you. So, my place or yours?"

His voice was so tender it sent shivers down my spine. The thought of being with him made me throb in places other than my heart. Did he want to live with me? "My place. I know my apartment, and I'll be more comfortable there."

"Okay, your place it is."

I thought about my parents. They were planning on staying with me when they came in. I couldn't have Alex there with my parents. That would be way too weird. "My parents planned on staying with me, so you can stay until they get here."

"Your parents can stay at my place or with us. I

want to be where you are. We're in this together, got it?"

I wondered what my parents would think. My mom would love Alex's place, since it was "posh" and mine wasn't, but they would most likely want to be with me too. "I'll ask them when I speak to them."

Lauren asked if we were all set before she settled the champagne tab with Alex. Apparently he was the passengers' favorite person. I could only smile when I heard her say again that I was a lucky woman.

Lucky . . . I hadn't felt that way lately. Dr. Griffin had said I was lucky when I woke after my accident. I guess if I thought about it, I was. I was alive and loved. "Thank you. I'm . . . truly very lucky." I felt Alex's lips on my forehead. I rested my head on his broad shoulder and fell asleep.

Chapter 3

"BABE, WE'RE HERE." ALEX GENTLY shook my shoulder.

I opened my eyes to darkness. "We're in New York?"

"Yeah, I got your stuff. Let's go."

He placed my purse in my hand and guided me out of our seats. I felt his hand on the small of my back as we walked. When we entered the airport, he laced his fingers with mine.

"We need to go through customs and then baggage claim," he said.

Alex held my hand through customs. At baggage claim, I listened to the beat of the conveyor belt as it went around and around. Before long, Alex said he had everything. He put my hand on the handle of the cart, placed his over mine, and we pushed the cart through the airport. I wondered how we were going to get home. I realized I'd never called Julie to tell her I was coming back today. I figured we would take a cab until I heard Julie shriek my name. She practically body-slammed me and told me Alex had sent a text to Brett saying I was with him.

Alex said, "Whoa, Julie, take it easy. You're going to

knock her over!"

I laughed, regained my balance, and hugged her back.

"Shut up, Alex. You've been with my best friend and I haven't, so back off, pal!"

Alex chuckled. "Okay! Just don't break her."

I pictured Alex with his hands up in surrender. I wished I could see it, but I knew that was what he was doing.

"Yo, man, how the hell they hangin'?" Brett was just being Brett: low key and funny.

I adored him. I pictured the guys "bro hugging" as I heard backs slapped.

Brett touched my shoulder and kissed my cheek. "Hey, Aubrey, glad you're home. Your BFF is making me crazy!"

I heard a smack and then Brett said "ow." I smirked. Julie hit Brett for that comment. They must be really happy.

"Aw, come on, hon. You know I love ya." Brett sounded so cute.

"I know. I love you too. Now let's get outta here." Julie was almost giddy.

Julie and Brett were in love? I was happy for them, but I'd lost so much time with them. I shouldn't have left. I wondered what else had changed. As I thought about all the good times we'd had together, shadows formed. I didn't see much of anything. I lowered my head because I didn't want anyone to see me sad when they were happy. I felt selfish and a little ridiculous. I should be happy.

Familiar arms wrapped around me, and a hand on

the back of my head pulled me into a muscular chest. "Are you okay?"

I nodded and shrugged. "Yeah, I guess. I can't wait to see the doctor and get this corrected for good." I held Alex tighter.

"Let's go home." He kissed the top of my head, took my hand, and we left the airport.

The ride home was comfortable. The guys talked about what Alex needed to do when he got back at the club, and Julie talked to me about work. I wished I was still there. When the car stopped at my apartment, Alex helped me out of the car. The guys grabbed our bags while Julie and I waited on the sidewalk. When the guys had everything, we went upstairs.

I reached into my bag and grabbed my apartment keys to give to Alex. I held them out. "Here you go."

He didn't take them. "I think you can unlock the door, don't you?"

Julie gasped. I nodded. He was right; I could do it. I felt for my door key and held it with my right hand while my left found the keyhole on the knob and the deadbolt. I unlocked them both and grinned. Alex put his hand on the small of my back as we stepped through my door.

I kicked off my shoes and felt my carpet under my feet. I walked toward my sofa and dragged my hand along the microfiber fabric.

Brett kissed my cheek. "We're gonna take off now. Glad you're both back."

Julie did the same and told me she'd call me later. I sat at the end of the couch next to the end table, where the phone was, so I could call my parents. My mom answered, and she was happy I was home. She asked me if I was with Alex, and I told her yes, and that Julie and Brett had just left. She sounded relieved.

"Mom, I was wondering something. You don't have to say yes, but Alex suggested that you and Dad stay at his apartment. It's closer to the medical building."

Silence.

In her best "Mom" voice, she said, "If we stay at his apartment, where will he stay?"

"He'll be staying with me." I scrunched my eyelids closed, which was silly since I was twenty-five years old.

"I take it you had a nice flight?" I heard the smile in her voice.

"Yes. If you don't want to stay at his place, you can stay here." I felt like a teenager asking if I could go to a boy/girl party.

She cleared her throat. "No worries, dear. We'll stay at his place as long as you're sure he doesn't mind."

"No, he offered. Thanks, Mom. I'll see you on Wednesday, and we can work out the details."

We hung up, and I exhaled. Apparently I had been holding my breath.

Alex sat next to me. He pulled me into his arms and kissed my cheek. "We all set?"

"Yup. My mom said that she and my dad will stay at your place. Do you think we can go together to pick them up when they arrive?"

"Of course we can. Whatever you want, babe."

My back was against his chest, and my head rested on his shoulder. Alex felt like home, my home. I thought about everything that had happened that year and what the future held. Life had become one big unknown, but one thing I knew for sure was that I was in love with that man. I raised my chin and angled my face toward his. He lightly kissed me.

He rubbed the tip of his nose on mine. "Why don't we go to bed? It's late, and you're going to need your energy tomorrow." God, his voice was sexy as hell.

I nodded. I was tired, but I knew we weren't going to sleep. "Why will I need energy tomorrow?"

"Because I'm going to make love to you all morning. I'm going to make your body feel things it never has before, all afternoon, and then we'll get out of bed so I can take you to dinner."

"Hmmm."

He laughed. "That is all you have to say? Hmmm?"

I straddled his lap and brought my hands to his face. My palms rested on his cheek bones, and my fingers rubbed his temples. Alex moaned. I leaned in and brushed his lips with mine, then ran my tongue down his chin to his Adam's apple, which I gently sucked.

"Babe . . . what are you doing to me?" His Adam's apple bobbed up and down as he spoke, as did his erection.

"Shhh . . . Let me play. I've missed loving you."

I shifted my hips back and forth, creating the friction I needed for the time being, while turning him on too. My hands ran down his hard chest and then back to his shoulders. I let them rest on his biceps. "I love you so much. I've missed this. I've missed you." I tossed my head back which pushed my breasts forward. That did it.

He stood, and his hands went under my ass to support me. I wrapped my legs around his waist as he walked. I heard a light click on.

"Take off your shirt, Aubrey."

With his hands still under me, I reached for the hem of my T-shirt and brought it over my head. My breasts were freed from my bra before I even felt him undo the clasp. My man definitely had skills. He laid me on my back on my bed and rid me of my jeans and thong.

I lay there completely naked. I felt the bed shift and assumed he was taking off his pants. I felt his hands on my legs as he bent them and pushed my knees back.

"Relax, it's my turn," he said.

I relaxed my legs, and he dipped his head between them, sending a wave of pleasure through me. He moved his lips over mine—well, my lower ones—and I felt myself pulse and swell underneath his tongue.

"Alex . . . uh . . . what . . ." I was unable to form a coherent sentence.

"Mmm mmm." Apparently he couldn't either.

That humming sent me over the edge. I'd heard of "hummers," but I didn't think it was delivered by a man. Maybe it wasn't and maybe that wasn't his intent, but it felt amazing. "I need you inside me . . . Please . . . now . . ." I was turned on, and I needed relief from the pressure building inside me.

I felt just his tip push into me and pull out again. I tried to move my hips closer, but he held them in place.

"I've got you sweetheart."

He thrust inside me, and I saw stars, which was pretty cool since I was used to seeing blackness. He let go of my hips, and we moved together as if music was on. Our bodies danced as one. I wasn't going to last, and I needed him to be ready with me. I squeezed my hand between our legs and caressed him. He groaned, and I stopped, thinking I'd hurt him.

"Don't stop, that feels amazing. Damn, Aubrey, do you know how hot you are? How good you are? How good you feel?" His lips were on mine, demanding and loving at the same time. His tongue mirrored his hips.

I was ready to explode. He pulled back, I opened my eyes, and I saw his face. He looked at me, and I saw his gorgeous face. I smiled and said, "Your eyes are the most beautiful shade of blue, like the depths of the sea."

"Mmm mmm, thank you. Wait . . . You can see me?"

"Yes. Please, love me, Alex. I want to watch you, and I don't know how long this will last." I thrust my hips, praying for my sight to stay.

"I love you so much, you know that?" His voice was so pure, and I knew his love was too.

My heart filled. I watched him reach his climax, not even worrying about my own. I wanted to see the pleasure in his face. I saw his feelings pour out of him. His eyes never left mine. No words were needed, just our eyes locked together. *Please let this last . . . don't think of anything bad . . . don't think of that kiss . . .* I memorized every feature of his face. He faded, and my tears flowed. Alex tried to pull out of me.

"No. Please just stay." I closed my eyes and sighed.

"It's gone again, isn't it?"

My vision was back to black, but I still pictured him over me, looking at me and loving me. "Yeah, but now your beautiful face was the last thing I saw."

"Does your head hurt?"

"No, I'm fine. Really." I heard him exhale and then what sounded like a stifled cry. I touched his cheeks and brought his head to my chest. "Alex, I'm okay, really." I ran my hands down his back and back up to the nape of his neck. "Thank you for being here. Sorry I got upset. When my sight comes back like that, I get so excited and then terrified that it will never happen again. I will it to stay, but it never does."

He kissed my chest. "Let's think positively. Your surgery will be a success, and we'll see the world together. I'll take you places you never dreamed of. We'll see the beauty of the waves, the aura of the moon, and the beauty of our family. We're in this together. I want forever with you." He brought his lips to mine and kissed me as if we were tasting each other for the first time.

We were side by side and still naked. Although we weren't physically connected, I knew our souls and hearts were. My head rested on his smooth, taut chest. I loved the way I fit there. He talked about "forever" and "our family" again. I'd never wanted anything more.

We spent the next day getting ready for my parents—after we made love all morning. We stopped at the grocery store to pick up a few things I knew my parents would enjoy, and we headed to his apartment. As we walked in, I realized I hadn't been there since the accident. The smell of citrus hit me.

"It smells so clean in here." He must have had a cleaning person take care of his place while he was in Paris.

"I had it cleaned while I was gone."

I smirked. I was right. He wanted to sit on the balcony and have a glass of wine, which sounded like heaven. We were just about to order Chinese take-out when his phone rang.

"Alex Logan. No, that delivery wasn't expected for two weeks. No, they can't leave it now. We don't have the storage for it."

I listened and assumed it was someone at the club. The thought of the club made me shiver.

"Mike, just tell them to take it back and deliver in two weeks. Yeah, I'm serious."

I could tell Alex was getting frustrated. *Who's Mike?*

"Isn't Brett there? Fine, I'll be there soon. Tell them to wait for me, and if they leave, they've lost my business. I'll set them straight." He hung up, and I heard the sound of his keys being picked up off the table. "Babe, I need to get to the club. Want to come? We can grab an early dinner afterward."

My heart raced. I needed to go to the club at some point, but I couldn't see what was going on or who was there. That was petrifying. My expression must have spoken volumes.

His arms wrapped around me. "If you don't want to, I understand. You can hang here, and I'll be back, with dinner, within the hour."

I needed to go. It was late afternoon, so no one would be there. "I want to be with you. Okay, I'll go."

His fingers curled between mine, and he kissed my knuckles. "What's wrong?"

I turned toward him. "I just haven't been back to the club since . . . you know."

"I know. It kills me that I . . ." Alex sighed. "That I caused all of this." His voice got softer as he spoke.

I found his cheek with my palm. "I told you, you didn't cause this. You need to believe that, Alex. We both played a part in what happened. That's not what I'm worried about. Do you think Leah will be there? She looked so smug that night. I hate her." I crossed my arms. I was getting more and more aggravated. I really did hate her. Not dislike. Honest-to-goodness hate. "I was so mortified. She was so pleased with herself when you kissed her. I get that you're a hot guy and a great lover, but you're *my* lover, *my* hot guy! She thinks she's a beautiful piece of ass that everyone wants, and that night, you proved her right."

Alex cleared his throat.

"Okay, what?"

"Are you done?" he asked.

I chuckled. "Yeah, I'm done." I wasn't close to being done. I wanted to rip her perfectly coiffed hair out of her brain-lacking head.

"First of all, thank you for calling me hot and a great lover." He kissed my palm, and I felt his smile. "I'm not, nor do I want to be, with her. You're the beautiful one, not her. To me, you're the most beautiful woman, my beautiful woman. I only want you, and I'll repeat that over and over until you believe me."

"I believe you. I suppose we should leave and get this over with."

His lips touched mine, and I relished the taste and smell of him. He took my hand and led me outside. We got in his car and headed off to the club.

He turned on the radio, and we listened to a playlist

he had loaded. We listened to "Talking to the Moon," and the words resonated with me. He had put that song on my tablet, and I loved it. I pictured him talking to the moon, hoping that I'd hear him. He'd told me that he had also talked to the waves.

He must have noticed my expression. "I like these songs too. They remind me of you."

I nodded and noticed the car was stopped. We must be at the club. "I do know you only want me. I want you and only you. I always have."

I felt him unbuckle my seatbelt, then the next thing I knew, I was hoisted onto his lap. My ass was backed up to the steering wheel.

He pulled my face down to his. He didn't kiss me, but he whispered onto my lips, "I will love you until the day I die."

I felt tears push against my eyes. That whisper was so hot that I felt it in my jeans. It may be fall and cool outside, but I was overheating. "I love you so much that it hurts sometimes."

He kissed me, and I grinded on him. I didn't care where we were. He gripped the back of my head, tangling my hair in his fingers, while his right hand moved under my sweater and over my lace bra. I swear the man had magic fingers. I moved my hips faster and felt like a teenager dry-humping in a car. But we weren't teenagers. We didn't have much room in his Maserati, but we didn't need it.

"I want you. I need to be inside you." His voice was rough, like he was ready to come apart. "I need to feel you around me. I'm hungry for you."

Oh my God! I was going to have an orgasm if he

didn't stop talking. My movements became slower and more deliberate. He licked my neck from my shoulder to my ear. He bit the top of my ear, which made me squeal, and then he pressed his tongue in my mouth.

"What do you want, Aubrey?"

"I want—"

Before I could answer, his phone rang. I suddenly remembered where we were and why we were there.

"Shit." He must have pushed his hands-free link because I heard the conversation. "Yeah?"

"Dude, get your ass in here. This guy's a prick. Mike tried to reason with him before I got here," Brett said.

"You can't handle him? Hey, how did you know I was here?"

"I just pulled up and you uh . . . looked . . . busy. So I thought I'd try to handle this, but he wants you."

Brett saw us? Was Julie with him? I needed to get off of Alex and out of his car. I shifted and his hand settled on my hip, preventing me from moving.

He sounded more annoyed. "Yeah, I'll be right in. What the fuck is with this guy? I should fire them and cancel the whole order."

Alex hung up, and I stayed stock-still. I felt his face in my hair and his mouth near my ear.

"You and me in my office as soon as I'm done with this guy. I want you on my desk, naked. Understood?"

All I could do was nod. Naked? In his office? I prayed his office had a dead bolt and a chain. Bad enough that Brett saw us doing the bump and grind. I was mortified. "Alex, who's Mike?"

"He's a bartender. I hired him when I went to Paris.

I didn't want to leave Brett and Tyler a man down. It freed up Ty to help with the business side of the club."

We walked into the club, and Brett greeted us. He kissed my cheek and told me Julie was at the bar.

It sounded noisy. "Is it crowded in here?" I asked.

Brett told me there was a decent crowd, and I felt my face redden. How many people saw us in the parking lot?

Alex must have sensed my embarrassment. "I parked in the back. No one saw us, except for Brett."

Alex laughed and walked me over to Julie, who pulled me into a hug. Alex kissed my cheek. He told me he'd be back in ten minutes, and then we would meet in his office. With a smack on the ass, he guided me to an empty barstool. That smack and the thought of his office made me damper than I already was.

"So, Miss Aubrey, I heard you were getting a little Maserati action . . . or was it the Maserati's seat getting the action?" Julie giggled.

"Oh, look at who we have here," said a nasty voice. "So you're back trying to reclaim your man? Well, just so you know, you're a little late. He was well taken care of while you were gone." She whispered in my ear, "He's better than I remembered. His lips are like velvet against mine. Let's just say we did things that would make your head spin."

My blood boiled. God, I hated her. Julie started to say something, but I cut her off. I slid off my stool, hanging on to the back to stabilize myself. Leah was taller than I was by about five inches since I didn't have heels. "Julie, is Leah in front of me?"

I heard Leah huff, and I pictured her rolling her eyes

and crossing her arms.

"Yes, directly in front of you."

"Does she have heels on?"

"Yup, about four inches. Your head reaches her chin. If you reach out about ten inches, you could touch her. I got your back, so go ahead."

"Want to know what color bra I'm wearing too?" Leah sounded disgusted.

I grinned. "No, that won't be necessary." My palm connected with what I thought was the majority of her cheek. I heard Julie laugh.

Leah gasped. "You blind bitch! You want to go rounds with me?"

I thrust out my chest, trying to portray a tough girl. I was just about to challenge her when I heard him.

"What the hell is going on here?" Alex sounded pissed!

"Nothing I can't handle, honey," I said.

"You wish, you bitch. Julie, get your hands off me and let Helen Keller fight her own battles." Leah was trying to sound fierce.

"You call her a name again, and you're out of here for good, got it?" Alex ordered.

I couldn't resist calling Leah out on her lie. "Alex, should you talk like that to the woman who took such good care of you while I was away? The one you did things with that would make my head spin?"

"What the hell are you talking about?"

I wasn't sure who that question was directed at, so I decided to answer. "I'm talking about your lover here, the one who satisfied your needs while I was in Paris."

"Leah, what the fuck? Why did you lie to Aubrey?"

"Alex, this homely bitch slapped me. I want to know what you're going to do about it!"

"That's it. You're done. I never want to see you here again. Do you understand? If I hear that you even tried to get in, I'll press charges on you for trespassing so fast your head will spin. Now get the fuck out!" Alex's voice scared me a little.

Note to self: don't piss him off. I heard sniffles. Was she playing the "poor me" card?

"Tyler! Get your . . . whatever she is out of here. If you want to see her, do it on your own time. She isn't allowed in my club again."

Leah said, "Wait until Daddy hears. He won't be happy, and I'm sure your father won't be pleased either. We're supposed to be together. You aren't supposed to be with her." Leah sniffled like a child who didn't get her way. What would she do next? Throw herself on the floor and throw a temper tantrum? I wished I could see that if she did.

"I should be with you? Well, you can forget that. It won't happen . . . ever." Alex sounded exasperated and ticked off. "I'm in love with Aubrey. Get that through your thick skull. As far as our fathers are concerned, it'll be a cold day in hell when I let either of them dictate who I spend my life with. Now get the fuck out of here!"

Holy crap, I'd never heard Alex so upset. I was having second thoughts about adding to this situation. I heard Tyler tell her to "come on," and then there was silence.

Brett was the first to break the quiet tension.

"Damn, I missed a cat fight. Shit!"

Julie laughed. "No, hon, you didn't. Aubrey slapped Leah. That was the end of the fight." We both laughed.

"Come on, Rocky, let's get out of here. I can't leave you alone for a minute." Alex chuckled.

I was relieved he wasn't mad at me. "Okay. Where to?" I had been hoping to have desk sex, but I figured that mood was broken.

We went out for a quiet dinner and decided to make an early night of it. We were picking up my parents the next night, and we were both exhausted.

Chapter 4

My parents' flight was on time, and we brought them directly to Alex's place. My mom loved everything about it: the doorman, the size, the view. She raved for over an hour. My dad was just happy to have a bed. He was tired and hadn't slept much on the plane. He complimented Alex's apartment, but he wasn't in awe like my mom. After we got them settled in, Alex and I went to my place.

Alex was quiet on the drive. He held my hand on his right thigh. His thumb caressed the back of my hand. The silence was deafening.

"What's wrong?" I hated silence. Sounds were the only thing to keep me company.

"What do you mean?" He lifted my hand and kissed it.

"You're quiet, like you're deep in thought. That's all."

"I was just thinking about how grateful I am. You've made me beyond happy. I never want to be without you. Promise me, please."

"I promise. You don't have to worry about that." I never wanted to be without him either.

"I want you to know that whatever happens next week, we're in this together. No. Matter. What."

I couldn't help but smile until I thought my face would crack. "I got it. No matter what, it's you and me, together."

"Good, I'm glad you agree with me. You know, since you had no choice." He chuckled.

I didn't say anything. I knew I'd had no choice, but him telling me that was hot as hell. His voice did things to me that were unexplainable. When he spoke, it triggered something straight from my heart to between my legs. I shifted to try to relieve the pressure building. It didn't work.

"Uh, everything okay over there, squirmy?" Alex chuckled.

"I'm not squirmy." I wondered what it looked like I was doing. If I could've reached between my legs and applied pressure where it was needed, I'd have been fine.

"Whatever you say. You seem uncomfortable. Whatcha thinking about?" He cleared his throat. He must know that I was feeling his words between my legs.

Two can play at this game. "Well, if you need to know, I was thinking about how great it'll be having sex with you blindfolded. I'm going to rock your world. You'll never be the same." I trailed my fingers up and down his thigh while my other hand traveled from my chest to my neck and back down again. I leaned my head back so my face pointed toward the ceiling. I moaned and exaggerated licking my lips. "Yeah, it's going to be so good." I threw in some moans inspired by Meg Ryan in *When Harry Met Sally*. "I could explode right now just thinking about it."

His right leg shifted, and the car came to an abrupt stop.

I grinned. "Are we at my apartment already?" I knew there was no way we were.

"No. I decided to pull over before I crashed."

I tried to stifle a laugh. "Why would we crash? Is something bothering you?" I moved my left hand between his legs. "Why Alex . . . what have we here?"

"What has gotten into you? Never mind, I don't want to know. Get out of the car."

"What? Why? Where are we?"

His warm breath tickled my neck. "We're at my club. I'm going to have you on my desk. I should have done it yesterday."

I felt a release, and my panties dampened. Holy shit . . . I honestly didn't think we would do that. I heard his door open and close and then felt the breeze when mine opened.

"Reach to your right and give me your hand. I need to make sure you stay with me this time."

I couldn't help but snicker. Our fingers interlocked, and he held me so tight that I thought my knuckles would break. I didn't wiggle my fingers because I didn't want him to loosen his hold. I heard keys and a door open. I figured we were in the private entrance to the club. Alex stopped walking, and he turned me toward him. The next thing I knew, I was scooped up.

"Wrap your legs around me." His voice was deep and sexy as hell.

My arms rested on his shoulders, curved around his neck. I moved my fingers into his hair and played with it. He pulled back and kissed me. I felt us going up stairs. I prayed he was kissing me with his eyes open. I didn't need us tumbling down the stairs.

I heard another door open, and he stepped onto a flat surface. The door closed. He put me down on my feet.

"I'm going to undress you now."

I stayed silent and nodded. I felt his hands at the hem of my shirt, and then the fabric was pulled over my head. His hands caressed my breasts, and his thumbs rubbed my stiff nipples. "You're the most gorgeous woman."

My head went down. He tilted my chin up. I pictured him looking at me.

"I know you don't believe me, but you really are." His thumb slid over my cheek, down my face, and down my neck, making me shiver. "I love your face."

His lips traced the path of his thumb. I moved my head to give him better access to my neck, which he took advantage of. His hands moved to the back of my bra to unclasp it. He continued to undress me. I wanted him naked too. I needed him inside me.

The next thing I knew, I was lifted up and felt wood underneath my ass. His hands went to my ankles, and he moved my heels to the edge of the desk. I reached out and touched firm skin. Naked Alex was my favorite. Actually, he was my favorite, naked or not. His hands pushed my knees apart, and his fingers entered me, making me groan. I raised my hips to drive his fingers deeper.

He pulled his fingers out and made circles with his thumbs. In . . . out . . . around . . . over and over again.

I felt my legs quiver, and he stopped. He thrust himself inside me, and I moaned in surprise. He was an amazing lover, not that I'd had a lot of experience. I knew I'd never want or need to experience anyone but him.

My breathing became heavy, and I couldn't have spoken a coherent sentence if I tried. He pulled me off the desk to stand facing away from him. He ran his hand from the top of my legs, around my hips, to the top of my shoulders.

His chest was pressed against my back. "Bend over."

I didn't know what to think. I had no idea what he had in mind, but I did what he wanted. He bent with me and trailed kisses down my spine. He kissed the tops of my thighs and my legs shook. It was a good thing that the desk supported me or I'd have fallen because my legs couldn't hold me. His words, lips, and body were sending me over the edge.

He grabbed my hips and drove in and out of me. His hands squeezed my hips as he moved. My insides tightened. I knew I wouldn't last long. He must have sensed that because his pace increased.

"Aubrey, I hope you're ready because . . ."

I tried to stifle a scream, but I couldn't. I let go and cried out his name. He lifted my hips until my feet came off the floor. I tried to grab onto something, but it was useless. He was forceful and fast. I thought I would fly off his desk. If he wasn't hanging on to me, I probably would have.

He stilled and moved slowly. He gave me a kiss on my back, and I rested my cheek on the desk, trying to cool down. When we were no longer connected, I stood and placed my hands where my feet once were. I needed to steady myself.

He held my shoulders. "I've got you. I'll always have you, Aubrey."

He straightened me so that I stood in front of him, our bodies touching. One of his hands was on my stomach, holding me tight against him, while the other was on my chest. I leaned back and rested my head on his chest. I turned in his arms so I could run my hands up his abs to his pecs, and I kept going until my hands were around his neck. I closed my eyes and pictured his face. I felt our eyes connecting even though I couldn't see him.

"I love you Alex. I hope you know how much." I said that a lot, but after everything we'd been though, I would say it every minute of every day if I had to.

He kissed the top of my head and inhaled. He pulled my head to his chest, and my ear rested over his heartbeat. It was a smooth steady rhythm.

"I do know how much," he said. "I feel it in everything you say and do. I feel that way too, with everything that I am and everything I will ever be."

We hugged each other as if we needed the other's strength to stand. I realized how much I needed him.

"Come on. Let's go home and get some rest," I said.

We left the club and headed to my apartment. When we got there, we went straight to bed and held each other all night. Waking in each other's arms was the best way to start the day. I opened my eyes and prayed I'd see something, but I didn't.

"Good morning, beautiful." Alex kissed my forehead.

"Good morning, handsome." I couldn't wait to see him again.

He ran his fingers up and down my arm. "So I was thinking that I'd like to take everyone out to dinner tomorrow night."

"Who's everyone?"

"You and me of course." He kissed my hand. "Your parents, Brett, Julie, Mark, and Val. What do you think?"

"I think it's a great idea. Where should we go?"

"I'd like to see Anthony, so how about we go to his place?"

"Sounds like a plan."

After we had breakfast, Alex called our friends to invite them to dinner. Val said she'd get us a great table at her father's restaurant. We spent the day lying on the couch.

I wondered why he wasn't going into the club since it was a Friday. "Are you working tonight?"

He hugged me. "Nope. You're stuck with me all day and all night."

"Hmm, all day and all night? What will we do to pass the time?"

I giggled, and Alex tossed me over his shoulder as though he was a fireman. My equilibrium danced, and I got a head rush. I yelped, and he lightly spanked my ass. That made me laugh and Alex groan.

We spent the day and night making love. We took a break for dinner, and I called to check on my parents. They were excited about our dinner the next night, and Alex told them he'd send a car for them at seven p.m. I was sure that delighted my mom.

We walked into the restaurant and were greeted by a boisterous Anthony. He was back to his old self after his heart attack, and I was happy to hear him. I pictured Alex's face when he saw Anthony, and it dawned on me that he had been apart from everyone he cared about while he was with me in Paris. That thought made my heart heavy.

I started to walk away from him to give him time with his friends, but Alex walked farther into the restaurant. My arm stretched with him since he was holding my hand. I felt my arm slacken and sensed Alex in front of me.

"What's the matter, baby?" he asked.

"Can I talk to you outside a minute?"

"Yeah . . . Are you okay?"

I didn't reply. I didn't know if I was okay.

He squeezed my hand. "Everyone is here already. Let me tell Anthony to set them up with wine and let them know we will be right back. Stay here." He let go of my hand.

I nodded and felt all alone. I heard people and silverware on plates, but I was alone in my darkness. I wasn't sure how much time passed, but it seemed like forever.

"I'm back. Let's go outside."

His voice startled me, and I gave him a slight smile. He weaved his hand in mine, and before I knew it, the crisp New York air hit my face, making me shiver.

He wrapped his arms around me. "What's wrong? Do you not feel well?"

I shook my head. "I feel fine. I need to tell you something, and I wanted it to be just us."

"Uh . . . okay. Should I be nervous?"

"I'm sorry I left you and pulled you away from everyone you care about. That really wasn't fair. I never stopped loving you or wanting to be with you. I was scared, hurt, and selfish." I lowered my head. "I never thought you would follow me."

He held me and whispered, "To the ends of the earth. That's how far I'd follow you."

"Thank you. I think you're the only person other than Julie who would do that for me."

He put his hands on my face and tilted up my head. "I'm sure others would be there for you: your parents, hell, even Mark. But I'd beat them all to it. Someday you'll understand how much you're loved. I swear that if I ever meet the jackass that made you feel inferior and not worthy, I'm going to make sure he knows he hurt you."

He kissed me and led me back inside. At the table, everyone greeted us. I was glad to be back with the people I loved, even Val. She had been good to Mark, and he deserved it after what his ex, Jessica, had done to him. A waitress came to the table, and we placed our orders.

Julie told everyone about the last time she saw me and how proud she was of me for taking a stand with Leah. Brett laughed about it. My mom told me that ladies don't fight, but my dad said, "That's my girl." I grinned.

I heard silverware tapping against a glass, then I heard Alex clear his throat. "I want to thank everyone for being here tonight." He cleared his throat again.

I knew he hated public speaking, but he shouldn't be nervous around his friends and family. I felt his hands on my knees, which made me jump.

He turned me in my chair and took my hands. "I'm looking into your eyes, and I know you can't see me, but soon you will. I'll repeat this to you then."

I felt my eyes well up with tears.

"You're the love of my life, Aubrey Ryan. I don't know how or why, but you were brought into my life, and I've never been more thankful for anything. You're my best friend, my lover, and I don't want to be without you ever. I want to travel the world with you, have a family with you, and grow old with you. You're my life, my reason, and my world. My heart beats stronger when we're together. You give me hope. Aubrey, will you marry me and be my wife so we can start *our* future?"

I heard a gasp, which I assumed was my mom. I was stunned. I hadn't expected that at all. Everyone was silent. I was sure they hadn't left, so they were probably waiting for my answer. I moved my hands to his face. I felt worry lines on his forehead and around his eyes. My fingers went to his lips, and they were in a straight line. He wasn't smiling.

"Alex, I love you more each day. You're the love of my life too." I took a deep breath. "Yes, I'll marry you. I'd love nothing more than to be Mrs. Alex Logan." I felt his cheeks raise into a smile.

He hugged me, and then I was in the air being spun around. The room burst into applause. Then his lips were on mine, and I heard hooting and hollering erupt in the restaurant.

He set me down and whispered, "Thank you."

Alex released me, and I instantly felt cold. He took my hand and placed it on what felt like a ring box. He positioned my fingers so I could open the box. I slowly opened the box and felt the ring. I raised my head. I wanted to see him so badly it hurt.

"Let me." He took the box. "I'm holding our engagement ring. I'd like to place it on your finger; may I? I want the world to know that you're mine."

"I'd like that." I was beaming. I felt the cool metal slide on my left ring finger. I felt it and couldn't believe the size of the stone. I wasn't sure if it was a diamond. "It's beautiful, Alex." I couldn't see it, but that didn't matter. I loved that he'd called it "our" engagement ring.

"I'm glad you like it." He sounded relieved.

He could've put a rubber band on my finger, and I would have loved it. Before I could sit down, Mark, Val, and Brett surrounded me with congratulations.

Julie practically mugged me. She grabbed me and rocked me back and forth, full of enthusiasm. "Let me see the ring. Oh, Aubrey, it's gorgeous, it really is. I'm so happy for you!"

My parents came up to me next, and I wondered if they had known about Alex's plan.

"Congratulations, honey!" My mom sounded happy.

I heard my dad say to Alex, "Treat my baby girl right, you got it?"

"Yes, sir."

My dad kissed my cheeks and hugged me. "I'm happy for you. He's a good man."

I rested my head on my father's shoulder. "Thank

you, Daddy."

Brett told us that our meals had arrived, so we sat back down. I didn't know how they expected me to eat when I just got engaged! The food smelled amazing, but I just sat there.

"Your plate is directly in front of you," Alex said. "The veal parmesan is at six o'clock, the ziti at two o'clock, and a roll at ten o'clock. There's a pat of butter on a small plate to the left of your roll."

The table was quiet, except for the sounds of people eating. I set my fork down and tried to absorb all that had happened. That was the best night of my life, aside from the first night I met Alex.

I felt his hand on mine. "You okay?"

"I'm better than okay." That was the truth. He loved me beyond what was considered unconditional. "I love you so much."

His lips were on mine and his hands threaded through my hair. I heard our friends hoot, followed by some of the customers. I didn't even care that we were in public. When I was with Alex, it was just us. I felt Alex's lips curve into a smile, and he chuckled against my lips. His hand rested on my neck.

Brett broke me out of my trance, "Yo, dude, your future father-in-law is right here. Want to take it down to a G-rating please? Not to mention I'm trying to eat!"

Everyone laughed. I wished I could see them. Picturing how happy everyone was was enough for me.

When Alex and I got back to my apartment. Alex opened the door and carried me inside.

"What are you doing?"

The door closed, and Alex kept walking with my legs over his arms and my arm around his neck. "I'm practicing," he said. "You know, threshold and all."

I put my head on his chest and giggled. "Are you going to do this every day?" I heard my bedroom door close. Then I was lying on my bed with Alex's breath near my ear.

"If you would like me to carry you in every day, I'd love nothing more," he said. "You carry my heart every day; I'll literally carry yours. I'd do anything for you."

"I think you've proven that, Chance. I mean, Alex." I laughed, but he didn't. "What's wrong? I was joking." I felt the bed shift as he moved away from me. I reached out to him and found him lying on his back. "Alex? What did I say?"

He exhaled. "Nothing really. You know I couldn't stay away from you, right? But if it meant that you could move on and be happy, I would've stayed away. I'd have died, but I'd have done that for you."

"I didn't want you to do that. I didn't mean anything by calling you Chance. I was just kidding. I know you would do anything for me. I'd do anything for you too. But you leaving me isn't an option, got it? You're stuck with me for life."

He rolled, and our chests touched. His hand went into my hair. "Tonight, you made me the happiest I've ever been in my life."

"Well, you shocked the hell out of me. I can't believe we're engaged. I really hope the doctor can help." I put my head on my pillow and sighed.

"Me too, babe. It'll all work out. I wasn't kidding

when I said I'd get you the best medical help there is. I'd spend every penny I have to make sure you're okay."

"It'll be fine," I said. "You keep your pennies in the bank. I have faith that things will work out." I leaned in and kissed him. I'd never needed anything or anyone the way I needed Alex. He made me feel like one of the beautiful girls who got all the hot guys. "Thank you."

"For what?"

"Choosing me." I smiled and felt a tear leak from my eye.

His finger wiped away the tear, and he moved my hair behind my ear. "I think my mom chose you for me. I think she sent me to check on things that night. Usually Tyler or Brett would have looked in on the speed-dating. You could be here with one of them now."

I shook my head. "No way. I would have left alone. I was ready to leave until you came along."

"I guess we're both lucky then." He kissed my forehead. "Let's get some sleep."

I rested my head on his chest and listened to his heartbeat. I fell asleep happier than I'd been in a long time—no, the happiest I'd ever been.

Chapter 5

ALEX WORKED AT THE CLUB over the weekend while I spent time with my folks. I didn't feel any insecurity with Alex, which was rare for me, and it was calming. I saw some shadows while I was with my parents, but I didn't say anything about them because they came and went so sporadically. I didn't want my parents to get their hopes up just to be let down. We were going to see the doctor on Monday, so I decided to wait to see what he had to say.

It was wonderful knowing Alex would be coming home to me every night. Spending time with my parents was nice, but falling asleep in Alex's arms was the best. I was a little nervous about the tests the doctor would conduct. I didn't sleep well on Sunday night. When I woke on Monday, I was nervous.

"Babe, are you okay? You tossed and turned all night." Alex sounded worried.

"Yes, I'm fine. I'm just a little nervous about the tests." I did my best to sound positive.

"Are you sure you don't want me to come with you?"

"No, I'll be fine. My parents will be here soon. I

should get ready."

Alex kissed me. "I'll get ready with you."

We both jumped in the shower and actually showered.

My parents took me to get some tests done at the doctor's office, and then we spent the entire day at my place. My mom did my laundry and made some meals so I'd have them in the freezer while my dad ran to the grocery store for me. I couldn't wait to be able to do all of that for myself. They were meeting friends for dinner, so after they left, I waited for Alex to come home. I figured we could grab something to eat.

I sat on the couch and grabbed my tablet. I felt for the music app to listen to some songs Alex had put on it for me. I was getting sleepy, and I laid back and listened. Bruno Mars was playing when I heard my door open. I sat up and looked toward the door, but I didn't see anything.

"Hey, babe, I brought Chinese. I hope you're hungry," Alex said.

I was starved. "What time is it?"

"Seven. I'm sorry I'm late. I wanted to get dinner, and I brought you this." He placed a flower in my hand.

I brought the orchid to my nose. "I love it. Thank you."

He gave me a chaste kiss. "Let's eat so I can get you into bed. I have been thinking about you all day. If you weren't with your parents, I'd have come home hours ago just to take you quick and then go back to the club."

"You can have me anytime." I winked and yawned.

"How were your tests? I wanted to text you, but I wasn't sure if you would be asleep after your appointment. I'm sorry I couldn't be there with you."

"It's okay, I understand. My parents were with me, so it worked out. The tests went fine. I just hope they drew some conclusions."

After we finished eating, Alex's lips landed on mine, and I was no longer tired. Our tongues explored each other's mouths. His hand went under my shirt and gently squeezed my right breast and then my left. He removed my pants and lifted my foot onto the back of the couch. With no warning, no foreplay, he was in me. I was more than ready for him. I felt every inch of him—he didn't lack in that department. I moved my hips with his and arched my back. My legs wrapped around his waist.

When his hands went under my shoulders, I realized I was still half dressed. I felt for his shirt, but he was totally naked. I didn't know how he'd done that without me noticing, but I didn't care. My hands explored his glorious muscles. I brought my hands to his back and felt it move with each thrust. I trailed my fingertips down his spine to his lower back.

"I need to come, Aubrey. I can't hold on." His pace increased.

"Do it, Alex. Let me feel you."

His thumb went between us, and he rubbed me. It felt amazing, and I convulsed around him, tightening to the point where I couldn't take it anymore.

"Please now, it needs to be—" My breathing hitched.

We came, and he collapsed on me. He trailed kisses

on my neck as he pulled out of me and took my hands. "Let's go to bed. We have a big day ahead of us tomorrow."

I nodded.

I woke in Alex's arms. I felt so safe. I was terrified I would get horrible news later.

Alex pulled me in tighter. "Good morning, babe." He softly kissed my lips. "You ready for today?"

I tried to smile. "Yes, I think I'm ready. I'm nervous, though. What if—"

"No what ifs okay?" he said.

We got ready and went to Doctor Fisher's office. I'd completed the tests the day before that would determine whether or not I'd be a good candidate for the surgery. I couldn't wait to hear what he had to say. I was nervous, excited, and terrified. I wanted to be "whole" for Alex and for us.

The doctor came in, sat at his desk and flipped through papers in a manila folder. "Well, Aubrey, I have good news and bad news. Well, not bad news. Different news. The good news is, your swelling has gone down considerably and there isn't much fluid behind your eyes. I don't think you need surgery."

I was completely stunned.

"Since the swelling and fluid are low, I'm surprised that your vision hasn't returned. I have a few questions for you. Are you opposed to discussing it with everyone here, or may I continue?"

"Um . . . you can discuss it. We're all family," I said.

Alex squeezed my hand.

The doctor asked, "Have you ever been prone to anxiety or have you experienced emotional trauma that caused you to have panic attacks or high anxiety?"

I shifted a little, shrugged, and almost whispered, "Yes. I've had a few panic attacks. Why?"

"Have you ever heard of Hysterical Blindness or Conversion Disorder?"

"No." What the hell was he talking about?

"Doctor, can you please explain it to us in layman's terms? I don't understand what's going on. Does Aubrey need surgery or not?" Alex sounded as scared and confused as I was.

"Aubrey, you have some fluid but not so much that requires surgery. We'll keep an eye on it, but right now, an operation isn't necessary. You've taken longer than normal to heal, but every patient is different. Conversion Disorder is when emotional or psychological stress manifests by temporarily shutting off the receptors that enable you to see. It causes you to show psychological stress in a physical manner, for example blocking your visual impulses from your eyes to your brain. It usually occurs when someone experiences emotional turmoil due to an accident or other traumatic event."

Alex cleared his throat. "I said laymen's terms." He sounded aggravated.

"Yes, I apologize. In simplest terms, your brain has shut off your ability to see as a protection mechanism. I know you hit your head, and that's why you initially had swelling and fluid. But if your blindness was due to your injury, you should be able to see by now. Dr. Beaumont wrote that you have had flashes of light and temporary vision improvement. Is that true?"

I couldn't believe what I was hearing. I was blind because I had psychological issues? I felt so stupid and like a total head case.

"Aubrey, honey, the doctor asked you a question." My mom sounded like the teacher in a Charlie Brown cartoon.

"I'm sorry, what?"

Dr. Fisher said, "Has your vision returned at any time?"

"Yes, my vision has returned on occasion. I'm sorry, but I'm confused. Dr. Beaumont told me I was blind because of the fluid." I was getting upset.

Alex rubbed my hand and kissed the back of it, trying to calm me down. He must be afraid that I was going to flip out. *Great, he probably thinks he has a weirdo for a fiancée.*

"I understand that. The CT scan you had in Paris wasn't wrong, it showed fluid, but our test didn't show as much. Are you opposed to seeing a therapist?"

I let go of Alex's hand and stood. "Are you telling me I'm blind because I need therapy? I can see but my brain won't let me because I'm messed up? Is that what you're saying? I've missed everything around me and seeing the people I love for months because of this . . ." I was breathing erratically and getting the shakes. I thought my chest would explode. I tried to catch my breath. "Because I have anxiety attacks? That's why I'm blind?" I felt Alex's arms around me. I buried my head in his chest and cried.

Dr. Fisher explained, "This is just a theory and one I'd like us to explore."

All I heard was the beat of my heart. I tried to calm

my breathing. *Perfect! This is exactly why I'm blind, because I have issues that I can't deal with.*

"Baby, you're going to be okay." Alex wiped my tears and kissed my cheeks.

I nodded and took a deep breath and then another.

Alex said, "Okay. Please continue, Dr. Fisher."

I sat back down. I wanted to crawl on Alex's lap and into his arms.

"Like I was saying, initially your blindness was caused by the trauma to your brain. But now, I believe it could have more to do with your anxiety. Something deep and emotional can add to your condition. One of the fellows here at NYU did his Fellowship Thesis on how stress and emotional suffering can affect a person's health. If it's okay with you, Aubrey, I'd like for you to meet with him and a therapist, Dr. Russo. Then, if need be, we can determine how to proceed."

I had no idea what to think.

My dad said, "Thank you, doctor. We'll go home and discuss everything and get back to you."

We left NYU and went back to my apartment. I didn't say a word the entire ride home. I couldn't believe this was happening. Brett called Alex while we were in the car and said that he was at my place with Julie and Mark. They wanted to hear what the doctor had said. I appreciated their concern, but I didn't want to talk about the visit. I felt like such a loser.

We walked into my place. I was greeted by Julie's hug and a kiss from Mark. Julie must have noticed my expression because she immediately wanted to know what was wrong. I couldn't say anything. My eyes filled, and tears spilled down my cheeks.

"Oh my God, Aubrey, what did the doctor say? What's wrong?" Julie sounded as though she was crying too.

I shook my head. "It's my fault . . . that I . . . that I . . . can't . . . that I can't see."

"What? What are you talking about? What happened?" Julie hugged me again. "Let's go to your room and talk."

I heard my mom say that she would start dinner. Brett was talking to Mark and my dad. I heard the TV click on. I was glad that everyone's attention was off of me. Then I realized I hadn't heard Alex

"Alex?" I stretched my arm out, hoping he'd take my hand. He didn't. I lowered my arm. "Julie, is Alex here?"

"I don't see him."

"Brett, where's Alex?"

"He stepped out." Brett sounded as though it was no big deal; I had a feeling it was.

"Okay." Before Julie and I went into my room, I asked Brett to call Alex and tell him I needed him.

I smelled Alex's cologne when I walked into my room; it smelled like home. He was my home. I felt the carpet and the cool cotton of my comforter. I loved my room. Julie held my hand as we sat on my bed.

"Okay, spill. What the hell is going on?" she asked.

I made nervous eights on the comforter with my fingers. "Have you ever heard of Hysterical Blindness or Conversion Disorder?"

"Um . . . no. Why would blindness be funny?"

I couldn't tell if Julie's question was serious or if she

was trying to make me laugh. I wiped my tears, but I knew there would be more. "Apparently, extreme anxiety and stress can cause blindness. The doctor said that initially my blindness was caused by the trauma to my head, but according to the scans he took, the amount of fluid and swelling shouldn't affect my sight. He said that I don't need surgery. He believes that my anxiety is causing it. It's psychological."

Silence.

"Jules?" I knew she was still there because she was holding my hand.

"I don't understand. So the emotional, not the physical, trauma you sustained is the reason you can't see?" Julie sounded angry.

I sighed. "Apparently, yes. This is all on me. Since my sight has returned on and off, that pretty much confirms it's not physical. He wants me to talk to some medical fellow who did a study on it or something. I'm such a freak!" I dropped my head in my hands.

"Oh no, you're not! This is not all on you! I get that you have issues with anxiety, but you don't just dream up scenarios that cause you to panic. What you saw sent you into this nightmare. Fuck, Aubrey, it's because of—"

I shook my head. "No! Don't blame him."

"Are you kidding me? The last thing you saw was him and that skank. You don't think that maybe seeing what he did made your brain protect you by blocking your vision?"

I spun my engagement ring on my finger and was about to say no when I heard him.

"Julie's right."

"What?" My heart sank. God, how much had he heard?

"This has everything to do with me and my mistake," Alex said. "That's what you think, right, Julie? Do you think it's better that I leave? Is that what she needs? Do you want me to leave her?" Alex sounded pissed, hurt, and ready to pack it in.

My head was reeling. He couldn't leave me. The thought of it made me sick.

Julie's voice was furious and loud. "It doesn't matter what I think, does it? I knew something would happen. I knew that this would come back around. I didn't want to be right, Aubrey, I really didn't. I told you that first night . . . shit. God damn you, Alex! I swear, I don't care if you're her fiancé or not. If you hurt her, I swear I will—"

"Julie, why are you yelling at Alex?" Brett sounded mad at Julie.

I burst into tears . . . again. I was so tired of crying.

"Aubrey, why are you crying? What'd you do, Logan?" Mark sounded angry. When did he come in?

Did everyone forget that I was there? "Shut up! Just shut up! You guys are talking about me like I'm not even here," I said. "Mark, stop yelling at Alex. He didn't do anything. Julie, you need to apologize to Alex. I need you all to leave. I need to talk to Alex alone."

They kept bickering, and then the door closed and it was very quiet. They must have left. I never heard Julie's apology, but I really didn't think I would.

I tried to catch my breath. My heart was breaking. I was so afraid to ask, "Are you here?"

"Yeah, I'm here. Listen, Aubrey, if I'm a constant

reminder of what brought all of this on, then maybe I shouldn't be here."

I tried to gather myself by taking a long, deep breath. "I need you more now than I ever have. Please don't leave me."

I felt for him. My hands landed on his chest, slid around his back, and tightly held him. His arms wrapped around me, and he squeezed me as if he was afraid to let go.

"Alex, I need you to come to the doctor's with me. I want you there when I talk to this guy and the psychologist." I was scared too. If the therapist said that Alex was to blame, I didn't know what he'd do.

"Okay, if you're sure, then it's me and you. I'll help you get through this. God, I'm so sorry. Can we call the doctor now? I have her card. I'll pay whatever it costs to get you an appointment for tomorrow so we can get this resolved. We'll figure out what this is and how to fix it."

All I could do was nod. Alex called and made the appointment for tomorrow afternoon at two o'clock.

I was nervous, which didn't help. "Please don't go. Please just hold me."

His arms were around me. "I'm not leaving you ever. I'll be here if you need me. But right now, I want you to rest." He kissed the top of my head and got up. "I need to make sure that everyone out there is okay and Julie doesn't have Brett's head in the freezer or anything. I'll tell them what's going on."

"Thank you." I grinned, lay back on my bed, and closed my eyes. I was exhausted.

When I woke, my apartment was quiet. I felt around

my bed; it was empty. I laid there thinking about when my anxiety started. I took deep breaths and tried to calm myself. I thought of the yoga class I took and how they talked about finding your "center." I closed my eyes, relaxed, and took deep breaths.

I thought of Alex, his love for me, and our future. I pictured white orchids in a bouquet, shapes of clouds, waves on a beach, and a perfect full moon. I imagined pushing a little girl on a swing and Alex playing catch with a young boy, both of them wearing Yankee hats. Alex looked over and smiled at me. He loved me and our family.

I felt like I was beaming, and I opened my eyes. I squinted at the light in the room. I sat up and swung my legs over the side of the bed. I looked around my room. It was just as I had left it, my luggage on the floor next to the dresser.

I walked to the door. I prayed Alex was close; I needed to see his face. I opened the door. Everyone was still there and eating dinner. I walked toward the table. I willed myself not to think of anything that would make my vision go away. I was going to enjoy my sight for as long as I could. I kept breathing and pictured the little girl on the swing.

My mom had prepared a beef roast, potatoes, and a salad. It smelled so good, but it looked even better. I couldn't believe how great lettuce looked.

"There she is! Did you sleep okay, babe?" Alex stood, probably to help me.

"Please don't get up. Sit down and finish your dinner." I looked at his gorgeous face.

Alex replied, "It's okay, I can get up for a minute. Wait . . . how did you know I stood? Oh my God! Can you see me?"

I looked around, and everyone stood at once. I beamed. "Yes, I can see all of you. Mom, that color suits you. Dinner looks delicious. Daddy, you look great. Mark, you need a haircut." I winked. "Brett, you and Julie look like twins. Do you shop together? And Val, you look beautiful, as always." I turned toward Alex, put my hands on his face, and stared into his dark blue eyes. "And you, mister, are still the most gorgeous man I have ever seen." I looked at my hand and saw my ring for the first time. "My ring! It's . . . it's perfect."

He pulled me into him. "God, I love you, Aubrey."

"I love you too. I'm hungry. I'd like to see what I'm eating for a change."

Alex pulled out my chair for me. I sat and looked at all the food. No one said anything as I helped myself.

I cut a piece of beef and savored it. I may have moaned. I glanced up and saw everyone looking at me. "Eat, people. Your chewing won't make me go blind."

"That is not funny, Aubrey Ryan!"

I looked at my mom and smirked.

Brett chimed in, "You know, Alex, when you go to the doctor's tomorrow, you should ask if what we were told as young boys really does cause blindness."

Alex threw a roll at him. "Really, dude? We're eating here."

We all laughed. I looked around the table at the faces I hadn't seen in months. Then I panicked that it would go away, and everyone's faces faded. I looked at Alex. He was absolutely stunning and perfect. His hair was messy but sexy. He was mine and no one else's. I got nervous at the thought of someone else with him and not me. He looked in my eyes. I didn't want to lose sight of him.

"It's fading, isn't it?" Alex sounded as sad as he looked.

I nodded, and the blackness returned. "Yeah, that's the part I don't understand." I slumped back in my chair and felt my ring. It was a perfectly cut circular diamond nestled in a platinum band. Alex really knew my tastes.

"I have an idea." Alex sounded determined. I heard his chair move. "We're going to write all this down: when your vision came back, what you were doing, what you were thinking of when it went away, and anything else we can think of. Then when we go to the doctor, we'll be really prepared."

My dad chimed in, "That's a fantastic idea."

Alex and I sat on the couch together after dinner. My mom, Julie, and Val cleaned up the kitchen, and the guys sat at the table playing cards. I heard my dad say "gin." I loved that everyone was together and getting along so well. Alex and I went through each time my vision returned. Alex asked me to tell him all the times I could remember.

"Well, tonight, I had a dream about our family. When I woke up, I could see."

"You dreamt of our family? We had our own family?" He sounded happy.

"Yeah, I was pushing our daughter on a swing, and you were playing catch with our son." I felt my face redden.

His lips touched mine. "I hope that comes true and

our daughter looks like her beautiful mother."

I smiled, and he kissed me again.

"Okay, when else?" he asked. "But so far, that's my favorite moment."

I grinned and placed my hand on his leg. I needed to touch him. I thought about it for a while. "Well, there were the flashes I had at the park with Chance, uh, you." I shook my head. I still couldn't believe it. How did I not know?

"I'm going to write down Chance because we need to see if there's a pattern."

"Okay. I also had flashes of light with Chance in the car, and I saw shadows when I was at lunch with Chance." I tried to remember more. "Oh! When I was on the phone with you, I saw my bedspread. And then the morning of the day I went to Chance's apartment for dinner, and then when I was with you that night." Alex was silent. "Alex, is everything okay?"

"Yeah . . . I forgot that you regained your sight when you were talking to me on the phone. You didn't tell me." He sounded defeated.

"But I did call and tell you."

"No, you didn't. You called Chance. You didn't want to share that with me. I wish you would have. Maybe I'm the problem here. Julie could be dead-on."

"No, you're not the problem. I don't know why I didn't tell you." I rubbed my temples. "Can we go lie down? I'm getting a headache." Silence. "Alex . . . did you hear me? Will you lie down with me?" I hoped he wasn't upset with me.

"Yeah, of course. Come on." He sounded so crushed. He held my hand while we said good night to everyone.

My mom asked what time we would be going to the doctor's tomorrow. I told her my appointment was at two p.m., but I asked if she'd mind if I just went in with Alex.

"If that is what you want, dear." She sounded hurt. "Your father and I are here for you too. I know we aren't Alex, but we're your parents and we do love you." She had perfected that tone over the years.

"I know, Mom. I'm sorry. If you and Daddy want to come, then I want you there. I didn't think you would want to just wait in the waiting room." I hope she understood that I didn't want her or my father in the doctor's office with me.

"Of course we want to be there." My mom guided me away from everyone. "I understand that you love Alex. He's clearly head over heels in love with you, and I couldn't be happier that the two of you will be married someday. He's a good man. But I just want to help you. Your father and I both do. I didn't mean to make you feel obligated to have us there, though."

I nodded. "I do want you and Daddy there. I just don't know what's going to happen. I feel as if every time I think everything will be okay, something else happens. I'm just nervous."

My mom hugged me. "I know, honey. We will meet you there."

Chapter 6

ALEX AND I WALKED INTO Dr. Russo's office at one forty-five p.m. My parents arrived shortly after. We sat in the waiting room, and no one said a word. The waiting and silence made me more anxious than I already was. Alex held my left hand, shifting the diamond back and forth. He had to be nervous too.

"Are you okay?" I asked.

He lifted my left hand and kissed it. "Yeah, I'm fine. Just losing my patience sitting here. It's been over thirty minutes."

I was going to say something when I heard the nurse call my name. I told my parents to wish me luck. Alex let go of my hand as I stood.

"What are you doing? Aren't you coming in with me?"

"Do you still want me to?"

I smirked and turned toward his voice. "Don't ask dumb questions, Mr. Logan."

"Okay, future Mrs. Logan. Lead the way."

"Really, you want me to lead the way? You're funny."

"Okay, I'll lead this time, but next time you're doing it. I can't do everything all the time."

"Haha, you're a funny guy." I loved that he was normal with me. He was a treasure.

The nurse opened a door and said that Dr. Russo would be with us in a few minutes. Alex and I said thank you at the same time, and we laughed. I wasn't as nervous as I should be.

He led me into the room. "We're standing at the door which I will call six o'clock. There's a desk in front of us at twelve o'clock, a black leather couch at three, and there are a few chairs and a book case at nine o'clock."

"Thank you." I kissed his hand, and he kissed the top of my head.

I heard the door close. "That is a good way to explain things to her."

Oh my God, I knew that voice. I spun around.

"Aubrey, I can't believe it's really you! What happened?"

"Garrett? What are you doing here? Why are you in here?" I felt my heart race, and Alex squeezed my hand.

"So, you're Garrett." Alex's voice was curt. He sounded pissed.

I moved my opposite hand to Alex's forearm. I didn't want him lunging at Garrett. Alex blamed him for a lot of my issues.

I heard the door open again, then an unfamiliar female voice. "I'm Dr. Russo. You must be Aubrey. I see you've met Dr. Reed."

Dr. Reed? When had he become a doctor? I stood there and didn't say a word.

"Alex Logan. It's a pleasure to meet you, Dr. Russo."

I felt Alex shift. He must have shaken her hand.

"It's a pleasure to meet you both. Mr. Logan, are you related to Aubrey? Generally, these sessions are limited to the patient and, if requested, immediate family."

I didn't know why that mattered. If I wanted him there, he'd be there. End of story. "He's my fiancé."

"Congratulations, Aubrey." Garrett sounded sincere.

I felt as though I would be sick.

Dr. Russo asked, "Do you two know each other?"

Alex answered for me. "They were friends once, until he screwed her over."

Oh my God! I can't believe Alex said that. "Yes, I know Garrett—I mean, Dr. Reed." I'd have shot Alex a dirty look, but I didn't want to make him feel bad.

"I don't think he should be in here." Alex sounded even more pissed. "What do you think, baby? Whatever you want to do is fine, but I think he needs to get the hell out of here."

Dr. Russo said, "The study Dr. Reed completed could be helpful to you, Aubrey, but I think it would be best if he left."

So far, that session was not helping my anxiety. "I just want to get better."

"I hope you do get better. Dr. Russo has my thesis. If she has any questions, she knows how to contact me. I wish you the best, Aubrey." I heard the door close.

"Are you okay, Aubrey? Again, my sincerest apology for Dr. Reed's presence."

Alex guided me to the couch.

"Aubrey, I want to go over a few things with you," Dr. Russo said. "It says in your file that you sustained a head injury that caused your blindness, but you have intermittently regained partial or full vision. It also says that you experience panic or anxiety attacks. That's what I want to focus on. Can you tell me how long you have been having anxiety issues?"

"Since I was in middle school. So about ten or so years, I guess."

"Mmm hmm, and do certain things trigger these episodes?"

I didn't know what to say. "Well, they usually happen when someone hurts me . . . emotionally. Or when I'm nervous or feel uncomfortable." I hoped Alex didn't hear me, although I knew he did.

Dr. Russo asked, "Nervous about what? Friends? School? Work? Relationships?"

I tried to remain calm and confident. "I wasn't nervous in school because of the work. I excelled in my classes. In middle school, I was teased and it stuck with me." I shrugged. I squeezed Alex's hand. "As far as relationships . . . let's say mine have never been easy." I shifted in my chair.

"Have you had many relationships?" Dr. Russo sounded so matter-of-fact.

I didn't say anything. I sat there, probably looking stupid.

After I stayed silent for too long, Dr. Russo said, "I'm sorry, Mr. Logan, but it might be better if you weren't here. If Aubrey's not comfortable opening up around you, then your presence will impede our progress."

"I'm comfortable, and I want Alex here," I said. "He knows everything about me; we don't have secrets. He knows my past, and he's my future." I wanted to not only reassure Alex but to get through to everyone in the room, including myself.

"Fine, then let's return to my question. Have you had many relationships?"

"What do you mean?" I was embarrassed.

"With men, how many intimate relationships have you had?"

"Two."

"I see. Let's talk about them," Dr. Russo said.

Holy hell! Seriously? Let's not.

"Was your other relationship healthy?" Dr. Russo asked. "Did he make you feel anxious or nervous? Was he emotionally or physically abusive?"

"No, Dr. Reed wasn't abusive. I felt anxious at times, but nothing that I care to remember."

Silence.

"Dr. Reed?" Dr. Russo said. "Dr. Reed was your other relationship?"

I didn't think it could get any worse. "Yes, he was. We were . . . we did . . ." Yup, it just got worse. I couldn't form a coherent sentence. Panic.

"Are you sure you're okay to continue?"

"Yes, I'm fine. I'm sorry, I wasn't expecting these questions." I sat up straighter, trying to regain some form of composure. "Garrett and I were close friends—at least I thought we were. I thought we loved each other, but when we slept together, that was the end of us. We weren't friends anymore, or anything else for that matter. We were over."

"And how did that make you feel?" Dr. Russo sounded so blasé.

"Used."

I heard Alex mutter "asshole," and I moved his hand to my lap and tried not to smile.

"I have Alex now, and everything is wonderful, except for the obvious." I waved my hand in front of my eyes.

Dr. Russo cleared her throat. "I want to talk about the night you lost your vision. Is that okay with you?"

No. "Okay."

"Can you tell me what you did that day?"

"Um . . . My friend Mark was moving, so I went to his new place and helped him." *Please don't make me say more.*

"And after that?"

Shit. "After that, I went home and . . ." I took a deep breath. Alex let go of my hand to rub my thigh. "I realized that I had made a big mistake. I hadn't been truthful with Alex about something. He found out and left me." A tear escaped my eye, which I wiped away.

"And then?"

I took a breath. "I went to his club to find him. I found him sitting at the bar doing shots. He was upset." I lowered my head, and tears fell. I needed to just blurt it out before she asked. "He kissed his ex-girlfriend in front of me. I panicked, ran out of the club, got pushed, and hit my head on the ground. I woke up in the hospital, blind."

Alex spoke. “Dr. Russo, this is my fault, isn’t it?”

Dr. Russo sounded so calm when she said, “Mr. Logan. We’re here only to see why this is happening. Aubrey, I think that we should meet twice a week so we can work through the issues causing your anxiety. Going forward, it may be better if we met one on one.”

I stood. “I will not leave here with you thinking that Alex is the cause of this. I’m the cause. I lied to Alex. That led to the events the night of my accident, so blaming him is wrong.”

Alex was at my side. “Baby, you don’t have to—” Alex sounded worried and protective.

“Yes, I do. I need to say this. Dr. Russo, there’s no way I’ll attend any more sessions if Alex isn’t with me.” I let out a long breath. “I love Alex, more than I’ve ever loved anyone. There will be no discussing that any further, or I’ll find another therapist.” My breathing accelerated.

“Aubrey, please try to relax,” Dr. Russo said. “Take a deep breath. I am not blaming Alex, or anyone. I’ve read Dr. Reed’s thesis, and I agree that we need to work through some emotional trauma together. Aubrey, your file says that you’ve had moments of sight, can you please tell me when your last one was?”

I sat back down. “It was last night. I was with Alex, a couple of friends, and my parents. It was the longest it has lasted.” I beamed at Alex as he sat next to me.

“What were you thinking about when it went away again?”

“I started wondering when it would go away. That made me nervous, and then it went away.”

“Hmmm . . . Do you take any anti-anxiety

medicine?"

"No, I don't."

"I'm going to send you home with a prescription to calm your nerves. You may experience some drowsiness or lack of appetite, but I'd be surprised if you experienced any side effects. We'll start you on the prescription every day, but I'd like to get you to the point where you only need to take it prior to an event that you know will bring on anxiety like, for example, flying on a plane."

"Thank you, doctor, I appreciate that."

"Honestly, I'm surprised your primary care physician never prescribed you any."

I nodded and told her that I'd never told him about my anxiety.

"Alex, here is the prescription. Please have it filled and have her start the medication immediately," Dr. Russo said. "Aubrey, I don't want you to rely solely on the pills. You won't be on them forever. I'll teach you some exercises that will help you cope and deal with situations that bring on anxiety. I want you to think about what causes you anxiety and why. We'll deal with those triggers one by one. Once your anxiety is controlled, your sight might come back all at once. You need to be able to work through what you saw."

I stood up. "Thank you, Dr. Russo."

I didn't say anything. I looked down and then up, and I saw shadows. I shook my head a little and brought my fingers to my temple.

"You okay, babe?"

I looked at Alex. "Yeah, I see shadows. They're becoming clearer though." I stood there a few minutes longer. "There's my gorgeous man." Clear as day. I smiled and turned my head to see Dr. Russo. She was younger than I thought she'd be, probably in her thirties. She probably appreciated Alex's appearance.

"How are you feeling?" Dr. Russo asked.

"I'm good right now, but who knows for how long."

"Just breathe and try not to think about anything negative."

Dr. Russo shouldn't have reminded me. Not knowing when it would go away again made my heart rate pick up. I told myself not to think about it, but I naturally did. I lowered my head.

"Gone, right?" Alex sounded sad.

I hated that. "Yeah. Let's go."

We said good-bye, made my appointments for next week, and headed out. I couldn't wait to leave and go home. My parents were still waiting for us. I told them I'd explain everything when we got home.

Alex suggested he and I go to my apartment after we got my prescription. We got in the car, and it was quiet—too quiet.

"Are you okay?" he asked.

"Yeah, I was caught off guard, that's all. I truly didn't expect to be in the same room with Garrett today, or ever." I didn't want to be with him at all.

"I'm sure it came as a surprise. It did to me too. I'm proud of you for holding your ground. I know you don't want to hear this, but I feel horrible for what I did. I know I apologized and you forgave me, but it makes me sick that I'm partially to blame for this."

"If you recall, I'm not lacking in the blame

department either. Let's just move on, okay? That's the only thing that will make me better."

Alex kissed my left ring finger. "Let's go to the pharmacy, and then I'll take you home. I have to go to the club tonight. Would you like to come with me?"

"No, you go. I think I'll hang with my parents and talk to them. There really isn't a reason for them to stay in the States since I'm not having surgery. Then you can have your place back."

"You want me to leave?"

"I didn't mean it that way. Your place is just more comfortable and closer to the club. I love being with you."

He stopped the car and told me he was going to run in and get my pills. The car door closed, and I was alone. I closed my eyes and did some breathing exercises. I needed to talk to Julie about going to her Yoga classes. I'd just do the breathing, not the movements, or I'd fall on my ass.

We went back to my apartment, and it smelled wonderful. My mom greeted us and said she'd made some canapés and couldn't wait to hear about the appointment.

I smiled. I loved my mom for trying to help. "Sounds great, Mom. I'm going to go change, though. I want to throw on something more comfortable."

"Baby, I need to get to the club," Alex said. "I'll be back as soon as I can."

"Can you help me first?" I needed to get him in my room. I needed to get him inside me.

"Sure, whatever you need."

"We'll be right back, Mom." I went into my room

and heard Alex behind me. I stopped, and I felt Alex against my back. "Close and lock the door, Alex."

I heard the door latch and lock. I spun around, extended my arms, and my hands landed on Alex's taut stomach. I moaned and stepped closer, pushing his back against the door. I ran my hands up his body until my hands were in his hair. "I need you."

His lips forcefully found mine, but they didn't hurt. He felt incredible.

"Make love to me. I want you."

He carried me to the bed, laid me down, and kissed me. He trailed kisses from my jaw to my breasts. I arched my back. I needed him.

"We're not alone, babe," he said.

"I don't care."

Alex took off my pants and unbuttoned my blouse. He pulled down the cups of my bra, and his tongue circled my nipples. He bit down gently, which made me cry out for him.

"Shhh, I don't need your dad running in here."

I sat up and removed my blouse and bra. "I don't care. I want you in me now."

"Whatever you want, whenever you want it. I'll never deny you." Alex sounded beyond sexy.

Before I knew it, we were one, connected. We moved in unison. I knew it wouldn't—well, couldn't—last long. I grabbed his amazing ass and tried to push him in deeper as I raised my hips.

"You're incredible," he said." You feel so good around me. You're warm, tight, and all mine . . . forever."

I was going to explode from the ecstasy in his voice. "Alex, please . . . faster . . ."

That was all he needed. He drove into me until he had to stifle my scream with his mouth. Our tongues met, and I concentrated on the feel and taste of him. When he spilled into me, I felt a need I'd never experienced for anyone else. I didn't want it to end. I wanted him to stay inside me forever.

"Babe, you ready?"

No, I really wasn't. "I guess so."

He pulled out of me, and I sighed.

"We will continue this when I get back and your parents are gone. Then it won't be quick or quiet."

I smiled, and we got cleaned up. We walked out of my room, and I felt like we smelled of sex. Alex gave me a kiss good-bye and told me he loved me and he'd see me later.

Chapter 7

I SAT AT THE TABLE with my parents and went over everything. To say that my mom was surprised to hear about Garrett would be an understatement. She was happy my sight would return without surgery and told me they would stay as long as I wanted.

I didn't want them to do that. They had a life in Paris, and I needed to get back to living as normal a life as I could. "Mom, why don't you and Dad head back to Paris? It's not that I don't want you here, but Christmas is only a month and a half away, and I'd love for you to come back then. I hope by then my sight will have returned." I was trying to be optimistic.

"Actually, your father and I discussed that today. We bought an open-ended ticket, so we'll see when we can go. I want to help you with your wedding plans. Have you and Alex talked about a date?"

"No, not yet. I haven't really thought about it much. I want to see him waiting for me. I want to see my dress. I need to see everything. But when we do set the date, I'll call you so we can start planning."

"That sounds wonderful. Now back to what we need to do for you. Is there anything we can help with?"

"Not really. I just need to work through some things, and once I do, I should be fine. I still can't believe this is happening because of anxiety. Just thinking about that makes me anxious."

"I didn't realize that you had these issues. I'm sorry I didn't pay closer attention." My dad sounded sad.

I reached out, and he took my hand. "It's okay, Daddy. I didn't realize how bad it was either. It's been going on for so long that it just seemed normal."

"Well, we'll all get through this, and you have a wonderful man by your side to help you," my mom said. "Now let's eat before dinner gets cold."

After dinner, my parents left. I took my pill and got ready to head to bed. I grabbed my tablet and decided to read before I fell asleep. Since I was using braille, I only made it through a chapter and a half. I tried to continue, but I must have fallen asleep. I felt the tablet lift from my chest and the silk of my nightie raise. I smelled flowers . . . orchids. Alex.

I decided to try to not move to see what he'd do next. Soft petals started at the base of my neck and continued down the center of my stomach to the top of my panties. Then I felt it on my knee and up my leg, stopping at my hip. My skin prickled. He had to see me getting goose bumps. The flower moved to my cheek and down my neck to the spot that always got me. I flinched and snickered.

"You can't fool me," he said. "But if you want to pretend you're still sleeping so you don't know my next move, that's fine with me."

My eyes were closed. "I can't see your next move

anyways, so it doesn't really matter."

"Open your eyes. I want you to see how much you trust in us." He kissed my cheek. "I love you"—he kissed my eyelids—"and I'm going to make you the happiest woman on the planet, because that's how happy I am." He kissed my lips.

I took a deep breath and pictured our kids from my dream. I pictured Alex having a picnic with me and dancing in the park. I thought of all the things that brought me joy. I smiled and opened my eyes. He was blurry, but he was there. "It's working."

Alex looked at his manhood. "It always works, baby." He kissed me again.

I laughed in his mouth. "No, not that. I know that works. I meant my eyes."

Alex propped himself up. "You can see?"

I blinked a few times and took a cleansing breath. "I thought of you, us, and of my dream. Maybe that's my 'happy place.'"

"I got your happy place."

I giggled and took a deep breath. Alex took off my nightie and entered me. He looked into my eyes as I stared into his. I saw love. I saw my fiancé, the man I'd spend the rest of my life with.

Alex moved in and out of me slowly. His eyes never left mine. "I want to see your eyes as we make love. I want you to see me lose myself in you."

I ran my hands up his back and remembered his tattoo. I couldn't wait to see it again. I looked to my left and saw an orchid lying on a notebook. My heart raced as I thought about my journal. N*o, no, no, no don't think about that.* Tears escaped my eyes, and my chest vibrated under Alex.

"Babe, what is it? Am I hurting you?"

I shook my head. "No, the notebook . . ." My voice broke. "On the nightstand. Please get rid of it."

Without leaving me, he threw it in a drawer. "It's gone. Are you okay?"

I took deep breaths, and every time I did, I felt his penis bob inside me. *He's with me. He's not gone. He loves me, and we're okay. You can do this, Aubrey, everything is okay.*

Alex didn't move. I looked up and could still see his face.

"I'm okay. Just love me, please, Alex."

We made love, and everything was as it should be.

I lay in bed with Alex, and I could see him. "Thank you."

"I should thank you. You're unbelievable."

We kissed as if we were starved for each other. I loved everything about him. He was strong, and I was grateful for him. He rolled us to our sides.

I just stared at him. "I'm sorry I left you. Maybe if I hadn't, I would've found out about my condition sooner."

"It's in the past, Aubrey. I don't want you thinking about that. You don't know what would have happened if you'd stayed here." He sounded scared.

I knew he was worried about me losing my sight, but I felt calm and comfortable. I didn't know if it was the medication or the fact that I'd talked and breathed my way through an "episode," but I felt a sense of relief and serenity. "Hey, can I see your tattoo?"

"Oh . . . I should tell you something about that."

I lowered my brows. “Okay, can I still see it?” I wanted to kiss it again.

Alex slowly rolled over, and I stared at his shoulder. The orchid had his mom’s and sister’s names on two angel wing petals, but they were joined by another. I looked closer and sat up on my knees. My hand covered my mouth.

Alex looked back at me. “Do you like it?”

“When did you . . . Alex . . . my name. You added my name?”

“I needed the three women I love together.” He smiled and his eyes brightened.

My heart fluttered. “When did you add me? While you were in Paris?”

“No, when you were in the hospital. The day you kicked me out and told me you were leaving. I needed you with me, even if it was just ink. I know some people believe that if you tattoo the name of your significant other on your body, then the relationship will end, but we were already broken up. Anyways, I’m not superstitious, and I didn’t have anything to lose. “

“I don’t know what to say. Thank you doesn’t seem like enough.” I leaned down and kissed his tattoo. I looked at the leaf with his mom’s name, ran my index finger over it, and kissed it. “Your son is wonderful.” Then I looked at him. “Thank you.”

Another day passed without me losing my sight. I was scared to go to sleep, but I was happy when I woke and saw Alex. He was usually awake before me and would wait to see how I was. Since it was Thursday, I had an appointment with Dr. Russo. I couldn’t wait to see her and tell her that I could see. I didn't want to sound overly confident that my sight had permanently returned, but I didn't want to think about it going away either. If it was just a fluke, I'd really flip out.

Alex drove me to the appointment. I looked at the few trees. Their leaves had changed, and some limbs were bare. I loved the fall. We stopped at a red light, and Alex looked at me. Our eyes met. I could stare at him all day.

"I have a surprise for you." He beamed his megawatt smile.

"You do, huh? What is it?"

"You think you're a clever girl, but there's no way I'm going to tell you."

"Hmmm . . . Okay, Mr. Logan, when am I getting this surprise?"

"Well, future Mrs. Logan, I'll take you to it after your appointment."

I was surprised. "It's a place? Is it close? Have we been there before?"

"Miss Twenty Questions, I'm not telling you, but I'll give you an 'A' for effort."

The light changed. We were laughing when we walked into the doctor's office because I'd continued my inquisition. I looked up and saw Garrett in the waiting room. We stopped laughing.

"Hey, Garrett, how are you?" I asked.

"Hi, Aubrey. How did you know I was here? Did you get your vision back?"

"Yes, I did."

"Congratulations." Garrett seemed genuinely happy

for me. Garrett looked at Alex and extended his hand. "Logan."

Alex eventually reached out and shook his hand. "Reed."

"Garrett, would you mind coming into my appointment for a few minutes?" I knew I should have asked Alex before I spoke. I glanced at Alex to try to gauge what he was thinking, but he had no expression. He didn't even look at me.

Garrett did though. He smiled brightly and said he'd be glad to. He left to check to see if Dr. Russo was ready. I nodded and sat in a chair. Alex sat next to me and stared forward.

I turned toward him "Alex, please understand. I need him in there for what I need to say."

He looked at me. "Whatever you need is fine, baby."

Garrett came back to tell us they were ready. We walked in and were greeted by Dr. Russo.

"Aubrey, it's good to see you, and you too, Alex."

"It's good to see you too." I smiled.

"I'm happy to hear you say that. I understand you wanted Dr. Reed present today?" She sounded as if she didn't believe Garrett and needed to hear it from me.

"Yes, just for a few minutes, if that's okay."

"Of course. So tell me, how are you?"

I sat on the couch, and Alex sat next to me. Garrett and Dr. Russo took the chairs in front of us.

"I'm great. That's actually why I wanted Garrett here." I took a breath and counted to five in my head—that seemed to help. I cleared my throat and tried to sound as confident as I could. "Garrett, I wanted to thank you for all that you've done for me. If you hadn't written your thesis about the effects of anxiety and stress, I may not have ever been diagnosed correctly. I still might be blind. I don't think I'll ever be able to repay you for that. I also wanted to wish you luck in the future and hope you're as happy as I am." I grabbed Alex's hand, which he brought to his lips and kissed.

Garrett looked at my hand in Alex's and then back to me. "Thank you. I hope that your sight stays and your anxiety remains controlled. I'm happy for you and Alex, and I wish you both nothing but the best."

I stood, and Alex did as well. I dropped his hand and hugged Garrett. "Thank you." I returned to Alex's side.

He shook Garrett's hand before Garrett left the room. I wasn't sure if I'd ever see him again, but that was okay because I didn't need to. We sat back down to continue with Dr. Russo.

Dr. Russo scribbled on her notepad and then looked at us. "So, Aubrey, how did that feel?"

I thought about the question before I answered. "Liberating, I suppose. I don't know why, but I feel lighter in a way, stronger, I guess." I shrugged.

Dr. Russo nodded and wrote again. "Mmm hmm. Lighter how? What do you mean by that? Do you think you were afraid that you still might have unresolved feelings toward Dr. Reed?"

Alex sat up straighter and stared forward. I noticed Dr. Russo shift her eyes between me and Alex, who looked tense.

"No, I don't have feelings for him," I said. "I think

that I just felt unsettled."

"And now? How do you feel now?"

"Better now that he knows that he hurt me. I didn't think he cared. I feel better knowing that he knows what he did made me feel used. I don't know how else to explain it."

Alex decided to chime in. "If I may speak?"

Dr. Russo directed her attention toward Alex. "Please, go ahead."

"I think that what Garrett did to Aubrey not only made her feel used, but unworthy of accepting love. I think he did a head trip on her that affected her on many levels. She doesn't see the beautiful woman I see, and her confidence was shattered. At work, she's self-assured and knows that she's good at what she does. That's totally the opposite of the way she is with her personal life."

My mouth hung open. I kept looking between Alex and Dr. Russo waiting for them to say something else.

I was about to say something, but Dr. Russo beat me to it. "And what about what you did? What impact do you think that had on Aubrey?"

Alex's brow furrowed, and his face dropped. He rubbed his chin and looked uncomfortable. "When she witnessed my stupidity, it manifested into something bigger: blindness. But I love Aubrey, and I apologized. Garrett just dumped her and left."

"You used a past relationship to harm someone you claimed to love. How did that make you feel?"

Shit! I didn't know what to do.

"I'll never forgive myself for hurting her. I broke a promise I made." Alex looked at me and cupped my cheek. "I promise I'll never intentionally hurt you again. I'll make mistakes, but I'll never do it on purpose."

I leaned over, not caring that we were in the middle of a therapy session, and hugged him. "No more apologies. We both made mistakes. We're good, better than good." I moved my left hand in front of him. "See this? I said yes. I'm going to be Mrs. Alex Logan." I smiled and kissed him.

Alex looked into my eyes and nodded. Then he looked over my shoulder at the doctor and back at me, raising his brow. I winked and got off his lap, which I hadn't noticed I'd climbed on.

Dr. Russo looked at us and smiled. "Aubrey, I think it's wonderful that you have worked through some of your issues. I still think we should meet twice a week. Between the medication and your ability to now cope with impending anxiety issues, I think, in time, you'll be fine. But if you feel the need to see me between appointments, please don't hesitate to call. I'm proud of you and what you've accomplished in a short amount of time. I think you were figuring out in Paris why you had flashes of sight. Whoever was with you in Paris must have made you comfortable. You should surround yourself with people like them."

I smirked. I had been there with my parents and Alex, even if I didn't know it was him. "Do you really think I'll be okay?"

"I think you'll be more than okay. You gave yourself time to recover physically, and you're recovering emotionally. Trust in yourself, and I don't foresee any future issues. But like I said, I'm here for you if you need me." She looked at Alex. "That goes for you too.

Even though you haven't suffered any physical trauma, there's no doubt you have emotionally. I suspect you're afraid of losing Aubrey, so you pushed her away to protect yourself."

Alex said, "Thank you, doctor. We'll see you next week."

We left the appointment, and I felt as if a weight had been lifted off my chest. For once in my life, I felt as though I had control of my feelings. Alex opened the car door for me, and I slid into my seat. He walked around the front, and I appreciated the view. He wore loose hanging, button-fly jeans and a navy T-shirt that perfectly clung to his body. He was delicious, and I just wanted to taste him. I couldn't take my eyes off of him. He opened his door and got inside.

I couldn't believe Dr. Russo had said those things to Alex. I wondered if he'd held on to his grief over his mom and sister for so long that it was affecting him. I didn't think he'd ever really talked about his feelings with anyone other than me, and we'd just scratched the surface of what he felt. I wanted to bring it up, but he interrupted my thoughts.

"Ready?"

"For what?" I knew what I was ready for—him. His voice did that to me.

"Your surprise." He winked, and we took off.

I looked around, trying to figure out where we were headed. I thought maybe we were going to lunch, but he had already passed several restaurants. "Where are we going?"

He grinned at me. "You're not going to give up, are you?"

I giggled. "Can't blame a girl for trying."

"I guess not, but you'll see soon enough. Hey, you know what?"

"Hmm?"

"You're beautiful, and I'm extremely proud of you." Alex kept his eyes on the road, but he grabbed my hand and kissed my knuckles, licking them lightly.

I hoped we were going somewhere with a bed. "Thank you. It's because of you, well, because of Chance."

"What is?"

"My flashes of sight. It's because you were with me in Paris. I don't care if you were Chance, Alex, or Santa Claus—it was you. You knew what I needed, and you gave it to me." The car slowed to a stop. I looked out the window and noticed we were near Creekside Park. "A picnic?"

"I can't get anything past you." Alex chuckled.

I looked at the joy in his eyes, and I felt like melting. "I love picnics with you."

"Well, that's a good thing because here we are and that is what we're doing."

We got out of the car, and Alex walked around to the trunk. He took out a blanket and a basket and one of his sweaters. I took the blanket, and he carried the basket and held my hand. The park was fairly empty except for a few runners. Alex found a spot, took the blanket, and laid it on the grass. It was early November, and it was chilly outside.

He set the basket down and handed me his sweater. "I figured you might be cold, so I brought you my sweater."

I put his sweater on over my jacket. Even if I wasn't cold, I wanted to be in his sweater. It was comforting and smelled of him. "Thank you. You think of everything."

Alex opened the basket and took out a bottle of sparkling grape juice, a cheese and fruit platter, and sandwiches. He spread out the food and poured the faux wine. "I know it's not the real thing, but since you can't drink because of your medication, this is the next best thing." Then he reached into the basket, took out a white orchid, and handed it to me.

"Thank you. My favorite." I brought my nose to the flower and glided it across my cheek. I looked at him, and his eyes were shining brightly.

Alex opened and poured our wine and set the glasses on top of the basket. "I'm so happy that you can see and that we worked through everything. I told you I'd do this again once you could see. Can I have your ring, please?"

I gave it to him reluctantly even though I guessed what he was about to do. I didn't want to ever take it off.

He shifted, got on one knee, and took my hands. "Aubrey Ryan, you are the love I have always dreamed of, my life and my future. There isn't anything I wouldn't do for you. I want us to share everything, have children, and grow old together. I'd go to the ends of the earth a million times and back for you. We'll make mistakes along the way, but we'll learn from them and become stronger together. I trust you with my heart. Will you trust me with yours and be my wife?"

Even though we were already engaged, it felt like a new proposal. I felt the love pouring from him. "I will trust you with my heart, and I promise to take care of yours. I'd love nothing more than to spend the rest of my life with you. Yes, I'll be your wife."

I watched as he slipped the ring on my finger, and I couldn't help but get choked up. I looked into his gorgeous eyes. He smiled and hugged me until I fell back on the blanket. He hovered over me, his arms supporting him, and our chests brushed together. That was enough to make my nipples stand at attention. He dropped his lips to mine, and I savored him. My head spun with desire.

He lowered onto me and rolled us to our sides. Moving his right hand through my hair, he whispered, "You've made me whole."

"I'm so glad you came up to me at that dumb speed dating event, and I'm even more grateful you came to Paris to be with me."

He rolled onto his back, and my head rested on his shoulder. After about a minute, he said, "An elephant."

"Uh . . . are you hallucinating?" I snickered. "What are you talking about?"

He pointed at the sky. "That cloud. See it? It looks like it has a trunk like an elephant."

I looked and couldn't help but smile as I remembered him describing clouds to me in Paris. "Yeah, I see it. You know what else I see?" I turned to look at him.

"No, what's that?"

"The man I'm going to make love to for the rest of my life. The man I'm going to do things to that he'll never forget." I ran my index finger from his temple to his chin.

He sounded sexy as hell when he replied, "I never forget anything you do to me, and I look forward to doing you for the rest of my life."

We laughed and carried on with our picnic.

Chapter 8

My parents were leaving that afternoon, so we had breakfast together. My parents were a little sad to leave. Well, my dad was. I think my mom was happy to be going back because compared to New York, living in Paris was an everyday vacation.

We dropped my parents off at the airport and headed over to the club. I was excited to see Julie, Brett, Mark, and Val. I couldn't wait to hang out together like normal people. It was Friday, so happy hour would be busy. Normally that would make me anxious, but I just had to look at my left hand to see that I belonged to Alex. I still wore the stunning bracelet he'd given me too. I felt as though I should get Alex something, but I didn't know what. I'd have to think about that. He didn't seem like the jewelry type. He wore a nice watch, but that was about it.

We pulled into the back lot, and I remembered what we'd almost done the last time we were there. The thought started a pulsing between my legs. I smiled and opened my door. Even the cool air didn't tame my thoughts. Alex came over and looked at my chest.

I followed his eyes and noticed my nipples were

erect. "What? It's cold out here."

"Whatever you say, baby." Alex chuckled, grabbed my hand, and led me into the club.

We said hi to Tyler, and he told us that everyone was upstairs. We walked up, and I stopped at the top of the stairs to appreciate what I was seeing. Brett's arm was on the back of Julie's chair. She looked gorgeous as always, and they both looked happy. Mark held Val's hand on the table top. Everyone looked content. I had awesome friends. I smiled at the thought of them all.

"You okay?" Alex asked.

I'd totally forgotten he was next to me. "Yeah, I'm fantastic. Let's go sit with our friends."

We walked up to the table, and everyone stopped talking and looked at me. They were probably trying to figure out if I could see them. It had to be weird for them too.

I smiled. "You all can stop staring at me now."

Julie jumped up. "You know what this means? We're going to dance until we drop tonight! I'm so excited for you!" She grabbed me for one of her bone-crushing hugs.

I laughed. "I wore my dancing shoes, so damn right we're going to dance."

Alex chimed in, "First we drink and toast to my beautiful fiancée."

Brett coughed into his fist, "Pussy whipped."

We all laughed, except for Alex. "Fuck you, man. You have it worse than I do. If Julie told you to wear a thong, you would."

"Only if it's her pink lace one. That one's the most comfortable."

Alex just stared at him with a dumbfounded expression. We were dying of laughter. The waitress brought us our drinks, and we could hardly thank her because of our hysteria.

Alex grabbed his glass and raised it. "To Aubrey getting better, to great friends, and to never, ever seeing Brett in Julie's thong."

Our hysteria came back, and I could hardly drink. I thought I'd either choke or the drink would come out of my nose. I looked at Mark joking around with Alex and Brett. I was about to ask Val how things were when Mark stopped laughing. His face dropped as he looked past me. I turned around to see a beautiful woman strolling toward us. Jessica.

Mark threw his arm around Val, who looked as though she was going to be sick. She had seen pictures of Jessica and knew who she was. I could relate to what she was feeling. Val looked into my eyes and silently pleaded with me to do something. I had no clue what that should be, so I did the only thing I could think of.

I stood up and intercepted Jessica. "Did you need something? This is a private party." I couldn't help but sound annoyed. I needed to protect my friend.

Jessica looked over my shoulder at Mark and Val. "I'm not here for you, whoever you are. I need to talk to Mark." She waved as if she was dismissing me and went to step around me.

I moved as she did. "I'm Aubrey, and my fiancé owns this club. It is my business because Mark is one of my best friends, and you aren't invited to this party."

I looked at everyone. Mark was looking down and Julie was ready to pounce.

Alex stood and came over to us. He stood behind me with his hands on my shoulders. "Like Aubrey said, this is a private party. If you need something, say so. If not, please go back down stairs. I have security in the club, and I would prefer not to call them. If you keep this up, I will. Why don't you head to the bar? Your drinks are on me."

"Who the hell are you? I'm not here for a drink. I'm here to talk to Mark." She was getting aggravated.

"I'm Alex Logan, and this is my club. As has been stated, this is a private party."

Mark said, "It's fine, man. I'll talk to her. Thanks for trying." Mark walked away, and Jessica followed.

My heart broke for Valerie, who guzzled her drink. I couldn't believe Mark went with her. I was disgusted, and apparently it showed. Alex and I watched Mark and Jessica go downstairs. Alex looked as if he wanted to kick Mark's ass.

I tried to calm his impending blow up. "Hon, he probably didn't want to make a scene, that's all. Don't be mad at Mark."

"Yeah, I know. But it's not fair to Val."

We looked at her, and she stared at us. We sat and tried to act as normal as possible.

Julie was the first one to break the silence. "What the hell was that? I get that they were in a relationship, but Mark should have told her to go to hell. He's being a douche right now."

I was a little surprised. "Jules, he loved her. Cut him some slack." *Where did that come from?*

Val spit, "Would you cut Alex some slack if that was Leah?"

"Val, don't," Alex warned.

"Really, Val? You want to go there?" I tried not to sound bitchy, but it didn't work. "No, if that was Leah, I wouldn't cut Alex slack because he didn't love Leah. He had sex with her." That thought made my stomach turn. "Mark loved Jessica. There's a difference."

"Baby, don't get upset. It's not good for you." Alex sounded protective, and I loved it, but it wasn't helping.

"Oh, I'm not getting upset. I'm already upset. I can't believe you would throw Leah into the mix. I'm sorry, Val, but one has nothing to do with the other. You don't even know what they're talking about. Take it from me, overreacting isn't the answer. Nor is throwing Leah in my face. I was trying to help you." My voice accelerated.

Brett chimed in, "Who wants a drink?"

"I do." I grabbed my purse and jacket and headed toward the stairs.

Alex was a few steps behind me. "Aubrey, slow down."

I kept walking.

"Babe, stop for a second."

I stopped and turned toward him. "What!"

He put his hands up. "Look, Val's just upset. I'm sure she didn't mean anything. You know it's just you for me."

I relaxed my shoulders which were up to my ears. I exhaled. "Yeah, I know. When Val gets like that, I'm reminded of the first time I met her and she was mean to me because she wanted you. I don't know, maybe she still does and Mark is her consolation guy."

"I'm whose consolation guy?"

Shit. I hadn't seen Mark walking toward us. "No one's. Where's Jessica?"

"She left." Mark sounded relieved and sad.

"What did she want?" I asked.

"She wanted money. Apparently, the guy she left me for cleaned her out. So she can't pay her rent and wanted me to help her or let her crash at my place." He shook his head in disbelief.

Alex asked, "She moved back to the city?"

Mark shrugged. "Apparently. Great way to find out, right?"

"What did you tell her?" I asked.

"I told her no. That's not my problem. I'm happy with Val, and I don't want or need her anymore. I reminded her that she was no longer mine by her own choice. She's not my problem." He shrugged, but it obviously bothered him. Mark was a nice guy, and he probably felt badly for her, no matter how she had treated him.

"I'm glad to hear that because Val is pretty upset," Alex said.

Mark looked at me. "What happened? What's going on?"

I looked from Alex to Mark. "Val is really upset. We had some words, but don't worry about it. Everything will be fine." The last thing Mark needed to worry about was Val and me being at odds.

Mark hugged me. "Thank you both for trying to get rid of Jessica. Let's go back upstairs. We're celebrating tonight."

I looked to Alex for some sign of what he wanted to do.

"Mark, you head up. Aubrey and I will be there in a minute."

Mark nodded and walked away.

Alex turned to me. "You can't possibly think I'd take anyone's side over yours. Val is a good friend of mine, like Mark is to you. She shouldn't she have said what she did, but you can't really be mad at her for it."

"What?" Was he kidding me? I was getting pissed, not at Val, but at Alex. I glared at him.

Alex held my face. "Look at me, Aubrey. I mean really look at me."

I crossed my arms, cocked my hip, and glared into his eyes.

"You and me, forever. It's just you. Let's go back to our friends and continue our celebration. I've had enough of exes lately." He kissed my lips. "When we get home, I'm going to make love to you all night." He kissed me again, owning my mouth. He brought his hands to the small of my back and down to my ass.

I uncrossed my arms as he pulled me in tight. Our kiss ended, and I felt winded.

"That's just a prelude of what's to come," he promised.

I smiled. "Then let's not make this a long evening."

He grabbed my hand, and we went back to the table to sit with our friends.

Val spoke first. "Aubrey, I'm sorry for what I said. I didn't mean it. I really didn't." The sadness in Val's tone and look in her glassed-over eyes proved to me that she wasn't lying.

"It's okay. I understand, I guess. Let's just make a pact not to bring up exes, okay?" I hated being in situations like that. I just wanted it all forgotten. I liked Val, and the fact that she made Mark happy was enough for me to try to forgive her. Plus I knew Alex would want her in the wedding party.

Brett asked Alex, "Hey, what did your old man say about your wedding plans?"

He took a sip of his drink. "I haven't told him yet."

I lowered my head. We'd had too much going on. "Are you going to tell him? Don't you want him to know we're getting married?"

"Yeah, I'll tell him. Actually, we can go see him on Monday and tell him together."

That wasn't what I wanted to hear. I didn't really want to be included. I liked Jack, but his relationship with his only son made me sad. I'd never understand how a parent could just turn away from his son. Not that Alex had helped the situation. It was just an odd dynamic.

"Oh my God, this party is going stale! Let's dance. Come on, girls!" Julie motioned for Val and me to get up. She looked back at the table. "If our guys don't want us grabbing other partners, they'd better get their asses on the floor too."

We all laughed and followed a bouncy Julie to the dance floor. Her hands were waving above her head to the beat of the music before we even got to the dance floor. A few women tried to approach Alex, but he didn't pay attention to them. I thought about getting him a shirt that said TAKEN, but that probably wouldn't do anything.

Alex grabbed me around the waist and pulled me into him when "Ain't No Other Man" by Christina Aguilera came on. Julie pulled me and Val away from the guys, huddled us together, and told us she had an idea. I was nervous about it, but Val loved it. Before I knew it, Julie had turned us into a girl group. We danced and sang for our men who just stood there looking at us. They all had shit-eating grins.

The dancers on the floor moved out of our way, and we gave something like a private performance that they'd see in a different type of club. Shockingly, I totally got into it. I didn't know if it was the events of the past few days or if I was just a woman in love dancing for her man. We all had our own way to get our man's attention. Julie grinded her ass on Brett, Val teased Mark with her boobs, and I had no choice to do anything other than grind against Alex. He'd pulled me in close and put his leg between mine.

Alex's hands supported my back as he dipped me. His head went to my chest, and he kissed me between my breasts. My hands went into his hair. He grabbed the back of my head and smashed his lips on mine. His tongue shot in my mouth like a dart. My hands went from his abs to his shoulders and back down. I was about to rip off his shirt when I realized where we were. I pulled away, and he looked at me. I smiled and licked my lips as my eyes trailed the length of his body. He grabbed my hand and pulled me off the dance floor. We didn't care about the people staring at us. We needed to be together.

He brought me to his office, slammed the door shut, and slammed me against it. I think that if I wasn't so hot with need for him, it would have hurt. We kissed, and he unbuttoned my jeans. I helped him pull them down, and he took off my shirt. I had a g-string on, which he ripped off of me until I stood in only my bra. I reached for his T-shirt, but he had it off before I could do anything. His pants and boxers followed suit, as did my bra.

He lifted me, and I wrapped my legs around him. No foreplay was needed since we were both more than ready. He thrust into me, and I yelped. I was ready for him, but he hit me so deep. My yelp seemed to be a "do it harder" signal. He pulled my hair so my head tilted back, and his mouth traveled over my breasts, not showing any favoritism. We moved with each other, and I lifted myself up using his shoulders. I was about to come, and if I didn't support myself, I was sure I would land on my ass.

"I got you, baby. You're so tight around me right now, you don't even have to hang on."

Those words groaned in my ear were enough to send me over the edge. My legs shook, Alex leaned back, and I arched against the door. With his left arm around my back, his right thumb rubbed me right above my entrance and then below it. I couldn't hold on anymore.

"Alex . . ." I couldn't say anymore.

He thrust into me and grunted. His warmth filled me, and my head collapsed on his sweaty shoulder.

I saw his tattoo out of the corner of my eye. I looked into his eyes. "December twenty-first."

"What about it?"

"Our wedding. I'd like it to be on December twenty-first."

His eyes filled, and he closed them. "That's my

mom's birthday. I think that would be . . . perfect."

I kissed his forehead. "Then that's when it will be."

We put ourselves back together, but my thong stayed on Alex's desk. We went back downstairs where our friends were still dancing. Alex pulled me into a corner and hugged me. I tipped my head up so I could see him.

"Does my hair look okay, or do I have the 'JFL'?"

He looked confused. "JFL?"

"Yeah, the 'Just Fucked Look.'" I couldn't believe he'd never heard that expression.

He laughed. Without looking at me, he said, "No, you're perfect. Let's go dance."

The song was slower, and one that meant a lot to us. It was "Talking to the Moon" by Bruno Mars. We swayed back and forth.

His thumbs made circles on my lower back as he held me. "I talked to the moon a lot before I followed you to Paris. When you were in the hospital, I'd go to Jones Beach and talk to the waves, hoping that you could hear me somehow."

"Is that why you told me to listen to the wave in your message?" I remembered him saying it. I'd never been quite sure why.

"Yeah, I didn't know what else to do. I'd just go stare at the water. I needed to get to you somehow, and I didn't know when you would hear my message or if it would mean what I wanted it to. I was desperate, so I took a chance."

"And you became Chance, Chance Love." I laughed, and he smirked at me. "What made you think of using Love for a last name?"

"I panicked. I didn't think of a last name, and then when you asked, the first thing I thought of was *L'Amour*. I was pretty proud of myself that I had the sense to come up with that."

I put my head down and laughed. He picked me up and spun me around. When he put me down, we were both laughing. We noticed our friends leaving the dance floor. I wanted to dance more, but we'd taken a break from dancing and they hadn't. Not that I'd rested on our break, but I felt energized. We followed our friends back to the table. Tyler brought us drinks and sat with us.

"Dude, so where did you and Aubrey run off to? I turned and you were gone." Brett had a shit-eating grin. He totally knew where we were.

My face instantly heated.

Julie looked at me and raised a brow. "Really? You don't look JFL. Were you standing?"

My mouth dropped open, and Alex laughed, along with the rest of the table.

Brett said, "What the hell is JFL?"

Julie leaned in and told him. He laughed and clued in the rest of the table as I lowered my head in embarrassment.

"You're a lucky man!" Brett lifted his hand to high five Alex, but Alex just shook his head.

Mark whispered something to Val before he said to the table, "On that note, we're outta here." Mark and Val stood.

"Hold on just a minute. Aubrey and I have an announcement," Alex said.

Everyone went silent. Alex was like E.F. Hutton.

When he talked, people listened.

"Aubrey and I have set a date. We're getting married on December twenty-first."

Julie squealed and clapped. "Yay! When are we going gown shopping? I'm in the wedding, right?"

I loved her enthusiasm. I looked at Alex and quietly asked him if we could have everyone at the table in the wedding. He nodded.

"Yes, you're my maid of honor," I said. "Val, I'd love for you to be my bridesmaid."

The girls got up and hugged me. We spun around in a circle as if we were girls on a playground.

Alex looked at the guys. "Brett, you're the closest thing I have to a brother, and I'd like you to be my best man. Ty and Mark, I'd be honored if you would also stand up for me as groomsmen."

All the guys did the handshake, bro-hug thing. I looked at the group and realized I was short a bridesmaid.

As if Julie read my mind, she said, "Don't worry Aubrey, I can handle two at once." She winked.

Tyler looked at her and then at Brett. "Right on!" They high-fived and threw their arms around Julie.

Brett looked at Tyler. "Just remember she's mine."

"Yeah, I know. You don't have to take all the fun out of it."

Val asked Alex, "Wait a minute, wasn't December twenty-first your mom's birthday?"

"Yeah, it was." He looked at me. "Hey, how did you know that?"

I shrugged. "It was on the program at the benefit

you and your dad had."

Alex nodded, and we walked out of the club. We laced our fingers and walked to his car. He opened my door, but before I could get in, he pulled me into an embrace. He held my head under his chin and smelled my hair. I felt safe, wanted, loved, and needed. Everything that I'd always wanted and needed from a man.

"I love you. I'll say it often and every chance I can," he said. "I hope you never get sick of me saying it." His arms tightened.

"Never. I'll never, ever get sick of hearing that. The same goes for you. I love you more every day."

"Come on, let's go home." He let go of my hand and walked around to his side of the car.

I watched him slide into his seat. All I could think about was how happy he made me. Despite all the obstacles we'd encountered in such a short time, he was mine. There was no doubt about it.

Chapter 9

WE WENT BACK TO HIS place and got ready for bed. I watched his muscles flex as he undressed. Alex was the only man I knew who could make taking socks off look sexy as hell. I couldn't take my eyes off him.

"See something you like?" Even his voice was amazing.

"No, not really. Same old thing. Seen it once, seen it a million times." I walked into the bathroom, took off my clothes, and threw on a T-shirt I had taken out of his drawer. I brushed my hair since it was coated in product, washed my face, and leaned over the sink to brush my teeth with his toothbrush.

I looked in the mirror and saw him. He leaned against the door frame, his right arm on the wall to support him. His arms, tight stomach, and chest begged me to go over and lick them. I continued brushing.

"So are you calling me old or are you just bored with what you see?" His eyes met mine in the mirror.

I tried not to smile. I rinsed my mouth and wiped my face with a hand towel. I turned to look at him.

"No, you're not old." Then it dawned on me that I didn't know his birthday. "When is your birthday?"

"August twenty-seventh. When is yours?"

I gasped. "I missed it. I'm so sorry. I wish I'd been with you. If I hadn't left, I would have been." I looked down.

He walked up and held my face. "You were with me. We were at the park looking at clouds. I spent my twenty-ninth birthday with you, and it was the best birthday I've ever had. Now, when is yours?"

"February sixth."

"You'll celebrate your first birthday with me as Mrs. Logan."

I smiled. "It's weird, isn't it? We're getting married without even knowing each other's birthdays. How did that happen?"

"We haven't really had a conventional relationship." His arms wrapped around me so his hands rested on the top of my butt. "How about we get to know each other? We can make it a game."

"Hmmm . . . I like games. What do you have in mind?"

He grabbed my hand and led me to the bed. "Have a seat." He left the room and came back with a handful of poker chips. He sat on the bed and put the chips in a pile between us. "The poker chips have a value on them: twenty-five, fifty, and one hundred. Pick a twenty-five and ask a question; pick a fifty and answer a question; pick a one hundred and you must do something the other tells you to do. Deal?"

I was nervous about what he would ask me and vice versa. "Okay."

"You ready, baby? You can go first." He mixed up the chips.

"Okay." I took a calming breath. I closed my eyes and picked a chip—twenty-five. I breathed a sigh of relief. "Um . . . how old were you the first time you had sex?"

He smiled. "Sixteen."

"Sixteen! Do you remember it?" I don't know why I needed to know that.

"That's two questions. But since you asked, yes, I do, and it wasn't anything to be proud of. It lasted about five minutes." He laughed.

I don't know why I'd asked that question. I knew we weren't each other's firsts, but his answer made me sad.

He smirked, closed his eyes, and picked a chip with a fifty on it. He dropped his head and laughed. "Hit me with another one. Maybe this wasn't such a great game."

I softly said, "Do you remember her?"

"Who?"

"The girl you lost your virginity to."

He lowered his brows, probably wondering why I wanted to know. I hoped he didn't ask because I didn't even know why. "Yeah, I remember her."

I nodded.

"Go, baby, pick." Alex was really enjoying his game!

Please not a fifty . . . Thank God, another twenty-five!

He shook his head. "This is not working in my favor at all!"

I laughed and tried to think of something I'd be interested in. "What's your favorite type of music?"

"That's easy. Anything that I can hold you close and dance to. But if I was alone, I guess it would be rock. Okay, my turn."

I beamed.

"What's that look for? You like rock too?"

"I do, but I love dancing with you. When I was younger, I'd watch ballroom dance competitions. The women had gorgeous gowns, and they just moved effortlessly. They were beautiful. I wanted to be like them."

Alex looked at me as if I had revealed where the Holy Grail was.

I shrugged and grinned. "Anyway, that never happened. It's your turn to pick."

Alex reached in the pile, and my nerves spiked. "Finally!" he said.

Alex had picked a twenty-five. I was nervous about what his question would be.

His eyes smoldered. "What did you first think of me when you saw me?"

I stared at him. How did he not know the answer? "Well, let's see. Considering your predecessors who spoke to me that night, when I heard your voice, my heart skipped a beat. I think it would have done that even if you were the first man I'd spoken to that night. I was stunned. I thought you were hotter than hot, and I had no clue why you wanted to talk to me."

He reached across the chips for my hand, which he brought to his mouth, and kissed my fingertips one by one. "That was the best thing I've ever done." He leaned over and kissed me.

His soft lips and light stubble made me melt. I felt

myself blush. I lowered my head because I didn't want to show my embarrassment.

He sat back down. "You don't get it, do you? It doesn't matter how many times I tell you." He lifted my chin. "Look into my eyes and listen to me, okay?"

I looked at him and got lost in the deep blue of his eyes.

"You, Aubrey Ryan, are beautiful. You're sexy and my dream come true. Now, stop asking ridiculous questions and pick a chip."

I let out a long breath, closed my eyes, and prayed for anything but a fifty. I put my right hand in the chips, closed my eyes, mixed them around, and picked. I looked at my hand—a fifty. Shit.

He looked at the chip and rubbed his hands. "Let's see . . . What should I ask . . . Hmm . . . What's something sexual you've always fantasized about doing but haven't done yet?"

I stared at him. I kept thinking that I wanted him to do whatever he wanted to me, but I couldn't put that out there. A light bulb went off, and I yelled, "Oh! I know."

Alex laughed and I giggled. *Way to blow a hot moment. I'm such a dork.*

I regained my composure, got on my knees, and leaned toward him. In the sexiest voice I could muster, I told him, "I want to blindfold you, cover you in chocolate sauce, and lick you like an ice cream cone. Then I want to make love to you, savor you, and enjoy every square inch of your amazingly hot body."

I hadn't intended to say anything after blindfold, but he smelled so sweet that I thought of dessert and chocolate. I sat back and looked at him. He looked shocked. Which was understandable since I was also shocked.

I tried to play it cool though. "I believe it's your turn." I grinned and winked.

"Shit, I don't know if I can move after that."

I laughed.

While looking into my eyes, he grabbed a chip. He looked at it, and a mischievous grin crept across his lips. He held it up. "One hundred, baby." His eyes got dark as he cocked a brow and looked into my eyes. "Go get the chocolate. Game's over . . . I win."

I didn't question his seriousness. The look in his eye told me he wasn't kidding, so I gracefully got up and went into his kitchen. My bare feet on the cool tile was what I needed because the entire thing was surreal, and I was sweating. I opened the refrigerator door and welcomed the blast of cool air. I found the chocolate sauce he liked on his ice cream and decided to warm it up to take off the chill.

Once it was ready, I steadied myself. Before I went into our room, I took a deep breath and quietly said, "You can do this, Aubrey. It was your idea, and you love each other." I walked into the room.

He was lying naked on the bed. The chips had been moved to the dresser, and he was alert and ready. I tried not to stare at my man's statuesque body, but that was a ridiculous notion. I set the bottle on the dresser and removed my T-shirt. I put some chocolate sauce on my middle finger and sucked it off. I looked at his dick, and it bobbed. Good, just what I wanted.

I folded the T-shirt and placed it over his eyes.

"Don't move."

I bent over and ran my tongue across his broad chest. I drizzled the chocolate where my tongue had been and slowly licked it away. I made a line with the sauce from his pecs to the wonderful V of his hips. I didn't lick it right away. I crawled between his legs, rested my hands on his thighs, and started at the V. I licked my way up while allowing my breasts to rub against him, making him groan and bend his knees. I kissed down to his waist. I pulled back and poured chocolate from his tip to the base of his erection, and I watched his abs flex. I moved my tongue around him, spreading the chocolate rather than licking him clean. My lips wrapped around him, and his hand fisted in my hair.

"I've tried not to say anything and not to move, but, baby, you're killing me."

I let him go, and in my sexiest voice, I asked, "Do you want me to stop? I wouldn't want you to die on me." I tried not to giggle.

"If you stop, I *will* die."

I looked at him through my lashes and noticed my makeshift blindfold was no longer on his eyes. "Well, okay then."

I continued on, and his hands became more forceful on my head. I thought he was going to explode, and I was ready. Instead, his hands dipped under my arms to lift me. He flipped us so I was underneath him.

"It's my turn."

I honestly thought I would orgasm just from the way his eyes penetrated mine. He touched me, and my hips buckled. I was so ready for him. I didn't want more chocolate; all I wanted was him. "Alex, no more games. I need you. Please make love to me."

That was all it took. He moved inside me, causing me to gasp. No other foreplay was needed. I grabbed his muscular back as we rocked in unison. I could tell he wanted to say something, but he didn't. I closed my eyes and felt every move he made. One last thrust, and he was satisfied, as was I.

He rolled off me. "Come on, let's shower and get cleaned up."

I couldn't help but feel proud of myself. The entire night was something I'd never have thought of doing. I stopped walking toward the bathroom and looked at him.

He turned toward me. "What it is?"

"Nothing. I'm just really happy."

He pulled me into a hug. "I'm happy too. I'm happier than I ever thought I could be." He tipped my face up. "That's because of you. Now let's shower so I can make you happier."

The rest of the weekend went by in a blur. We spent most of it inside talking about our wedding. We decided to have a small ceremony at a chapel near Creekside Park and the reception at Anthony's restaurant. We didn't want anything lavish. We just wanted to be surrounded by family and close friends.

We woke up at the sound of his alarm clock. I glanced over his shoulder and saw it was seven a.m. I moaned and rolled away. He must have turned it off because it stopped the annoying beeping sound.

I felt him breathing into my ear. "Baby, you awake or are you moaning because you're dreaming of me?"

I smiled. "I'm awake thanks to that annoying sound. Why is it set so early?"

"I wanted to call my dad's office and go see him."

I perked up and felt wide awake. "Why?"

"I need to tell him that he's going to gain a daughter-in-law soon." Alex kissed my shoulder.

"I hope he's happy about that."

He pulled me toward him. "How could he not be? You're the best thing that's ever happened to me. I think he saw that at the benefit."

I stared into his eyes. "What if he doesn't?"

Alex looked at my chest, which was rising a little quicker than normal. I closed my eyes and counted slowly to calm myself. I focused on my breathing. *Calm down. Breathe. It's okay, Aubrey* . . . I rolled away from Alex and wrapped my arms around my chest. I felt Alex's arms over mine, holding me tightly.

He kissed the back of my head. "It will be okay. I promise you. He doesn't have a reason not to like you. He saw us together, so it's not like this will be a surprise. No matter what, it's me and you. If he's not happy about it, that's his issue."

"I want him to be happy. He's your family. He'll be my family." I didn't know if he heard me.

Alex threw his right leg over both of mine with his arms still wrapped around me. His chin rested on my shoulder. He was like an Alex cocoon. "Together, okay? Always together."

I nodded. "Okay."

"I'm going to jump in the shower and then call my dad. I have this problem though, and I was hoping you could help me with it." He ran his tongue from my shoulder blade to my ear, making me giggle.

"A problem, huh? What would said problem be?" I could tell by his tone that his problem would make my bad morning get a hell of a lot better.

He rolled on his back, and I propped myself on my side and looked at him.

His hands went to his bare, beautiful abs. "Well see, it's like this. When I'm in the shower and the hot water runs over my muscles, they ache. I try to massage them, kind of like this." His hands moved up and down his torso. "Then once I relieve the ache here . . . I try to massage the rest of me." He looked into my eyes. "That's where you come in. I think about you, and I feel the need to have you rub my . . ."

I licked my lips in anticipation.

"Back." He beamed.

I reached for a pillow and smacked him in the head. Then I swallowed hard and looked at his boxers, feeling a throbbing between my legs.

He rolled me over and pinned my hands above my head. "What'd you think I was going to say?"

I was so embarrassed. "Nothing. I didn't think anything." I tried to turn my head so he didn't see me blush.

He rubbed against me until I looked at him. "I'm just kidding, I know what you were thinking because that's what I was thinking. Now get up and come relieve the ache in my . . . back."

"You're not funny, Logan. What makes you think I want to relieve your ache?"

His eyes roamed my body from head to toe. "Well, okay. If you don't want to, then don't worry about it."

He wants to play games? Okay, let's play. "You're right. I don't. Let me know when you're done in there, and save me some hot water."

I got up to leave the bedroom, and he followed me, scooped me up, and tossed me over his shoulder. I shrieked and laughed. I may have even snorted he had me laughing so hard.

He smacked my ass. "You think you're so clever."

I put my hands on his back and rubbed his muscles as he turned on the shower. "Alex, put me down."

"You want me to put you down? Sure thing."

I squealed when he put me down in the shower with my pajamas on. The water wasn't what I'd consider "shower temperature." It was downright cold! "Oh my God, Alex!"

I moved as close as I could to the back of the shower to get away from the frigid water. He got in and pulled me close to him. I became unaware of the water temperature as I pressed against a naked Alex. My forehead was on his chest, and I noticed his nipples were hard. I gave the right one a little bite and then did the same to the left one, making Alex groan. He grabbed my face and kissed me. Our tongues danced, and he lifted my cotton shirt over my head. He tossed it on the shower floor and then did to my nipples what I'd done to his. I threw my head back and gasped. He stopped and held me. Our bodies were so close that the water couldn't pass between us; it just fell over us like a waterfall.

"What's wrong?" Usually at that point, he'd be trying to get between my legs in one way or another.

"Nothing is wrong. I just need you."

I snickered. "I know, and I need you too."

"I just can't believe how much we've been through, and yet I have you in my life and in my shower." He smirked, and his eyes refocused on my body.

I still had my pajama bottoms on, so I slowly removed them. I wasn't trying to be seductive, but they were soaked and sticking to me. I hoped I could show some form of grace and not fall. I managed to get them off and pushed them into the corner of the shower with my foot.

He reached the shampoo and washed my hair, which he followed up with conditioner. He grabbed the bar of soap and turned me so my back was pressed to his chest. He washed my breasts, stomach, between my thighs, down my legs, and back up again. I watched his hands washing me, and it was the most sensual thing I'd ever seen. I never thought something so simple would turn me on so much. I wanted to turn around and throw my legs around his waist. I felt his hand between my shoulder blades.

He carefully pushed me forward. "Bend over. I need to do your back."

I bent over and felt the soap go down my spine to the top of my butt and around my cheeks. His hands massaged me, and then his hands were on my hips. He must have put down the soap. He pulled me back, and I felt him. He was ready, so I gave him the access he needed. I felt a kiss on my back before he slid into me. Neither of us spoke or made a sound. I heard the sound of the water running over us and splashing between our bodies as he thrust into me. He amplified his pace before he gave a final thrust. I clenched around him, finding my silent release. I didn't know why we were being quiet. The sex was so good we should have been screaming.

He pulled out of me and turned me around. "Never, Aubrey. I never want to be without you. Promise me that I never will be."

I looked at him and saw fear, or maybe doubt, in his eyes. I knew I hadn't done anything to make him have either of those feelings about me. "I'll never leave you. I'm going to be Mrs. Logan, remember?" I held up my left hand, and he kissed our engagement ring.

He turned the water off and slid the shower door open. He grabbed two towels off the heated towel stand and wrapped me up in one. I didn't understand his mood, and I wasn't sure if I should ask, either. We stepped out onto the bath rug, and I looked at my man. His towel was wrapped around his waist, and his muscles were firm as if he had just done one hundred crunches. I looked him over and smiled.

"Still like what you see?" he asked.

Still? I took his hand, led him to the bed, and pulled him down to sit with me. "Okay, what gives?"

His head went down, and his thumb swiped his chin just below his lip. He looked at me without really lifting his head and exhaled. "What do you mean?"

"Look at me."

His eyes met mine. There was something about them—was it worry?

"You've been acting weird all morning. You were joking with me, and then we got in the shower and you changed. What is it? Talk to me."

"I need to call my dad, and just thinking about it aggravates me. I don't know what he'll say, and if it's anything but positive, I'll be furious. I don't want him ruining us."

I looked at him as if he had just spoken a foreign language. "I thought you said he'd be happy for us? Maybe I shouldn't go with you." I turned away, but he grabbed my arm.

"My dad is just . . . well, my dad. I never know what he's going to say or do. He's spent the majority of my life being disappointed in me, and I guess that I'm worried you'll see that today. The past two times we've seen him were at functions. There were buffers." He exhaled.

"Your father couldn't say or do anything that would make me think less of you or look at you in a different light. You're everything to me. No one can ruin us." I hugged him.

He sighed into my hair. "You're right. Go get dressed, and I'll call his office."

Chapter 10

We were on our way to Logan Industries for our ten a.m. appointment. I couldn't imagine needing an appointment to see my parents. Sitting in Alex's sleek car, I looked at his pensive face. His right hand rested on the gear shift, so I placed my hand on his. He glanced over and gave me a nervous smile.

"Hey, relax. You're making me nervous," I said.

He kissed my hand then lowered it to his thigh. "I'm fine." He tried to give me a reassuring smile, but it wasn't working.

"Would it be better if I didn't go into his office? I can wait in the lobby." *Please tell me I can wait in the lobby.*

"No, you're coming with me. This is about us."

Damn. "Okay." My nerves were getting the better of me. I kept taking deep, deliberate breaths.

We pulled up in front of the building encased in black glass, and Alex turned his car over to valet. We headed to the elevator. As people hurried in and out of it, I felt as though we were entering the subway. Everyone looked professional in their business attire. I had on jeans and a sweater, as did Alex. For some reason, he looked better than I did. The only person dressed more casually than us was the bike messenger guy who had on a spandex riding outfit. I watched the numbers increase by floor. Fifteen—ding—Alex excused us through the crowd. I noticed some women's roaming eyes, which just made me roll mine.

We approached the door to Logan Industries, and Alex stopped and pulled me into a hug. He didn't say anything. He kissed the top of my head. I loved it, and he needed it. We walked in and were greeted by Darla. She gave me half a glance, but Alex got the majority of her attention. I remembered her from the benefit and how she'd wanted him to kiss her hand and he didn't. That thought made me smile.

"Mr. Logan, your father said to send you in when you arrived. I was unaware . . ." Darla looked at me. "What's your name?"

Alex chimed in, "Aubrey. Her name is Aubrey."

She gave me a once-over. "Yes. I didn't tell your father you wouldn't be alone."

"That's fine, he'll know soon enough. Thank you, Darla."

We continued down the hall. He had a beautiful office. It was different from Walker-Stone's. That reminded me I needed to call Brian. I was losing my train of thought. I heard a light knock, and a man's voice told us to go in.

Alex squeezed my hand, opened the door, and we walked in. Mr. Logan saw me first and couldn't hide his surprise and something else—maybe disappointment. I didn't know.

He stood and came to greet us. "Aubrey, nice to see you again. I didn't know you would be here." He looked at Alex and extended his hand. "Son." They shook hands.

"Hi, Dad."

"Have a seat, please."

Alex and I sat on the deep brown leather sofa situated on the left side of the rather large office. Mr. Logan's beautiful desk was in front of the wall of windows with a wet bar to the right.

His father sat across from us in a matching leather chair. "I'm glad you wanted to see me. I've been meaning to call you."

"Really, why did you want to see me?" Alex asked.

"Well, maybe this is better discussed in private." His father looked at me and then at the door.

"I can step out." I went to move, and Alex stopped me.

"No. You can say anything you need to, Dad. Aubrey and I don't have secrets." He looked at me and smiled.

Confidently, and with a little snark, he said, "Okay, if that's the way you want it . . ."

"I do. Just come out with it, and then I can tell you why we're here."

His dad cleared his throat. "I received a call from Jarrod Pierce. To say that he's extremely disappointed in you would be an understatement."

I knew that last name, but I couldn't place it.

Alex looked perplexed. "Why would I give a shit if he was disappointed in me?"

I felt my body tense.

Jack looked at me and then back at Alex. "Is it true

that you banned Leah from the club?"

That's where I knew that name; it was Leah's last name. Jarrod must be her father.

"Yes, that's right. It's my place of business, and she's disruptive. I don't understand why that would disappoint him. He should be thankful I stopped his daughter from sleeping her way through my staff."

He looked at Alex as though he couldn't believe Leah would ever behave like the slut she was. Then he glanced at me and blurted, "He also wants her to be a Logan. For her not to be near you makes that nearly impossible."

My eyes filled. Did Alex's father want her to be a Logan too? I needed to get the hell out of there, but I knew Alex would never let me leave. I glanced at him, and his eyes were daggers. I'd never seen that look on his face. He was furious.

"So you marry her then. That brings me to why we're here." Alex sat up straighter. "I have asked Aubrey to be my wife. We'll be married on December twenty-first. I hope you'll be happy for us. We'd like to have your blessing. It isn't necessary, but it'd be appreciated."

He looked shocked and then apologetic. "Congratulations to you both. Aubrey seems like a lovely young woman."

I felt extremely uncomfortable. Did he think I was good enough for his son? Did he think Leah was better? He didn't even know me.

He looked at me. "I think we need to talk about logistics, son."

"And what would they be?" Alex sounded

infuriated.

"Why don't I go wait outside?" I stood to leave.

Alex stood by my side. "No, I think we're done here."

His father walked over to his desk, opened the top drawer, pulled out a business card, and handed it to Alex. "Here's Matthew Garrison's card. He'll handle your prenuptial agreement. You *will* have an agreement in place. I'm sorry, Aubrey, but Alex will be worth more than a small fortune when I pass."

I swallowed hard, and my eyes filled. I started counting because I had a feeling an attack was on the horizon. Did he think I only was with Alex for his money? I didn't even know how much he had. I wondered if I should chime in and tell him I wasn't interested in any of the Logan money or businesses; my only interest was Alex. Funny thing was, Leah was the one who would need the prenuptial agreement, yet he preferred her as a daughter-in-law. The only thought getting me through the meeting was Alex knowing that I loved him for him and nothing else.

"No. We will have no such agreement. My marriage is not a business arrangement, and it won't be treated like one. Maybe if you'd felt that way about Mom, she'd still be here."

I couldn't believe Alex had said that to his father. I was breathing too much, and I was getting lightheaded.

Alex pulled me into his side. "Are you okay?"

I nodded. I didn't know if my voice worked at that point, and I didn't want to embarrass myself.

He kissed my temple. "Let's get out of here." Alex looked at his dad. "Thanks for making my visit everything I hoped it wouldn't be." With his arm around me, we started for the door.

"Son, wait."

Alex's head dropped. He turned around. "What?"

"I'm happy for you and Aubrey. Apparently her sight has returned, and I'm happy for that too. I'm sorry if I dampened your announcement. But please think about what I said. It's your future, son."

I couldn't look at Jack anymore, so I focused on Alex's chest.

Alex motioned between us. "It's our future. I won't let you or anyone else tell me how to live or what I need to do. Aubrey is my life. Accept it or don't, I really don't give a shit."

Alex opened the door and led me through it. We walked past Darla to the elevator. Alex pushed the down button and the door opened. I was happy that it was empty. Alex moved to the back wall and leaned on the brass bar running across it.

He elbowed the wall. "Fuck!"

I was startled. "I'm sorry." My voice was shaky. I didn't know what else to say.

"What are you sorry for? You didn't do anything. I'm the one who's sorry for my jackass of a father. I suppose I should have expected it, since he's all about protecting the family business, but he knows I don't feel that way. It never dawned on me that he would spring this on us. But for you to apologize . . . I won't have it, okay?"

I nodded. I felt as though I did a lot of that lately.

"How are you feeling? I was so worried you were going to have a black-out moment."

"Honestly, I thought I would too. Thankfully, I had taken my pill, and I've been practicing my relaxation techniques." I was happy I had an appointment with Dr. Russo tomorrow. I wanted her to help me recognize triggers before I felt as though I needed a paper bag to breathe into.

The elevator door opened, and I couldn't wait to leave. We exited the elevator and went to get Alex's car. Darla must have called down to valet because it was waiting for us. The valet went to open my door when Alex stepped in front of him.

"I got it," Alex said.

And my door was opened by my man. After Alex closed my door and tipped the valet, he got in. He took off as quickly as he could, darting through NYC traffic.

I put my hand on his leg and felt his muscles tense as he pressed the accelerator. "Hon, are you okay?"

"Yeah, I'm sorry. He just pisses me off, ya know? I mean, be happy for me once in your fucking life. I excelled in sports, and he didn't give a shit. I have a successful club, and that's not good enough. I bring my beautiful fiancée to his office, and he mentions another woman and then a prenuptial agreement. My mom would have never done that. Some days I wish it had been him in the car, and not my mom and sister. That makes me just as awful as him, right?"

"I'll sign."

"What?"

"I'll sign whatever your dad wants. I heard everything you said, but whether you like it or not, he's your dad. He's all you have left. If it'll make things better, I'll sign the agreement. I'm not with you for your money. Having you and your love makes me the richest woman alive, so I'll sign."

He pulled into the small lot next to the club. "No. There won't be an agreement. The thing you will be signing is the marriage license. He's not all I have left. I have you and our future family. I know you aren't with me for money. You've never made me feel that way."

Deep down, I was a little relieved that Alex didn't want me to sign anything. That would have made me think he didn't trust me or us; we'd promised to always trust one another. "Okay, but I want you to know that if you need me to, I will."

He opened the car door and walked around to mine. He closed my door and backed me up against it. His hands threaded through my hair as his lips crushed mine. I felt his tongue, so I opened to him. I closed my eyes and savored his taste. I breathed him in and prayed that everything would work out. Our tongues danced together, and I felt a growing need for him. I wanted to cross my legs, but Alex was standing between them. He broke the kiss and rested his head against mine.

"Me and you, right?" He sounded desperate, like he did when he told me he was Chance.

I smiled. "Forever."

"Good answer. Now, I need to check on a couple things in here. I won't be long. No one is here except for a few staff members."

"I think I'd like to call Brian and talk to him about my job."

"I think that's a great idea. Whatever you want to do, I'll support you. If you don't want to go back to

Walker-Stone, I could use you here." He winked.

I laughed. "Why, Mr. Logan, what are you proposing?"

"Well, I've heard that some secretaries like to help their bosses relieve tension." He winked and smiled that smile I loved.

"Hmmm, is that so? Well, remind me to never let you hire a secretary. Let's go in and see if I can relieve your tension."

We practically ran into his office. He reached for the bottom of my sweater and removed it. My bra quickly followed. His hands roamed all over me. He picked me up and laid me down on the couch. He unbuttoned and unzipped my jeans, pulled them off, and stood. He looked at me as if he didn't know what to do.

"You're stunning. Do you know that?"

I looked at him. "Take your shirt off."

He did.

"And your pants."

He did.

I stared at every inch of my man. "Now that is stunning." I licked my lips and reached for him.

He lay on top of me. "I want you so much. Every day, I need you more. You're my addiction."

I licked my lips. "What are you going to do about it?"

He made a sound that sounded like a growl. He removed my thong and his boxer briefs. "I'm going to love you eternally."

I melted. "Good, now come here."

We made love, and we held on to each other. I

loved that part of love making. There's nothing better than being held by the man that holds my heart. I kissed Alex and asked him if he still had work to do since he hadn't done a thing except make amazing love to me.

"Yeah, I need to go check on deliveries and bar stock."

I started to move.

"Wait, just a few more minutes." He kissed my cheek and the corner of my lips. He pulled me close and breathed into my hair. "I need to hold you a little while longer." He brought put his ear over my heart. "Let me listen to the beat of your heart, okay?"

I had never felt more connected to anyone. I knew something was bothering him, which bothered me. I figured it had to be his dad. "Are you okay?"

Not moving away from my chest, he said, "Yeah, I'm perfect. You're perfect. I was thinking that I'd like to go to the cemetery to tell my mom and sister about us."

"Okay."

"I want to introduce you to them. I prayed for my mom to bring you back to me, and then to God to make you see again. I'd have given you up for you to have your sight back. I was so afraid when my dad brought up all that bullshit today. I didn't want you to have an episode."

I pulled back and looked into his eyes. I studied him. I saw the worry, but more importantly, I saw the honesty. "I'd love to go to the cemetery and see your mom and sister. I wish I could've met them. I don't want you to worry about my vision anymore. I want to live with you and for you." I closed my eyes and traced his face with my fingers the way I had when I couldn't see. I opened my eyes, and he was studying me. "You'll never lose me, and I'd give up my sight to be with you. My heart will always be yours." I gave him a soft kiss. His lips made me feel safe and loved.

We laid there for a few more minutes until we heard his cell phone vibrate. Alex went downstairs, and I sat at his desk to call Brian about my job. He told me that of course I could come back. Thanks to the increase in business, Mark wouldn't be affected by my return. I would go back to work next week.

I went downstairs and watched Alex move effortlessly through the club. He spoke to a member of the cleaning staff, and then he moved to the bar where Tyler and Brett were. I was transported back to the first night I met Alex, and I thought about everything that had happened.

I walked up to them and heard Brett say, "I don't get your old man. Doesn't he realize how awesome she is and how great you guys are together?"

Alex shrugged. I needed to do something to bring him and his dad closer. I walked up to the guys, and Alex grabbed me around the waist.

"How'd it go with Brian?" he asked.

"Great! I start back next week."

"That's fantastic, baby. Are you ready to get out of here?"

"I am, but I had an idea. I wanted to know what you thought about it." I swallowed hard. "How would you feel about having an engagement party here at the club?"

Alex beamed. "That's a great idea. I'd love to announce that I'm marrying the most amazing woman."

I laughed. "I'd love to announce to all the women that you're off the market!"

Brett chimed in, "That may take more than an engagement." He laughed and abruptly stopped when he saw the rest of us weren't laughing. "What?"

"You're such a douche." Tyler threw a bar towel at him.

"How about if we have it two weeks from Sunday? Will that give you enough time to plan?" Alex asked.

"Sure, I'll talk to Julie. She'll help me." I was excited. Even though the club would be closed, everyone would catch wind that we were engaged.

He pulled me into a hug. "Invite whoever you want. Just give me a number for the caterer. I'll have Mike bartend."

"Let me know who you want to be there." I didn't want to exclude anyone, but aside from Brett and Tyler, I didn't know who he'd want to invite. "What about your dad?"

Alex rubbed the back of his neck and tilted his head. "No. I don't want him here. I'll invite him to the rehearsal dinner and wedding, but I don't care if he comes to those either."

I kissed him. "I'll go call Julie and tell her. I suppose I should go gown shopping soon too."

"Can I come?" He looked at me with puppy dog eyes.

"No, you can't come." I shoved his shoulder.

"I'd like to pay for everything. Do you think your

parents would mind? I don't want to offend them," Alex asked.

"I can talk to them about it. We've had so much going on lately that it never dawned on me to talk to them. But I'd like to pay for some of it too."

Brett interrupted us. "Hey, Aubrey, make sure Julie doesn't get any ideas while you're gown shopping."

My heart sunk, and I had no idea what expression I had. What did that mean? He didn't want to get married? I knew Julie did. I didn't ask any questions because I didn't want to know the response. Whatever the reply, I'd feel obligated to tell Julie. I walked away and sat at a nearby table to call Julie. She said she would come over after work to work on a guest list for the party.

Chapter 11

ALEX BROUGHT ME TO MY place, and he headed back to the club. I didn't know if I was going to tell Julie what Brett said, but if I did, I didn't want her so close to his apartment or the club. Alex stopped at the grocery store on our way to my apartment, and then we went to the liquor store. I figured we might need to eat and drink.

I made a salad and some bruschetta. I wanted to change into something comfy, so I went in my room to pull out a pair of yoga pants and a sweatshirt. I looked in the drawer and felt relieved that I could pick out clothes all on my own. I opened the drawer in my nightstand to grab a hair tie and saw my journal and Alex's good-bye note. I wanted to test myself, so I removed the notebook and crumpled up paper. I sat on my bed and stared at them. I remembered when that book was supposed to hold the key to my success as a writer, but it led to my demise as a girlfriend.

I took a deep breath and opened the book. Page by page, turn by turn, I read what I'd written about Alex. It did sound pretty horrible in the beginning. Then I read my last entry about how in love I was and how happy Alex made me. I closed the book and held it. I'd made it through without an episode, and I was proud of myself. The buzzer rang, startling me. I put the book down and went to let Julie in. After I buzzed her in, I opened the door and went into the kitchen to pour us some wine.

Julie bustled in, her body full of energy and her hands full of magazines. "Your maid of honor is reporting for duty." Julie was all bubbly and practically singing when she spoke. She came into the kitchen, gave me a kiss, and threw her arms around me. "You're getting married!"

I giggled at her excitement. "Yes, I am. Are you hungry?"

She grabbed a glass of wine and my hand and dragged me into my living room. "Ta da!" She pointed at my coffee table, which was covered in what appeared to be every bridal magazine published that month.

"Oh my God, Julie, did you buy out the store?"

"No, I stopped at every newsstand on the way here. I wanted to make sure you had all your options. Look at this one. The gowns featured here have been worn by celebrities. Aren't they incredible?" Julie flipped through pages while explaining the different gown styles: princess, mermaid, A-line, and so on. She looked at me. "Do you know what style you like? I mean, you have a kick ass body, so I'd go with something straight, strapless, and hot. Alex will pop something when he sees you in something like that. That's what I'm going to get when I get married. I've always wanted to be a princess, but I don't know about all that fluff. Maybe I'll get a gown that can be converted from poufy to short and sassy."

I just stared at Julie as she rambled. I had no idea what I wanted. Most little girls dream about their wedding, but I didn't think I'd ever find my prince, so I'd never daydreamed much about the specifics. I could tell that Julie, on the other hand, had thought about it in great detail. "How about we have dinner before we start checking off which ones I like?"

"Lead the way! Let's eat. I can't wait to get started!"

I went into the kitchen and poured another glass of wine for myself. Julie did as well. I took the salad out of the fridge and the bruschetta out of the oven. I carried the wine to the table, and Julie grabbed our plates. As we sat and ate, I still didn't know what to do about what Brett'd said.

"Oh hell! I totally forgot, how did it go with Alex's dad?" Julie asked.

I put a forkful of crisp lettuce in my mouth and looked at Julie. I just kept chewing.

"Uh oh, it didn't go well? What's his problem?"

I swallowed, took a sip of wine, and said, "Well, my future father-in-law had a lot to say. Let's see, what should I start with? The part where Jack told us Mr. Pierce was upset because his beloved daughter Leah was exiled from the White Orchid, or the fact that Leah was expected to be Mrs. Alex Logan, or that Alex should have me sign a prenuptial agreement?" I took a bite of my bruschetta. I looked at Julie. "How's that for a 'welcome to the Logan family'?"

"Are you shitting me? What did Alex say?"

"To which part?"

"To all of it. Who does that? What an arrogant prick."

"Well, Alex told his dad that if he wanted Leah to be a Logan, then he should marry her. Then he basically told him to stick the prenup up his ass."

Julie took a big sip of wine. "Thank God. I'm telling you, if Brett asked me to sign anything like that, I'd tell him to go to hell."

I looked at my salad and moved the pieces of lettuce and tomato around with my fork. That was twice that she'd mentioned a future with Brett.

"What's wrong, Aubrey? I'm sure dealing with his dad isn't easy, but Alex is all about making you happy. You don't have anything to worry about."

"It's not that. How do I say this?"

"Okay, spill it. What the hell is going on?" Julie asked.

"Do you and Brett talk about getting married?"

"No, not really. I mean, we love each other, so it's inevitable, right?" Julie looked at me, and her smile vanished. "What? What aren't you telling me?"

I wiped my lips with my napkin and cleared my throat. "I think you should talk to him about it."

She looked sad. "About getting married? Why?"

"When I was with the guys today, I said I was going to call you to help me plan the wedding and that you'd help me with gowns. Brett said . . ." I couldn't do it. She was going to be crushed.

"And Brett said what?" Her voice was low and sad.

My eyes filled with tears. "Brett said to make sure you didn't get any ideas."

"He did?"

"Yeah. Jules, I'm really sorry. Maybe he was just

kidding. I mean, Brett is the comedian of the bunch." I had no clue what to do. My best friend was hurt, and I couldn't help her.

"No, it's fine. If he doesn't want to marry me, that's fine. But he won't have me either. When it comes to Brett, I don't want just a boyfriend. I want everything."

Shit. "Please don't do anything without talking to him first." I knew she was itching to grab her cell phone and tell him to go to hell.

"Oh, I *will* talk to him, don't worry about that. Now let's grab more wine and look at gowns for you."

We went back to the couch. Julie didn't miss a beat, but I felt horrible and didn't know what to do.

Julie picked up a magazine. "Oh, look at this one. It's beautiful, and it's a Vera Wang. I think you would look gorgeous in a sheath style. It's a perfect silhouette for you."

"Isn't Vera Wang expensive? I mean, it's a stunning gown, but I don't know."

"Yes, Vera Wang is expensive, but I'm sure your parents or Alex would buy it for you. Just look at the intricate beading, and the chiffon is to die for. Did you guys pick a venue?"

"Yeah, we're getting married in the small chapel next to Creekside Park, and the reception will be at Anthony's."

Julie stared at me.

"What?"

"You're marrying one of New York's most eligible bachelors, and you're getting married in a chapel and having a small reception at a restaurant?"

"Yes. Since the guest list is small, Anthony is

rearranging the restaurant to include enough tables and a small dance floor. It will be intimate. What's wrong with that?"

"Nothing, I guess. I'm just surprised. This is society news. If you're going to do that, then you need to have a gorgeous gown."

I shrugged. "Okay, we can go look at them and I'll try them on, but if it's too expensive, I'm not buying it." I put my hand on the magazine Julie was tagging with little Post-it notes. "Are you okay?"

She closed the magazine, tossed it on the table, and flopped back on the couch.

"I'm sorry I told you what Brett said. I just wanted you to know. Maybe what he said doesn't have anything to do with you. Maybe because he was married before, he doesn't want a big wedding. I bet that's it. He probably wants to get married but doesn't want all the hoopla."

"Yeah, maybe you're right. I'm still going to ask him about it. I should go. It's getting late."

I looked at the clock and saw that it was almost ten. I walked her to the door. "You're okay, right?"

"Yes, I'm fine." Julie kissed my cheek and told me she was leaving the magazines for me.

I cleaned the dinner dishes and heard a knock on my door. I wiped my hands on a towel. I figured Julie had forgotten something, but when I opened the door, there was Alex. "I passed Julie on her way out," he said. "She let me in. She didn't look good, and when I asked her if she was okay, she said no."

"What do you mean she didn't look good? Wait, she said no?"

He walked into my apartment. "I think she was crying. I noticed her wiping her eyes when she saw me. Did you two have a fight or something?"

"She was crying? I knew she wasn't okay. I should have made her stay here." I was starting to get upset.

Alex kissed me. "What happened."

"Brett happened, that's what."

He looked confused. "I just left Brett, and he seemed fine."

I mumbled, "He won't be fine for long."

"He won't be fine for long? Why?"

"Well . . . don't get mad, okay?"

"Why would I get mad?"

As quickly as I could, I said, "Because I told Julie what Brett said about making sure Julie didn't get any ideas about getting married." I walked to the couch to hide behind a throw pillow.

He stared at me. Then his expression changed. "Oh my God, Aubrey, why would you tell her that? He could've been kidding." He paced and looked really worried. "You know he was married before. Maybe he just isn't ready."

"She should know. I'd want to know." I looked at him. "If you didn't want me forever, I'd need to know."

He scooped me up and carried me into the bedroom. "I do want you forever." He stopped and stared at my bed. He set me down and went to the note lying next to my journal. He picked it up and read it. When he turned to me, he looked sad. "Why do you have this?"

"I went to get something today, and I found it. I didn't look at it."

"I'm throwing it away. It isn't something I want for the scrapbook."

"Okay, will you take my journal too? I don't need it anymore."

Alex sat on the bed and stared at the notebook. "This was your dream, wasn't it? I ruined that for you."

I shrugged. "I guess. I mean, yeah, I wanted to write a romance novel, but I have you, and that's even better. You didn't ruin it. You are it." I sat next to him and stared at the notebook and then at Alex.

"Can't you still write it?"

"I suppose I could. I really never knew if I could actually do it or not. It isn't important anymore."

"You know, I never did read the other pages." He looked at me and raised his brow.

"Can you not? Or at least not in front of me?" The thought of anything that I wrote in my journal made me uncomfortable, especially if he read it while he was with me.

"Okay. I don't need to. I still feel badly that I only read the beginning. I didn't read how I'm the love of your life and best lover in the entire world."

I glanced up, and he smirked at me. "You don't have to read it because you already know that. I tell you all the time." I rested my head on his shoulder.

He tossed the book on the floor, shoved the note in his pocket, and kissed me. "I want to hear it again."

I pulled back and looked into his eyes. "You're the love of my life and the best lover. Now shut up and make love to me."

His kisses lingered, his touch was slow, and he made me crazy for him. His fingers moved in and out of me, and I lifted my hips. He stared at where his fingers were and gently blew on me. I was ready to lose it. He glanced at me, smiled, and threw me a wink. I laid my head back and enjoyed everything he was doing to me. Before I knew it, he was inside me. His arms supported him, and my hands went into his hair. I needed his lips on mine. We made love like we never have. He consumed my body with his and took his time savoring me. Neither of us said a word because we knew what the other needed. It was the most satisfying thing in the world.

I was woken by soft kisses trailing across my shoulder blades. I smiled and tilted my head back to see my man. He swept my hair around my neck so I could see him.

He kissed my cheek. "Good morning, beautiful."

I snuggled into his arms. "Good morning. I could get used to waking up like this."

"Then move in with me."

I turned to face him. My eyes went right to his bare chest and then looked into his eyes. "What did you say?"

"I said move in with me. We're going to be married soon, and we spend every night together, so why not? We should decide where we're going to live after we're married anyways. What do you think? Would you want to live in my apartment, yours, or a house?"

"I haven't really thought about it. I guess your place. It's closer to the club and it's much nicer than mine. You would probably be more comfortable there."

"I'm comfortable wherever you are. What about the house idea?"

"I don't know. Maybe when we start a family. But then you'll be farther away from work, and I won't see you as much, especially with your hours." I pictured myself in a house with kids and no husband around. I didn't like that at all. "I want to be where you are, so whatever is easier."

He rested his hand on my head and played with my hair. "We don't have to decide that now, but will you move in with me?"

I nodded, and he devoured my mouth. It was as if we were starving and needed each other more than air. I didn't know how to explain what I felt when I was with him except for safe. I knew that he'd be with me whenever I needed him, as I'd be for him, and that he loved me.

We broke apart, and he rubbed his nose on mine. "You make me so happy. I can't wait to have you with me every day for the rest of my life. You just made me a very happy man . . . again."

He rolled me over and was lying on top of me when his cell phone rang. I shifted to let him get it off the nightstand. He ignored it and kissed my neck. Then "Girls Just Want to Have Fun" played on my phone, indicating as call from Julie.

"That's Julie. I need to get that."

Alex moaned and rolled off me. He grabbed his phone, which had started ringing again, and looked at the screen. "Shit, it's Brett."

I grabbed my phone, got out of bed, and took it into the kitchen. I pushed the green button. "Hi, Jules." I tried to sound perky, but I had a feeling that would be a wasted effort.

She sniffled. "Aub . . . rey . . . it's . . . o . . . ver." She was trying to catch her breath between each syllable.

"Sweetie, what are you talking about?" It had to be Brett. I didn't even know why I asked.

"It's Brett . . . We . . . b-bro-broke . . . up . . . We . . ." Julie was sobbing, which was very un-Julie like.

"Julie, honey, where are you? Are you home?"

"N-no, I'm in my c-car."

She's driving? "Pull over, and I'll come to you. Where are you?"

"I was on my . . . on my way to your place."

"Please be careful. I'll put coffee on, okay?"

Alex walked out of the bedroom, totally dressed, and looked at me. He heard me say, "No, he's leaving. Don't worry about it." Julie ended the call. I looked at my phone and felt horrible.

Alex drew me in close. "Brett sounds awful. I'm going to his place. I gather Julie is coming here?"

"Yeah, she sounds devastated. I should have kept my mouth closed."

"Don't take the blame for this. Brett doesn't blame you. He'd have had to tell her at some point. Let's help our friends try to work through this and meet up later. We should start getting you packed."

"Can we do it after Thanksgiving?"

He kissed the top of my head. "Whatever you want, but not too long after that, okay? I gotta go and talk to my man."

After Alex left, I threw on some comfy clothes and

started coffee. I decided to make blueberry muffins from a mix. I figured Julie must have called in sick to work, and she'd need comfort food. I needed to call Brian as well. My buzzer rang, and I let Julie in. I could tell she wasn't in a good place just by looking at her. She had on last night's makeup, and her mascara was smudged under her eyes. Her hair was in a messy ponytail, and she was wearing yoga pants and a hoodie. I hugged my friend, and she started bawling. I let her get as much of it out of her system as possible before I let her go.

"I can't believe this," she said. "I can't believe I didn't know he didn't want to get married again. How could he not tell me?"

"Let's sit. Want some coffee? I made muffins too. They should be ready soon." I tried to sound as upbeat as I could.

"I'll have coffee, sure." Julie wiped her nose on her sleeve and plopped down on the couch. She grabbed the same throw pillow I had last night, and she just held it.

I poured us coffee. "Okay, talk to me. What happened?" I settled into the sofa.

"I went to his place when I left here last night. Naturally, he wasn't home from the club yet, so I waited in the lobby since I don't have a key. When he finally got home, he was excited to see me and mad that I hadn't called him so he could have the doorman let me in to his place. Anyways, we went upstairs and into his apartment, and he was all over me."

I nodded.

"So I stopped him and told him I wanted to talk, and he said that he wanted to fuck and then go to sleep. He said 'fuck.' Not sex or make love but 'fuck.' So, I told him no. I wasn't in the mood."

"And then what happened?"

"What do you think? He got angry and asked me what my problem was. I asked him what his was, and he told me that he was tired and had a long day at the club and just wanted to fuck me and go to sleep."

I braced myself for what was coming next.

"So I told him I'm not his fuck buddy and that I loved him and was hoping to build a life with him. He said his life is as built as it is going to be. He loved me and didn't consider me a fuck buddy. I was his girlfriend, and that was enough. I told him that wasn't enough and that I wanted to get married someday."

"And?"

Julie's eyes filled up and the tears spilled out. "And he said that . . . that I should find someone else because that isn't in the cards for us. I should never expect a proposal from him because there won't be one. Never, Aubrey. He didn't say not in the near future or this year or anything like that. He said never!"

"Oh, Jules, I'm sorry. Maybe he was just really tired?" I sucked at these situations.

"If he wasn't tired then, he's really tired now. We didn't sleep; we argued for hours. It was horrible."

My heart broke for her. "I'm so sorry. I shouldn't have said anything."

Julie shook her head and wiped away her tears. "No, I'm glad you told me. It's better to know than not to. I just didn't expect us to end. I thought he was my forever. I pictured me and you, our gorgeous husbands, and our children growing up together. I guess I was way off base."

My timer beeped, and I was glad. It gave me a minute to collect my thoughts. I went into the kitchen, took the muffins out of the oven, and put them on a plate with some butter. I walked back into the living room and noticed Julie staring at a bridal magazine on the coffee table. My heart broke.

She looked up and gave me a half smile. "I'm supposed to stand up with him at your wedding, and your engagement party is soon. I'm never going to be able to avoid him. You're my best friend, and he's Alex's. If I want to avoid him, I need to avoid you, and I can't do that." She wiped a tear away.

I hadn't thought about our wedding or the party. "I'm so sorry. Do you still want to be my maid of honor?"

"Of course I do!" She shook her head and composed herself. She sat up, reached for a muffin, peeled the top off, and ate. "Wow, these are good. Boxed, right? I know you aren't a baker." She laughed.

It was good to hear her laugh even though it was forced. "You know me. If it doesn't come in a box, it's not getting baked."

She nodded, and her lips slightly curled. "You know what? I'll be fine. I mean, I was fine before, right? I don't want to dampen this for you, so screw him. If he wants to be a prick, then he can be a prick. I don't need to pine over him. There are other fish in the sea. I just hadn't intended on ever having to swim in that water again. I really thought he was the one."

I shook my head. "No, you don't have to pine over him. But you should probably let yourself heal and work through this. Maybe you guys can reach a compromise."

"Screw that. I took the day off, so let's go out. We can go shopping and then to the White Orchid for drinks. What do you think?"

I was stunned. "You want to go to the club?"

"Yeah, Tuesdays are ladies nights, so why the hell not? I'm not going to wallow. I hope his sorry ass is there so he can see what he's missing." She shoved the rest of her muffin in her mouth, finished her coffee, and got up.

I stood too. "Uh, okay, if that's what you want to do. We can go to the square and walk around and shop. But I need to call work, and I have an appointment with my doctor at two o'clock today. But if you don't mind waiting, you can come with me and we can go out after that."

"No need to call work. I told Mark, and he said Brian is out of the office anyways, so it's cool. I have no problem waiting for you during your appointment." She kissed my cheek. "Meet me at my place at one, okay? I need to take a nap and then get ready."

"Sure, whatever you want."

"See ya, chica!" And with that, Julie was out the door.

I walked back to the couch, grabbed a muffin, and plopped down. What the hell was that? One minute she was a mess, then she was fine. I finished what appeared to be a magic, heart-healing muffin and went back into the kitchen to get another cup of coffee. I heard my phone ring and scurried into my room to retrieve my phone.

I pressed the answer button. "Hi."

“Hey, baby, how is she?” Alex asked.

I sighed. “I honestly don’t know. I’ve known Julie for a long time, and I’ve never seen her like this. At first, she was devastated, absolutely crushed. Then she flipped. She wants to go shopping and then to the club. What happened with Brett?”

“Apparently his ex-wife got wind of Brett being a partner at the club and filed amended alimony papers to get more money from him. I hooked him up with my attorney.”

Money, it was always about money. That was why I hated it. “Is that why he was so mean to Julie?”

Alex sighed. “I don’t know that he was mean. I don’t think last night was the right time to discuss their future. Before you say it, yes, he should have told her that. I’ll be at the club tonight with Brett. I’m sure he’ll want to fix this. We have an appointment today with Dr. Russo. You didn’t cancel it, did you?”

I lay on my bed and stared at the ceiling. “No, I didn’t, but I think I’ll be fine to go on my own. Julie will be with me—in the waiting room of course. Is that okay?”

“Of course it is. You can fill me in when I see you later, or if you need to, you can call me.”

“Okay. I figured Brett would want to fix things. I don’t know if Julie will though. She’s in a mood, and it can go one of two ways. I have a feeling it won’t be in a way that Brett will appreciate. But if he can’t give Julie what she wants, then maybe they should be over.” That thought was nauseating. “Can I stay at your place tonight? I can only imagine what will happen at the club.”

"No, you can stay at our place."

A smile grew on my face, and it felt so good after the depressing morning. "Thank you."

"No need to thank me. I'll talk to you later."

I put my phone on the charger and headed to the bathroom to get ready. While in the shower, I thought about everything and prayed that things would work out between Julie and Brett. I wanted them to be as happy as we were. I also hoped that their break up didn't come between me and Alex. I thought how it could weigh on my relationship. I couldn't let that happen.

After my shower, I went into my room, opened my side table drawer, and noticed that my journal was gone. My thoughts raced. I took deep breaths and figured Alex had taken it. He had said he wanted to read it. I tried to push that to the back of my mind and move on with my day with Julie.

Chapter 12

THE HUSTLE AND BUSTLE OF NYC never ceases to amaze me, nor would I want to change it. Business people sped to get to where they needed to go, tourists stopped to take pictures, and cab horns blared. I loved it. I was thankful I had my eyesight back.

Julie and I left Dr. Russo's office. I'd had a productive session discussing Jack's feelings about me and his money. Dr. Russo assured me that his response to our engagement most likely came from the business man in him. She said he was a father trying to protect his son, and I shouldn't take it personally. We also discussed my ability to handle situations and how to pre-empt feelings that would generally make me anxious. She told me she was proud of me, which made me happy.

We headed toward Fifth Avenue to do some "killer shopping" as Julie put it. We went into some high-end stores. Julie was in a purchasing mood and didn't flinch at the seven hundred dollar Gucci shoes that went with the dress she bought from Saks. It was gorgeous, black, form fitting, and it hugged her in all the right places. Julie decided to splurge on me as well as a welcome home gift. She bought me a form-fitting navy dress, although my upper curves weren't as abundant as hers and it was a little shorter than I'd normally wear. She also decided I needed a new pair of Jimmy Choos. They were natural-colored platform pumps, and they were pretty hot. I insisted on paying for those, which I knew I'd regret once I got my credit card bill.

We went to lunch, and I was glad for a couple minutes of down time to talk to Julie. "I spoke to Alex and told him we're going to the club tonight."

Julie looked up from her menu. "Oh yeah?"

She was so nonchalant it was unnerving. "Yeah, he said Brett would be there too." I hoped she'd no longer want to go, but I knew better.

She set her menu down and took a sip of water. "Is that bit of information supposed to deter me from wanting to go tonight?"

"No, I just wanted you to know. So you could . . . um . . . be prepared."

Julie looked at me. "You have known me forever, Aub. I don't care that he'll be there. I can't get over someone by avoiding them, right? Look at you and Alex. You tried to avoid him, and that didn't really work out for you, did it?"

"It's not the same thing."

She shrugged as the waiter came up. We both ordered soup and salad, and I asked for some bread. I knew she would be drinking in a few hours, and I didn't want her drunk.

We went back to my place and got ready. I called Alex and told him about my appointment and what Dr. Russo had said about his father's intentions. That didn't change his opinion on the matter. I couldn't wait to see him, but I was so nervous about how the evening would play out that I took my anxiety meds before hopping in the cab to go to the White Orchid. I looked at Julie, who was looking out the window.

"You don't have to do this, ya know," I said. "We can go back to my place and hang out. Maybe watch a movie?" I was hoping she'd tell the cabbie to pull over, but no luck. We pulled up to the club, and Julie plastered on a big smile and hopped out. I handed the driver our fare and slid across the seat to join her.

She looked at the door and then back to me. "Ready?"

No. "Yeah, let's go in."

We walked toward the bar, and my eyes found Alex even though he was flanked by women. My thumb went to my engagement ring, a nervous move I made to remind myself that I was his. He looked at me, and his face lit up. His eyes sparkled, and his lips broadened into a beautiful smile. His expression changed so much that even the women trying to come on to him noticed and looked to see what had gotten his attention.

He stood and walked over to us. He said hi to Julie and softly kissed me on the lips. "You two look beautiful. I have our table waiting, so why don't we head upstairs?"

I realized he wanted to get away from the bar. "Sounds great. Let's head up."

Julie remained where we were and started looking around. I was sure she was looking for Brett. Alex looked stressed. He squeezed my hand and motioned for me to look toward the dance floor. I saw Brett dancing closely with a redhead. I gasped, making Julie look too. At first her eyes looked sad, but then they narrowed. She was pissed.

"Come on, Jules, let's head up," I said.

She looked at me and smirked. "No, I want to stay down here. You guys can go. I'll be *just* fine."

I knew what that meant. She walked to the bar and ordered what looked like a lemon drop shot. After she downed one, she signaled to the bartender and downed another before gliding toward the dance floor. I noticed men look at her as she passed, and I was sure she didn't miss that. A gorgeous, tall blond man stood and held out his hand. She took it and let him lead her to the dance floor. She was dancing on the opposite side of the floor from Brett, but I knew that wouldn't last. I felt as though I was looking at a car crash I couldn't stop. Hand in hand, Alex and I walked closer to the impending accident.

He slowed his pace, causing me to glance at him. "This isn't going to be good, is it?"

He looked so concerned. I shook my head and felt like getting an airbag ready. Alex pulled me into him and looked over my shoulder at Brett. I looked around him at Julie. When Alex spun me around, I could see Brett again. The redhead he was dancing with looked familiar.

"Do you know who that is dancing with Brett?" I asked.

Alex said, "Nikki."

"Do you know her?"

He cringed slightly. "Yeah, she's a regular."

It hit me like a ton of bricks—she was the one who had been in the ladies' room. She was the one who told either Leah or Alex about my journal. "She's the one, isn't she?"

Alex looked down and then into my eyes. "The one?"

"The one who told you about me wanting to use you." Those words made me wince.

"She was involved, yes. Nikki isn't a bad person, but her loyalties were in the wrong place."

That was an odd thing to say. Why would she choose to be loyal to Alex over Leah? My stomach turned. "Is she one of your complications?"

Alex kissed my forehead. "It doesn't matter."

It mattered to me. I stopped moving and looked at him. "I see." I shook my head and went back to the current train wreck. I was too concerned with Julie to worry about my fiancé's past.

Brett looked over and smiled, but his face fell when he saw Julie and blond guy gyrating on the dance floor. He grabbed Nikki's hand and started toward us. "Hey, Aubrey." Brett kissed my cheek. "This is Nikki. Nik, this is Aubrey, Alex's fiancée."

She gave me a wry smile. "I know who she is." She looked at Alex. "Hey, sexy. No kiss for me?"

Alex shifted and changed the subject. "Brett, let's go get a drink. Nikki, please excuse us."

Alex, Brett, and I walked away, leaving Nikki on the dance floor. I watched Brett stare at Julie before he stopped and motioned for Nikki to join us. Alex shot him a look and kept walking. His fingers flexed on my hand.

We all went to the bar where Tyler was pouring drinks. "Hey, guys, what'll it be?"

We told him what we wanted and sat.

"So, Aubrey, are you happy that Alex has distanced himself from his friends for you?" Nikki asked

My mouth dropped. Nikki definitely didn't hold back. I didn't know what to do. I needed Julie. I was getting better at handling confrontations, but I liked having my wing-woman.

Alex wasn't fazed at all and came to my rescue. "That's enough, Nikki. Aubrey has never told me who I can and can't hang out with. I just don't have time for petty bullshit."

"Whatever you say. All I know is Leah didn't deserve to be kicked out of here. You've known her for years. She misses you and the club. This is where we all hang out, but I guess we'll have to find another place. Mr. Pierce isn't too happy either."

"I'm not rehashing this. She knows why she was kicked out. If you guys want to hang somewhere else, be my guest. No one is forcing you to come here."

Brett leaned toward Nikki and whispered in her ear. I glanced over at the dance floor and saw Julie walking toward me, alone. She walked up to the bar and stood next to me and Alex. Tyler smiled at her.

Giving her best smile, she said, "Hey, Tyler, can I have a Jack and Coke?" She didn't look or sound put off that Brett was three stools away canoodling with Nikki. "So are you guys ready for your engagement party? Is there anything I can do to help?"

I could tell she was trying to act normal, and I was about to answer her when Brett beat me to it.

"Julie."

She looked at him with her face blank. "Brett." Julie

looked back at me. "So, your party—"

"This is Nikki," Brett interjected.

What the hell was he doing? My heart raced. I looked at Alex for guidance, but he looked as stunned as I was.

Julie looked around me and saw Nikki hanging on Brett. Her face was impassive, but I knew she was hurt. "Yeah, I know who she is, but thanks for the introduction." Her voice was sad and flat.

"Weren't you two together, like, yesterday?" Nikki snickered and did an annoying hair flip.

Julie didn't dignify her question with an answer. Tyler placed her drink in front of her, and Julie took a long sip. "Want to go sit upstairs?"

I nodded and scooted off my stool.

Alex joined us. "See ya later, man."

Brett called, "Hey, Julie."

We stopped, and I looked at Julie. She closed her eyes before opening them. Then she delicately turned toward him.

"See ya 'round."

Julie didn't reply. She turned and led us upstairs. We slid into a booth.

Alex looked nervous but spoke anyway. "He's hurting too, you know."

Julie nodded. "Yeah, I can see he's really torn up."

I needed to try to do something, but I didn't know what. If Alex wasn't there, I'd have totally girl-bashed Brett. I needed a different diversion. I was going to mention the engagement party, but I didn't want to bring that up either.

Julie broke the silence. "So this is a different kind of night, huh? I really thought I'd come in here and party it up and show Brett what he's missing." Julie shook her head. "Guess the joke's on me."

Her eyes went to the dance floor. So did mine and my heart hurt for my best friend. Brett was in a lip-lock with Nikki. Julie looked as though she was about to fall apart.

Alex looked repulsed. "Ladies, if you'll excuse me."

I watched him walk away, and I was happy that we were okay. I needed Julie to be okay. Alex made his way to the dance floor and to Brett. His hand was on Nikki's ass. I watched as Alex pulled Brett away to talk. Brett glanced up to where we were, and his face dropped as Alex spoke. I wished I could hear what he said. Brett nodded and walked back to Nikki. He took Nikki's hand and led her away.

When Alex came back, he looked irritated. "You guys ready? I'll drive you home."

Julie stood, and I followed. We walked to the door to the private parking area. Instead of holding Alex's hand, I held Julie's. Alex opened the door for us, and before we crossed the threshold, Julie turned and looked back into the club. I didn't know what to say or do. I'd never been in that position with her. She was the one who always knew what to say. She shrugged, and we left.

Thankfully, Alex had driven his Porsche SUV. He opened the doors for us, but I shook my head and climbed in the back with Julie. Alex started the engine, and we pulled away. That was all it took. Julie burst into tears.

I rubbed the back of her hand with my thumb.

"Sweetie, why don't you come back to my place?"

Alex looked at me through his rearview mirror. I was sure he had other plans for the night, but I couldn't think about that. My best friend needed me.

"What do you think? My place?"

Julie nodded. "I just don't understand. He's going to sleep with her tonight, isn't he? Alex? Do you think he's going to . . . sl-sl-sleep with her?"

I felt horrible for her. I prayed Alex would say no, but he wouldn't lie.

"I don't know, Julie. He's hurt right now, and guys deal with hurt differently."

Julie and I stared at him.

He glanced back at me. "What?"

"Guys deal with hurt differently? So if that was us, I'd be going home crying and you would be getting it on with someone? Would you at least have the decency not to do it in front of me? You know what, don't answer that. I already know, don't I?" I was completely disgusted.

Julie wiped her tears. "Aubrey, don't."

We pulled up in front of my building, and I opened my door before Alex had a chance to get out. I waited for Julie to slide out, and then I turned to Alex.

"Thanks for the ride. I'll talk to you later." I shut the door. I was irritated. Maybe I was annoyed with Brett and his insensitivity, or maybe I was peeved with Alex's comment. Whatever it was, I just wanted to get inside my apartment.

"Aubrey, wait."

I turned and looked at my beautiful man. I didn't

care how mad I was, he was still the most handsome man in the world. I crossed my arms.

He put his hand on my elbow. "Hey, are you mad at me? I didn't mean anything by that. I wouldn't do that to you. I made a promise, remember?" He held up my left hand. "I love you. I don't know why Brett did what he did tonight. I do know that he's really hurt. Julie isn't the only one in pain right now."

"I'm sorry. I just don't understand guys. How could he do that? How could you do what you did to me? I need to go." I turned in haste to avoid his answer, stumbled on the curb, and almost fell. Alex's arms wrapped around my waist to steady me.

Julie came over. "Aubrey, are you okay?"

I stood stock-still in Alex's arms.

He turned me around and grabbed my face. "Look at me."

Our eyes met. "You have nothing to worry about, do you understand?" he said. "You have my heart and my soul. You're my life. Please let me stay with you."

"Okay." I looked at Julie. "Is that all right with you?"

"Yeah, it's fine. I'm freezing my tits off out here." She shivered and giggled.

There's my friend.

Julie and Alex ended up spending the night. I loved having both of my best friends there.

I woke up to soft kisses trailing up and down the back of my neck.

"Waking up with you in my arms has to be my best

dream coming true." His voice was gruff, and he sounded sexy as hell.

I rolled in his arms and looked at him. "You're my dream. I just feel horrible that Julie is in a nightmare. She has to be wondering if Brett is alone." *God, I hope he's alone.*

"I don't know, but I hope he is too. I know Nikki, and I'm sure she was willing and ready."

I felt a chill go down my spine. "I hate that you know that, and I hate that I know why you know that." I started to leave the bed, but Alex stopped me.

"Hey, that was a long time ago. She meant nothing to me, and you mean everything to me." He pulled me in and hugged me as if I was falling out of a plane and he was my parachute.

I held on as tight as I could. I loved when I couldn't tell if I was feeling my heartbeat or his. But I needed to check on Julie. I kissed him and got out of bed. I threw on my robe and walked into my living room to find an empty couch with a folded blanket and a note.

Aubrey,

Thank you for letting me crash here. I needed to know, so I'm going to Brett's. I know you don't agree with this, but I need to see it for myself. Please don't tell Alex. Just tell him I went home. I don't want him to think I'm a stalker. Thank you for everything. I love you and will call later.

Julie xoxo

"Shit."

"What's the matter, babe? Where's Julie?"

"She left." That wasn't a lie.

"Oh, I hope she's okay."

I muttered, "Me too." I prayed she didn't see Nikki. I looked over at Alex, who was making coffee in the kitchen. I wrapped my arms around him. "Do you have to go to the club soon?"

"Yeah, I wish I didn't. I'm still thinking I should sell it. I don't know. What do you think?"

"I don't want you to. It's yours. Not to mention it's where we met." I kissed him.

"Will you be okay today? What are you going to do today?"

"I'm going into the office. I need to talk to Brian and see what the plan is. I should have gone back yesterday, but I knew Julie needed me." My chest hurt. I wasn't anxious; I was just filled with worry for her.

Alex tilted my head up. "I know you're stressed over what Julie saw at the club, but if it's meant to be, it will be. I know that he loves her. I just hope they can find a compromise."

"I don't know. She's really broken up. I've never seen her like this. She's even waiting to see—" I snapped my mouth shut.

"She's waiting to see what? Is she at Brett's? Please tell me she isn't going there to see if he's alone."

I shrugged. "Go to the club so I can get ready for work. I'll call you later."

Alex's lips were on mine, and he pulled me into a hug. "I'm sorry this is happening."

"Me too. I'll see you later."

Alex left, and I got ready to go into the office. I walked to the subway and called Julie on the way. She didn't pick up, which made me nervous. I hoped she was already at work. The walk from the subway station to Walker-Stone was short, but it was getting colder. I wished I had taken a cab. The office seemed busier than normal when I got in.

Mark was by the break room. "There she is, my favorite copy editor!" Mark hugged me. He kissed the top of my head.

That probably wasn't the best office protocol, but I didn't care. I missed working, and I missed working with my friends even more. "Hey there, handsome. Is Julie here?"

Mark handed me a cup of coffee. "Yeah, she just got here. She doesn't look good. I asked her what was wrong, but she didn't want to talk about it."

"Probably better that you don't know because you'd want to kick Brett's ass. I'm going to go see her." I walked away from Mark, but he followed on my heels. I turned toward Mark. "She's really hurting over Brett right now."

Mark looked at me as if he was ready to come out of his skin. "What happened? If Brett hurt her, you're right; I'll want to go kick his ass."

"They had a disagreement. Julie thought going to the club last night would make her feel better, but it made her feel worse." I tried to walk away again, but he wouldn't let me get too far. "Brett was at the club, but he wasn't alone. Julie was devastated. She went by his place this morning to see if he was alone, and I need to find out what happened."

"Holy shit! You'd better tell me what happened. What the hell is wrong with these guys? First Alex pulls crap on you and now Brett?"

"Please don't bring up what happened with me and Alex," I said. "That was as much my fault as it was his."

Mark shrugged. "I don't like seeing my best friends upset. Alex is a good guy, but the jury's still out on Brett." Mark turned and walked to his desk.

I looked into Julie's office. She was looking out the window. I knocked on the open door. "Can I come in?"

She turned and smiled. "Hi."

"Hi, yourself. So what happened?"

Julie let out a long breath. "Nothing happened. I decided on the way there that I didn't want to know. I don't think I can take it. What pisses me off more than anything is how upset I am. I don't do this. I don't pine or get hurt. This is why love sucks."

My heart broke for her. "Love doesn't suck, Jules. Sometimes it just takes a little compromise."

"So I should, as Brett put it, 'fuck' him and be his girlfriend and nothing more? How long? Forever?"

"I don't know." I had no idea what to say that would help her.

Julie sat at her desk. "I know, and I can't do that. I thought that's what I wanted too, to be with Brett and have a great time. He told me he loved me. This isn't love, is it?"

I shook my head. "No, it isn't."

"Anyways, we have a meeting today with them about *Amoureux*."

That was news to me. "We do? Since when?"

"Since Alex just called me and said they would be here at one."

"Oh, okay. Are you going to be okay?"

"Yeah, I'm fine. I need to be professional. It is what it is."

I stood to leave, but before I did, I walked around the desk to give Julie a hug.

Chapter 13

I WENT BACK TO MY desk and tried calling Alex, but it went to voice mail. I was nervous about our meeting, and I wondered why he hadn't told me. I looking over the other pending projects on my desk, and before I knew it, a small white orchid plant was placed by my computer. I looked to my right and there he was, wearing black slacks and a deep blue shirt that made his eyes look even more amazing than they were. I beamed, and then Brett appeared. He looked good too, but he looked tired. I hoped he was tired because he'd been up all night worrying about Julie. I couldn't stomach thinking that he was tired because he was up all night with Nikki.

Mark was behind them. "I have the conference room ready. Right this way, gentlemen."

Alex took my hand and kissed it. "Sorry I didn't tell you about this. You'll understand once we get in there. If it makes you feel better, Brett just found out too."

"Okay." I noticed Mark and Brett talking, and Mark didn't look pleased.

Alex and I sat at the conference table across from each other, waiting for Julie and Brett to join us. Brett sat next to Alex, and Julie came in shortly after and sat next to me.

She pulled out her notepad and pen. "So, Alex, what can we do for you?"

Alex cleared his throat, stood, and walked around the table. "Nothing. I'm sorry to have deceived you all, but I don't have any marketing needs at this time."

Julie looked at him as if he had two heads. "Why are you here?"

"I'm here because this is the only place I could think of that you and Brett could talk without killing each other. Aubrey and I are getting married soon, and I'd like our best friends to get along. Our engagement party is coming up, and I don't need you two taking aim at each other. Aubrey doesn't need the stress. If you two can't find a common ground, then I'll take Aubrey away and elope."

"Alex! You can't force them to talk." His heart was in the right place, but the conference was about to go badly.

"No, it's okay," Julie said. "This is good. I have a question for Brett, and his hopefully honest answer will clear all this up."

Brett looked at us and then at Julie. He leaned back and looked nervous. "Okay, what do you want to know? Do you want to know if I love you? Because the answer is yes. If you want to know if I miss you, that answer is yes too."

Julie ran her hand through her hair. "No, actually. I need to know if you slept with Nikki last night."

"What? Why do you need to know that?"

"Tell me." Julie's voice was strong, but I knew the

wrong answer would devastate her.

Brett looked down and let out a deep breath. He looked right into her eyes. "Yeah, I did. Feel better now?"

Julie picked up her notepad and pen. She stood and looked at Brett. "No, I don't, but thank you for your honesty." She walked toward the door, stopped, and looked at us. "Alex, I appreciate what you tried to do here. Although I doubt this is the way you wanted it to go, I'm glad you brought us together. This way everyone knows how my ex-boyfriend, who claims to love me, shows his love. I promise your engagement party will be beautiful and won't be dampened by our issues. Same goes for your wedding." Julie looked at me. "I'll be your maid of honor, Aubrey. I wouldn't miss that for anything in the world." She turned and looked at Brett. "Don't worry, Brett. When you and I walk down the aisle that day, we'll be walking away from the altar, not toward it."

Julie left, and we all stood there staring at each other.

"I'd better go too. I'll walk you guys out," I said.

I kissed Alex good-bye and thanked him for trying. I sat at my desk and dropped my head in my hands. I was going to go see Julie, but her door was closed. Mark came to my desk, and I told him what had happened. It didn't brighten his mood toward Brett. When the day ended, I couldn't wait to get out of there. Julie and I walked out together.

"Want to come to my place? We can order pizza and watch a movie," I said.

"No thanks. I need a drink. I'm headed over to the club for happy hour. Want to come?"

I couldn't believe she wanted to go there. "Sure, I guess. I don't want to stay long, though."

We took a cab. The club was busy but not too busy. Brett and Mike were manning the bar, so I told Julie to grab a table and I'd get our drinks. Thankfully Brett was busy, so Mike made our drinks. I was about to grab them when I felt arms around my waist.

"Baby, do you know how sexy you look? Do you know how badly I want you on this bar . . . naked?"

A shiver shot down my spine. I left the drinks where they were and turned to see the face I loved. My lips were on his in an instant. "*Amoureux*."

He chuckled. "Yes, you're my lover."

"No. I want you. Let's go into Amoureux. It's empty, right?"

"Mike, take these drinks to Julie. Grab a beer for Mark and a cosmo for Val."

"Mark's here?" I looked over Alex's shoulder and saw him and Val with Julie.

"There, they're taken care of. Let me go take care of you. It sounds like you need some of this." He motioned toward his body.

I giggled, and with our hands together, we practically ran into the wine room. Alex lifted me and put me on one of the high-top wine tasting tables. His hands went to my thighs, and my skirt became a belt as he forced it up to my waist. He pulled my panties aside and put his fingers in me. His hand was on the small of my back, supporting me, while the others did things that threw me into complete bliss. I felt myself tighten around him, and my release surprised even me. I leaned forward and put my hands on his shoulders to support myself.

He looked into my eyes. "This is a tasting room right?" He held up the fingers that had just brought me sheer pleasure and put them in his mouth. He pulled them out slowly, making me wet all over again.

I could hardly speak. "Yes." I lowered myself from the table by hanging on to his shoulders. I decided to reciprocate the ecstasy he had shown me.

I went to my knees and massaged him. Once I had him naked, he was all mine. I'd never felt something as deep as I did for Alex. He was everything to me, and I would give him everything I had. I took him as deep as I could, and his hand went to the back of my head. I felt him harden as I tasted him. I never thought I'd like doing that, but with him, I enjoyed every minute of it.

Afterward, we put ourselves back together and rejoined our friends. Mark was with Julie at the bar, and Brett was still slinging cocktails. I couldn't understand how he could know Julie was there and not care. Mark asked Julie to dance while Val took a phone call, and Alex asked if I wanted to join them.

We walked to the dance floor, and I noticed women staring at my man. I gave a couple of them a flippant wave, and Alex laughed.

He spun me into his arms. "Our engagement party is next week. Can you believe it?"

"No, I can't. I really think we should ask your dad to come. He's family." I was torn because I knew that Jack didn't really approve of me for his son. But I could overlook that if it meant Alex would have his dad at the party.

Alex stopped moving. "This is really important to

you, isn't it?"

"Yeah, I guess it is. What do you think?"

"We can invite him, but if he says anything about a prenup or anything else negative, he's out of here."

I agreed and hugged Alex. I tried to find Julie and Mark, but Mark was dancing with Val. I looked toward the bar and noticed Brett talking to Julie. They didn't look as though they were arguing. They looked like strangers. It made me sad. Alex followed my eyes and gave my arm a tug. He motioned for us to go to our friends. We walked up, and Brett offered us drinks. He turned toward the liquor behind him.

I looked at Julie. "You okay?"

"Yeah, I'm fine. I don't want to talk about it, okay?"

"Sure, yeah, fine." I wasn't going to push her for an explanation if she didn't want to give it.

Brett gave us our drinks and told us he had to go up to the VIP area. We said good-bye, and then Mark and Val joined us.

"So next Sunday is the party. Are you guys excited?" Julie asked.

She was back to being Julie. It was so disconcerting.

"I can't wait." Alex sounded genuinely excited. "I'll make some calls tomorrow to caterers and my dad and make sure everything is perfect."

"Your dad? You're inviting your father?" Julie sounded confused.

"Yes. That's what my beautiful fiancée wants, so that's what'll happen." Alex kissed the top of my head.

"Hey, I think Julie and I are going to head out. I'm tired." I really was, and I wanted to get Julie out of there.

"Okay, babe, I'll have my driver take you."

Memories from our first night flooded my memories. "Thank you, that would be great. I don't feel like waiting for a cab. Will you come over later?"

"I wouldn't want to be anywhere else." Alex pulled out his cell and told the driver to come around front. He walked us out and then went back in the club.

I was alone with Julie. "You want to come to my place or go home?"

"I just want to go home. I'm fine, Aub, really I am. I just needed closure." Her voice was impassive.

"Did you get it?"

"Yeah, I guess so." Julie shrugged. "It's just hard, ya know?"

I hugged her. I definitely knew.

The driver dropped Julie off first and then me. I sat on my couch, grabbed the bridal magazines, and thumbed through them. My cell rang, and it was Alex.

"Hi there. Miss me already?" I asked.

"Always. I forgot to ask you if you were busy on Sunday. I want to go to the cemetery, and then we can grab lunch afterward."

"Sure, I'd love to. You're coming over when you get out of work, right?"

"I wouldn't want to be anyplace else," he said. "I've got to go. I'll talk to you later."

We hung up, and I looked around my apartment. I was happy to be home and engaged to the love of my life. I sat on my bed and tried to absorb what had happened over the past few months. Not too long ago,

I was sitting there looking at pictures of me and my parents and me and Julie. Now I had pictures of me with Alex. I lifted the frame and ran my finger down his face. Then I looked at the picture of the four of us: me, Alex, Julie, and Brett. I thought about calling Julie, but I didn't know what to say to her. I laid back and rolled to my side. I reached for the frame that held the picture of me and Alex.

The rest of the week went by in a blur. Julie and I worked hard on a new campaign. It wasn't as glamorous as Amoureux, but it was work. I was so happy I could see that it could've been a marketing campaign for condoms and I'd have been happy. Julie never really mentioned Brett, and I didn't either. On Friday, Mark came into Julie's office and asked if we wanted to grab a pizza with him. Val was working at the restaurant, so he would be alone.

"Sounds great to me. What do you think, Julie?"

She stared out the window with a pencil between her teeth. "Yeah, sure. Whatever."

"Did you hear what we said?"

"What? Yeah, of course I did. Pizza."

We grabbed a cab even though we were only going about six blocks. It was getting cold out, and I realized Thanksgiving was just a week and a half away. I had so much to be thankful for, even Garrett. We walked into the Italian restaurant, and the smell of garlic hit me hard. It smelled divine. We were greeted by the hostess and shown to a booth. Julie ordered our drinks, and Mark ordered two large pizzas for us.

Julie took a sip of water that was placed in front of

her. "So did you send out invites for the engagement party?"

I shook my head. "Alex took care of all that. Since it's so soon, he emailed or called everyone."

"He's really a good guy, Aub. I'm sorry I didn't think so at first. Apparently I don't have the best judgment."

"Yes, you do. People make mistakes, then they learn and grow from them. It's all good." I grabbed her hand. "Everything will be fine. I promise."

Our pizza came, and we devoured it. We laughed when we realized we were full and we'd left a whole pizza untouched. Julie and I looked at Mark.

"What?" he said. "It could be my dinner tomorrow."

"You date a girl whose father owns a restaurant and you worry about dinner?" Julie was a little snarky.

Mark rolled his eyes. "Her father owns it, not her."

"So back to your party . . . Is Jack coming?" Julie was obviously unimpressed by Mark's retort.

"I told Alex to invite him, but I don't know what he said." I needed to ask him about that. "We're going to visit his mom and sister this weekend."

Mark looked at me as though I was insane. "What? Where are you going?"

"To the cemetery. Alex wants to go, so I'll go with him. He wants to introduce me."

Julie's eyes filled with tears. "That's really sweet."

"Is it weird that I'm nervous? I mean, they aren't really there. But what if they don't like me? What if his mom sends some type of sign?"

Mark and Julie stared at me.

Mark gave me a wink. "My mom would love you, so I'm sure his will too."

I took a sip of my soda. "Yeah, maybe. I don't know. I just have this odd feeling about it."

I wasn't sure if I believed in signs, but I knew I wanted his mom and sister to like me. It was cold, and the weather would get worse over the weekend. All I could think of was a large snowball hitting me or me slipping on ice. I wished I could shake that feeling.

Chapter 14

ALEX DIDN'T SPEND THE NIGHT because he had errands to run before we went to the cemetery. He planned on picking me up at ten. I woke early due to my nerves. I felt like I did when I was younger and excited about the first day of school. I decided to call my parents. They agreed to let Alex pay for the wedding, but they wanted me to tell him that if he needed anything, they would be more than happy to contribute. I thanked them and said I would mention it to Alex.

I was looking for my hat and gloves when Alex came in. The front door nearly hit me in the ass since I was bending over in the closet next to it. I looked back, and Alex peeked around the door.

"Hey, babe. Sorry about that." He tried to stifle a laugh.

I stood and brushed off my jeans. "It's okay. I was looking for my gloves."

Alex closed the door and handed me a single orchid, accompanied by his beautiful smile. "For my beautiful girl. Thank you for going with me today. I'll take you out afterward."

I scrunched my brow and looked at my clothes. "Do

I need to change?"

"No, you're perfect the way you are." He kissed me, and I melted.

"Okay, where are we going?"

Alex put his finger to his lips.

"Another surprise, huh? Okay, as long as I'm dressed okay." I walked into the kitchen and put the flower in water. I was so bad at keeping them alive. "Would you like some coffee or do you want to get going?"

His hands were in his pockets. He looked nervous. "I'm ready if you are."

I threw my arms around his neck. "Are you okay? When was the last time you visited them?"

He stared into my eyes. "Before I went to Paris."

"I'm really sorry, Alex. I can't believe you left everything for me." I shook my head and looked down.

He raised my head. "I told you, I wouldn't have wanted to be anywhere else. I'd give my life for you."

Tears filled my eyes. "I'd give mine for you, too."

"Great. Now that we've got that cleared up, what do you say? Ready?"

I grabbed my gloves and put on my coat. "Ready."

He grabbed my hand and walked me to his SUV. After he opened my door, I slid in and watched my man walk around to his door. When Alex started the car, my nerves started. I was glad I'd taken my pill when I got up. He turned on the radio, and "Be Still" from The Fray played. I loved that song. We drove out of the city and headed toward Long Island.

"My mom always liked the country, so that's where

she and Ellie are," he said.

I took held his hand, which was resting on the gear shift. "I'm sure it's beautiful."

We pulled into the cemetery, and my heart rate accelerated. Alex drove us down a winding road. Fallen leaves swirled around. He slowed and stopped in front of beautiful headstones. I looked at them, and a tear ran down my cheek. Alex got out of the car, came around to my side, and opened my door.

I sat there and looked at him. "Are you sure about this?"

He took my hand and helped me out of the car. He kissed my head. "I can't wait for them to meet you. Come on." He grabbed a bouquet of white orchids from the back seat. "I always bring her a bouquet of her favorite flowers."

He held my hand and walked toward the headstone that read "Logan." There was an angel above Ellie's name and a heart above Angela's. I looked down and saw a bouquet of orchids.

Alex must have noticed it too because a sigh escaped him. "I guess my dad was here."

I guess they both did the same thing. I wondered if Alex had known that, but I didn't ask. "I'm sure he misses them." I moved closer to him and held his arm.

"Yeah, I know. I'm sure he does." He stared at the headstone. "Mom and El, this is Aubrey." His voice cracked. "She's going to be my wife. I wish you both were really here to meet her. She's an amazing woman. She's courageous, loving, smart, beautiful, and she's all mine."

I looked at him, and a tear left the corner of his eye.

I didn't know what to do or say. I cleared my throat. "It is a pleasure meeting you both. I'm sorry you're not here too. Alex has made me the happiest I've ever been. He gives me courage and strength, but most of all, he gives me love. The same love you gave him." I looked at Alex. He was smiling. "I want you to know I'll take care of him for the rest of my life. I'll hold his heart with tender hands. I'll encourage him no matter what. He's a successful man, but his greatest success is who he is; everything else is secondary. I love him more than I've ever loved anyone. I'll love him for the rest of my life. I want you both to know that." I kissed my fingers and touched the stone.

We heard twigs snapping, and we turned to see Jack behind us.

His eyes were watery. "I'm sorry to intrude. I think I left my hat when I was here earlier." He walked past us. It was on the ground not far from the orchids. He put it on and turned to us. "Aubrey, that was beautiful. I'm sorry for upsetting you when you came to see me. I see how much you love my son and how much he loves you. I just want you both to be happy."

I was stunned. I knew in my heart that Alex's mom had sent him. I had been worried about what sign she would send, but it was wonderful. I hugged him. "Thank you."

"I should be thanking you. I'm surprised you didn't walk away that day. If it isn't too late, I'd like to welcome you to the Logan family. I'm pleased that you'll be my daughter-in-law." He smiled at me and looked at Alex. "Son, I'm sorry for how I acted. I hope you can forgive me."

Alex looked as stunned as I thought I did. "Thank

you, Dad. I'm glad that you understand that Aubrey comes first to me."

His father nodded. "That's how it should be. I should have put your mother first, and I didn't. I've been thinking about that a lot lately. How different things could've been. I lost them and you at the same time. If I could change the past, I would, but if it's okay, I'd like to focus on the present and the future with my son back in my life."

Alex hugged his father.

I looked at the headstone and then to the sky. I mouthed, "Thank you."

"Aubrey and I are going to go to lunch. Would you like to join us?" Alex looked like a young boy.

Jack smiled. "I think that would be great. It's my treat. It's the least I can do."

Alex and I walked back to the car to follow Jack to a steakhouse he liked near Rockefeller Center.

Alex started the car and looked at me. "Well, that was unexpected."

I smiled and nodded. "Yes, it was. Sometimes the best things are unexpected. You were unexpected."

At the restaurant, we valeted the car and met Jack at a table. He ordered a bottle of wine with a pensive, nervous look. "So what's new in the wedding department?"

"Actually, Aubrey and I are having an engagement party next Sunday. I was going to call and invite you. We hope you can come."

"I wouldn't miss it. Thank you. Have you two picked a date?"

"Aubrey did, and I think it's a great choice. Tell him,

sweetheart."

I looked at Alex and then at Jack. "We agreed on December twenty-first."

Jack looked at me and smiled, and I saw his resemblance to Alex. "I can't think of a better date. Angela would have loved you, Aubrey. To think that I was pushing you both away . . . It's funny because I wasn't planning on going to the cemetery today. I was going to go yesterday, and I got busy. This morning, something told me to go."

I looked at Alex. "It was your mom."

He looked at me and then at his dad. "My mom?"

"Ever since you told me you wanted to go to the cemetery, I've been nervous. Like something was going to happen. Naturally, I thought bad things. I was hoping your mom would send some sort of sign, and then your dad showed up. I think that your mom sent us all there on the same day." I took a sip of my water.

"I think you're right," Jack said. "I think it was Angela. I can see why Alex loves you; you're easy to love."

After lunch, Alex told his dad we'd see him next week at our party. They shook hands, and Jack gave me a hug good-bye.

Alex threw his arm around me. "Are you ready for your surprise?"

I turned and walked backward out of the restaurant so I could see his face. "Yes, what is it?"

He spun me around and whispered in my ear, "You're always trying to get things out of me. When are you going to learn that I won't tell you? Before your surprise, I need to go to the club and pick something up."

"Then can I get my surprise?" I was practically bouncing. The day had been weighing on me, but it had become one of the best days ever, and I still had a surprise coming.

"Yes, Miss Impatient, then you can get your surprise." He chuckled.

"I have patience." I crossed my arms and pouted.

"Yeah, you have patience. That look will not make me tell you what I have planned, so forget it. Now, get in the car so you don't have to wait anymore." Alex winked as he opened my door.

We pulled away, and I felt at peace with everything that had happened so far that day. We pulled into the club's parking lot, which was empty except for a couple cars that I assumed were the cleaners.'

"Come on, babe."

Alex and I walked into the club and saw a few people sitting at the bar.

Mike came out from the back. "Hey, boss. Everything is all set."

Alex turned to me. "Surprise, baby."

He looked so pleased with himself, and I was beyond confused. "Um . . . thank you?"

Laughing, he brought me over to the people at the bar. He pointed at an attractive woman in her forties. "Aubrey, this is Mary. She works with Rob and Chelsea." He motioned toward the much younger couple.

"It's nice to meet you all." I looked at Alex. "I don't understand."

"You told me that when you were younger, you wanted to be a ballroom dancer. Rob and Chelsea are professional dancers, and they'll be teaching us some dances. Mary is their wardrobe designer. She has clothes for you that go with the dances."

I stared at him. "You did this because I told you I wanted to be a ballroom dancer? What if I'd told you I had wanted to be an astronaut?"

"I'd have bought you the moon."

I threw myself at him. My legs went around his waist, and I kissed his face.

Alex laughed. "I take it you like this surprise?"

I leaned back and looked at him. "Are you kidding? This is awesome! I can't believe you did this! I hope I can learn the steps."

He kissed me. "If I don't put you down, the only thing you're going to learn is how to have sex in front of people."

I giggled, and he set me down. He swatted my butt as I scurried off to his office with Mary. She informed me that the first dance we would learn was the jive. Mary pulled out an adorable blue dress covered in sparkles. It ended above my knees and had little cap sleeves. I slipped it on behind a makeshift changing wall. She handed me a cute pair of low-heeled nude dancing shoes. I put them on and twirled.

"Very nice. Mr. Logan will be pleased," Mary said.

I walked down the stairs and saw Alex sitting at the bar with Rob and Chelsea. He inspected me from head to toe.

I spun around. "You like?"

He put his arms around my waist. "Like? I love!

Let's do this."

Rob and Chelsea danced the jive once for us so we could see what it was like. It was really fast, and I pictured myself falling on my ass. Alex gave Mike, who was in the DJ booth, a thumbs up, and "Runaway Baby" by Bruno Mars played. We followed Rob and Chelsea as best we could while laughing between twirls. Alex even picked me up and tried to toss me around, but I couldn't contain my laughter, so it didn't work. We danced over and over again and I think by the twentieth time, we had it. Dancing was a lot harder than I'd thought.

"Okay, go with Mary and change for the next one." Alex was either excited or he wanted to get it over with.

"How many are we doing?"

"Two more. Now go," he said.

The next dance was the rumba, and I had on the skimpiest outfit. The dance was slow and seductive. I'd never do it with anyone else. Our hips moved together, and my panties could reveal my excitement. Chelsea told us we needed to think of making love when we danced the rumba. It was no wonder the rumba was easier for us than the jive.

For the last dance, I ran up the stairs and found Mary waiting for me with a long, flowing ball gown. It was cloud white and stunning. When I slipped it on, I felt beautiful. I walked down the stairs to the dance floor, and I saw that Alex had changed into a tux. We looked like a bride and groom, and I got goose bumps all over.

He brought my hand to his lips. "You're stunning, future Mrs. Logan."

I held my skirt out with my left hand and curtseyed. "As are you, Mr. Logan."

"Shall we?"

He walked me to the center of the dance floor for the waltz. Rob and Chelsea showed us the basic steps, but I was familiar with the dance. Alex nodded to Mike, and Frank Sinatra's "The Way You Look Tonight" came on.

I didn't move right away. I just looked at Alex. "Our song."

He grinned. "One of many."

We danced and held each other. I didn't hear Rob or Chelsea, and the music stopped, I think. But we kept moving.

Alex twirled me and pulled me into his chest. "I love you."

I felt as if my face would burst with my feelings. I was sure I was glowing because I was so happy. I looked at my handsome man. "I love you. I thought we were broken, and I'm so glad we aren't."

"No, we're not." He kissed the tip of my nose.

"Thank you for making my dream come true."

He dipped me and pulled me into a searing kiss. We separated, and he looked into my eyes. I thought I would melt into a puddle on the dance floor.

"You're my dream come true every day," he said.

"I don't think I'll ever be able to show you how much you mean to me, but I promise to spend my life trying to."

He smiled. "Come on, let's get out of here."

We went up to his office. I took off the dress and

hung it on the rack. I didn't see Mary though.

"Did Mary leave? I need to give her back these outfits," I said.

"No, you don't. They're yours."

I was stunned. "You bought me all of these?"

"I'll buy you the world if it makes you as happy as you are right now."

I shook my head. "I don't want the world. I just want you." I put my regular clothes back on.

Alex was already in his street clothes, and he had a mischievous glint in his eye. "Baby, we need to hurry because I thought of one more thing I need to give you."

"Really? What would that be?"

He took my hand and put it on the zipper of his pants. "Any questions?"

"Let's go."

Alex told Mike to lock up, and we were out the back door faster than ever. We got in Alex's car, and he drove us to his apartment. We practically raced into the building. The elevator opened, and an older couple and their Pomeranian got out. We got in, and Alex pressed me against the wall. The door was still open.

I panted, "Alex . . . the . . . door."

He pushed a button. The door closed, and before I knew it, my shirt was off. I stood in the elevator in my bra and jeans, and I couldn't have cared less if anyone else got in. We were in utter bliss in a world of our own.

The door opened at the twentieth floor, Alex's floor. He picked me up, and my legs wrapped around his waist. He didn't fumble with the key, and we landed on the couch. Alex unbuttoned my jeans and pulled them off, along with my thong. He shed his clothes and lowered himself on top of me. He pushed my hair off my face, and his palm rested on my cheek. My legs wrapped around him as he slid into me. I wasn't expecting it, and the move made my back arch. A cry flew out my mouth.

He turned us so his back was against the back of the couch and I was on top of him. "Let's rumba."

I didn't say anything. I just moved my hips in a circle, back and forth and up and down. My hips met his with every move, and his hands went from the small of my back to my hips while his lips found mine. When I picked up the pace, his tongue did as well. The kiss was more forceful than any kiss I could remember. I felt my legs shake, and his hand went into my hair. I shattered around him. We stopped kissing so I could catch my breath. I felt as if I was panting. I dropped my head to his shoulder and he held me.

Chapter 15

WALKING INTO THE OFFICE, I felt as if I was still on a cloud. I peeked around my cube at Julie's office and noticed the door was closed. I'd thought about calling her while I was on my way to work, but I didn't. I felt guilty about being so happy while she was so sad. I fired up my computer to check my schedule. I heard a knock on my cube wall, which always made me laugh. I looked over and saw Mark. He looked hung over and held a cup of coffee.

"Please don't tell me you and Val are having issues. I can only deal with one best friend being sad, and I'm not even dealing with that very well." I smiled at him, but he didn't return it.

"No, I'm not having issues with Val. I'm having issues with Jess." I opened my mouth to say something, but he stopped me. "Don't say anything please. I know she shouldn't be an issue. She called me last night and was really upset. I didn't know what to do."

I lowered my brow. "So what did you do?"

Mark sat in the extra chair in my cubicle and took a sip of his coffee. He didn't say anything.

I was uneasy. "Mark?"

"I talked to her. Well, I mostly listened while she talked. She's so sad about everything. I just don't know what to do. She lost her job and her boyfriend, or whatever he was. She lost her money. She's just sad. I don't know how else to say it." He shrugged, leaned back, and exhaled. "I don't have feelings for her anymore, but she needs a friend." He took a sip of his coffee and looked at me.

I knew my mouth was open, but no words came out.

"You don't have to say anything. You probably think I'm stupid for even giving her the time of day, but what would you have done?" Mark exhaled. "I don't know. I suppose I should tell Val, right?"

I put my hands up in surrender. "Please don't ask me that."

He half smiled. "Too late. I already did."

"Ugh! I think that being honest is the only way to go. God knows I learned my lesson. Don't be upset with Val if this sends her for a loop. You have to know it will upset her, but I think she knows the kind of guy you are. If you want to be Jessica's friend, then I hope Val understands that."

He nodded. "Just like you understood her friendship with Alex?"

My heart hurt a little because they had had a sort of "relationship." I nodded. "Yeah, like I did. It might not be easy for her. Just remember that."

Julie came around the corner with her coffee cup. "Hey, guys. What's going on?" She seemed as though she was in a good mood.

"Hey, Jules, how are you?"

She tilted her head back and forth. "I'm okay. Trying to get over everything. I'll be fine. How are you? How was your weekend? Oh my God, Aubrey, I totally forgot you went to the cemetery yesterday. Everything go okay?"

"The cemetery was sad and happy at the same time. I was glad to share that time with Alex and being close to where his mom and sister were buried was sad. Then his dad showed up."

Mark and Julie both looked concerned.

"It was one of the best parts of the day. Alex and his dad spoke, and I think they'll be fine. He's even coming to our engagement party. Then . . . Are you ready for this?" I beamed and spun in my chair.

Julie laughed. "Spill it! What did you guys do after that?" She winked at me.

"I think this is my cue to leave." Mark stood.

Julie hit his arm. "Shut it and sit down. So what? Dish!"

"Well, we went back to the club and . . ." I looked around as though I was about to tell them juicy news. "Alex had hired professional ballroom dancers to teach us. He even hired a stylist for me!"

Julie gasped. "You've always wanted to do that! He's the best!"

Mark chimed in. "He's a jerk."

"What? How does that make him a jerk?" I wasn't pleased by his statement, and by the look on Julie's face, neither was she.

"Do you know how horrible your boyfriend makes the rest of us look? Shit. I hope Val doesn't find out."

We all laughed, and Mark said he needed to get to

his desk. He kissed us both on the cheek and left.

"You really are lucky, Aubrey. I'm so happy for you I could burst."

"I want you to be happy too."

"I will be, I promise," Julie said. "Now I need to get to my office. I have a lot to do. I hate Mondays."

I usually hated Mondays too, but I was happy. I thought about the day before, and it had ended up being one of the best days I'd ever had. I picked up my phone and called Alex. I was looking at a picture of us when he answered.

"Hello there, future Mrs. Logan."

I couldn't help giggling. "Hi."

"What's up? Miss me already?"

"As a matter of fact, yes, I do. I was thinking about you and the amazing day we had yesterday. I just wanted you to know you were on my mind."

"Yesterday was pretty incredible, wasn't it? I love surprising you. I intend to keep doing so for the rest of our lives. I was thinking about you too actually. Everyone I invited to our engagement party has accepted. It should be a lot of fun. I can't wait to make the formal announcement that you will be my wife."

I closed my eyes and let the word wife linger in my mind. I pictured him in a tux and me in my white gown with Julie by my side. Then I pictured Brett next to Alex, and my daydream ended. "Yeah, I can't wait either."

"That didn't sound enthusiastic. What's wrong?"

"Do you know if Brett is bringing a date? I don't want anything to make Julie sad."

Alex was quiet.

"Alex? Did you hear me?"

"Yeah, sorry. He did ask if he could bring a date, and I told him yes."

Shit. "Oh." Yup, that was all I said. Julie was going to flip. I would have to tell her. I shouldn't have asked.

"Aubrey, what was I supposed to say? 'No, you can't bring a date because your ex-girlfriend will be there'?"

Yes. "No, I just wish he hadn't asked. I don't know how Julie will react. I'll tell her." Not a conversation I wanted to have.

"I'm sorry, babe. She knows he's already been with someone else, so do you think she'll really care?"

"I don't know. This sucks, ya know? I hate this. I've never seen her so sad. It breaks my heart, and there's nothing I can do to help her. I'll talk to you later. I love you."

After we hung up, I stood to go into Julie's office and almost ran into her. My hand went to my chest. "You startled me, Jules."

"Sorry. I take it that was Alex on the phone?"

I nodded.

"So Brett has a date for Sunday?"

Shit. How much did she hear? "Yes. I'm really sorry. I wish he'd wake up."

"I don't want him." Julie looked down. When she looked up, she had tears in her eyes. "I love him, but he slept with her. How can I love a man who would do that to me? He must be totally into her since he's bringing her to your party. If he wanted me back, that would be the perfect opportunity. He's not taking it." She wiped tears away.

I hugged her. "I'm so sorry. You still want to be there, right?"

"Yeah, yeah, of course I do. It'll be okay, I promise."

"Okay, if you're sure." I almost told her she could bring someone, but I knew she wouldn't. "Want to grab a drink after work? We don't have to go to the club. We can go somewhere else."

"Sure, that sounds great. But we can go to the club. I'd like to thank Alex for being the man we all dream of. Ironic, isn't it?"

"What is?"

"Alex. I mean, he's done some shitty things, but all in all, he's an awesome boyfriend . . . fiancé. Look at everything he's done for you. It still blows my mind that he was in Paris with you. What man does that? What man leaves his business, his friends, his life? A man who knows what it means to love unconditionally. I know I didn't give him a fair shake and I wanted to kick his ass after the Leah debacle, but he has to be the best man for you. I'm so happy for you." Julie pulled me into a hug. "I love you."

I was crying too. "I love you too."

We got ourselves together, and Julie went to her office. I sat down to edit some marketing copy Mark had sent me. I read the words, but nothing made sense. I knew it wasn't the copy—it was me. I put my forehead in my hands and my fingers in my hair. I was so frustrated I felt like pulling my hair and screaming. I tossed my pencil instead and leaned back in my chair to look at the ceiling.

"Stressed?"

For the second time, my hand covered my chest and I jumped. "Shit."

Alex stood at my cubicle wall. He had on his designer jeans that hung low, a rugged black leather belt, a baby blue T-shirt, and his black leather jacket. His hair was messy, very JFL, and extremely sexy. "I'm sorry. I didn't mean to scare you. Is everything okay?"

I shook my head. "No." I got out of my chair and fell into his chest.

His arms wrapped around me. "Sweetheart, what's wrong? Are you not feeling okay?"

My words went into his chest. "I feel bad for Julie. Brett's being mean to her."

His hands went to my shoulders, and he moved me so I was no longer plastered to his chest. He brought his palms to my cheeks, tilted my head up, and looked into my eyes. "I feel badly too, but I don't want you getting so upset. I can tell Brett to come alone if that's what you want."

Yes, that is exactly what I want. "No, he can bring someone. I just want them to get back together."

"Babe, Sunday is about you and me." He kissed my lips. "I don't want us to concentrate on our friends' messed up relationship, okay?"

"You're right. Sunday is about us. Have you talked to your dad?"

"Not since yesterday. I emailed him the party details. I need to go back to work, but I was in the neighborhood, so I wanted to pop in and see you. Did you speak to your parents about the wedding?"

"Yes, I did, and my mom agreed to let you cover the costs. She said if you need anything to let them know, and they would be more than happy to contribute."

"I'll talk to them about it when I see them. Want to meet me later for a drink? We can go home after that."

"Yeah, actually Julie and I are planning on going out. I'm not even going to ask if Brett will be there. It's Monday, so it shouldn't be too busy, right?"

"I'm trying out a new DJ. He has a following, so I don't know how busy it'll be. I wanted to see if having new music during happy hour would bring in more people. Today's the first night, so we'll see."

"Shouldn't you have brought in your marketing team for that? Do people even know?" I asked.

"We announced it over the weekend. If we don't get a good response, then I'll set something up with you guys. I have to go, though. I'll see you tonight. By the way, this is for you." He handed me a white orchid.

I didn't know where he'd been hiding it. I laughed. "Adding magic to your many talents?"

He winked and walked toward the door. I smiled and set the orchid on my desk.

Julie and I arrived at the club around six. Alex had been right—there were more people than normal.

"Man, this place is jumping. I guess your fiancé knows his shit," Julie said.

I looked at the bar. It was packed. Before I could walk toward it, I was scooped up from behind and spun around.

"Hey, beautiful. I have a table for you guys upstairs.

I don't know why you would want to sit at the bar when you have a VIP table reserved for you," Alex said.

I looked at Julie. "Shall we?"

Julie scanned the room. "Sure, lead the way."

We went upstairs. It was much nicer than the bar.

"I'll send someone over to get your drink order," Alex said. "I need to go check on the DJ and a few other things. See you guys in a few."

I looked at Julie, but she was staring at something behind me. I turned around, and all I saw was Alex's backside. "Um, Jules? Like something you see?"

"Yeah, your boyfriend has a really great ass."

We laughed.

"I can't wait until Sunday. It'll be like practice for your wedding!"

"This all happened so fast," I said. "If you think about what has happened in the past year, it's crazy."

"Sure is. But everything worked out the way it was supposed to, right? You found romance, your muse is amazing, and you're getting married! I'm so excited I could burst."

Julie was so cute. Even though her heart was crushed, she was still enthusiastic for us.

"Want to go and look for dresses this Saturday?" I asked.

"Finally! I thought you were going to walk down the aisle naked! Yes, let's do that. You have less than a month, so you'll probably have to buy something off the rack."

"No, she won't." Alex appeared. He must have

heard us talking.

"What are you talking about? Are you in the wedding gown business now?" Julie laughed.

I looked at him. "What do you mean?"

"No, I'm not in the wedding gown business, but I have a friend who will design whatever Aubrey wants. So your job is to make sure she gets what she wants. I don't care if she wants real diamonds on her dress. Got it?" Alex kissed my forehead and left.

"Okay, I'm officially jealous." Julie stared at the door Alex just walked through.

I waved my hand. "No, you don't need to be jealous."

"You can brush it off if you want to, but that is crazy cool."

Julie was right, it was cool that he would give me anything I wanted. I never really thought about Alex's money, except when his father brought it up. "At least I know it'll fit, right? Since I don't have to worry about mine, how about we go look for yours? What color do you want to wear? I can call Val and see if she can come too."

Julie's expression changed. "Sure. I really don't care what color. No, scratch that, yes, I do. I don't want to wear cotton candy pink or anything like that. What about black? I can rock black, and if Dumbass brings someone, I want to look hot."

"Jules, who knows? By then, your two could be back together."

"I don't think so. But let's not worry about it. I'm sorry I brought it up. I'm going to have to deal with him on Sunday anyways."

I gave her a sympathetic look. "I hate that he's bringing someone."

"Me too, but we can't do anything about it. If he wants to spend his life with a skank who will screw him when he wants, that's his choice. I need more than that. I didn't think I ever would, but after being with Brett, that's what I want." Julie laughed. "Ironic, right? I never wanted a serious relationship with the guys who wanted one with me, and now the table's turned. I guess this is my karma." She stared at her drink stirrer going around and around in her glass.

I looked up and saw Brett walking toward us with Alex. I tapped Julie's foot so she'd look at me, but she didn't. "Hey, guys," I said.

That got her attention. She looked behind her and then back to me. "Great."

I slid farther into the booth, and Alex sat next to me. Julie didn't move, and Brett just stood there. He looked sad. I wondered where Nikki was.

Julie must have wondered the same because she asked, "Where's your girlfriend?"

Brett shoved his hands in his pockets. "I don't have a girlfriend."

"Oh, that's right. You don't do commitment. Let me rephrase. Where's your fuck buddy?"

"Jules . . ." I said.

"No, Aubrey, it's true. That's what he wanted from me and I said no, so he found a slut to say yes. Isn't that right, Brett?"

Brett's expression remained blank. His eyes were almost hollow. There was no life in them at all. "I just came over to say hi. I'll see you guys later. For the record, Julie, I didn't want you to be my fuck buddy. I wanted you to be my girlfriend. Have a good night."

"I should go too." Julie's voice cracked.

"I'll go with you." I looked at Alex.

He slid out of the booth. "My driver will take you both home."

"Thank you. You're a good guy, Alex." Julie smiled as a tear ran down her cheek.

Alex placed his hand on her shoulder. "He's trying. He really is. He's not bringing anyone on Sunday, just so you know."

I was surprised to hear that.

Julie smirked and shrugged. "It really doesn't matter, does it? Thank you, Alex."

Alex kissed me and told me he'd see me later.

The rest of the week went by slowly. It was monotonous, and my nerves were getting to me. I had received a call from Mary. Apparently she was the designer Alex had referred to. She was coming over on Saturday to show me gown styles and fabrics and discuss my wedding gown. I asked Julie to come over Friday for a girl's night. We planned to hang out, watch chick flicks, and chat until we fell asleep. Julie was as excited about it as I was.

On Friday, Julie and I changed into our PJs and waited for the pizza guy. We were sitting on the couch when the buzzer rang.

I went to the door and pushed the intercom. "Hello."

A muffled voice came through the speaker. "Pizza

delivery for Aubrey Ryan."

"Come on up." I went to my purse to grab some money. When I heard the knock on my door, I opened it and found out that my pizza guy was Alex. I laughed. "What are you doing?"

"I wanted to kiss you good night since I wasn't allowed over here tonight. I intercepted your pizza guy." Alex walked in and set the pizza on the table. He looked at Julie. "Hi, Julie."

"Hey, Alex."

"Okay, I'm not going to hang around. I just wanted to say have a good night. Remember, the sky is the limit for your gown, okay?"

"Yes, sir." I walked Alex to the door. "Thank you for the pizza." I put my hand on his jacket zipper and unzipped it a little. I kissed his heart and zipped his jacket back up. "I love you."

He held my face, looked into my eyes, and kissed me. I felt it all the way to my feet. My knees literally became weak.

"You two have a great night." Alex pulled the door closed.

"You're a lucky lady, Ryan," Julie said. "Now how about that pizza?"

We cuddled together to watch the Hallmark Channel. By the time the credits rolled, we both had tears running down our cheeks. We looked at each other and laughed.

"We're a pair, aren't we?" I said.

Julie handed me a tissue. "I don't know what my problem is. I think all of this shit with Brett has me all messed up, or maybe it's my best friend who's getting married in a few weeks!"

"Can you believe it? It blows my mind! We'd better get some sleep because Mary is coming at nine."

We crawled into my bed together like we did when we were teenagers.

I turned off the lights. "Good night, Julie."

"Thanks for everything, Aubrey. I'm really happy for you. I can't wait to help with your wedding gown."

"I wouldn't want anyone else helping me. You're my family. Love you. Good night."

"Good night, Aubrey."

Mary was on time and accompanied by two assistants. One helped me try on different styles, and the other draped fabric over me. It was quite the production.

Julie sat in a chair and held signs like a judge in the Olympics. Only a few earned anything over a five. The last dress I tried on was a fit and flare, and the fabric was a combination of soft lace and tulle. It had a sweetheart neckline, and since it would most likely be cold, Mary paired the dress with a white faux fur shrug. I walked into the living room, and Julie started crying.

She stood and dropped her score cards. "Oh my god, Aubrey, that is perfect. You're so beautiful." She held up both her hands. "That's a ten! What do you think?"

I stepped in front of the mirror Mary had set up by my front door. I was stunned when I looked at my reflection. I felt my eyes well up, and I looked at Julie. "Yea, I think this is it. We should call my mom so she can feel like she's a part of this."

Julie grabbed my laptop and called her via Skype.

Mom started crying when she saw me. "You look perfect, honey, just perfect. You look beautiful."

Mary and I discussed where the embellishments would be. I told her I didn't want too many, and the gown really didn't need them. Once that was settled, Mary and her crew headed out. It was mid-afternoon, and I was spent. Julie decided to head home, and I headed for a bath.

I sank into the bubbles and let the hot water lap over my shoulders. My hair was up in a bun, and I lit some candles. I had my iPad playing the songs that Alex had transferred to it from the tablet he had given me. I sang along to some, and I didn't hear my front door open. When I saw a shadow and then Alex, I was startled. I moved so quickly that water spilled from my tub.

"Geez, Alex, you scared me." I looked at his black pants and gray, fitted, long-sleeved V-neck shirt. "But you look so hot you can scare me anytime."

"I love your outfit too. Those bubbles look amazing on you." Alex laughed.

"How about you join me?"

Alex didn't hesitate to strip off his clothes and slip in behind me. He wrapped his arms around me and kissed my cheek. "So how was the gown shopping?"

"It was great, thank you. I found the perfect one. Mary was awesome, and there's nothing better than having the gowns brought to me."

"You would be beautiful in a sack, but you deserve the best."

I leaned my head back and looked at him. "You're

the best, so if that's what I deserve, then I already have it."

He kissed me, and I turned around to wrap my legs around his waist. My arms slid around his neck, and my hands slid into his damp hair. We looked into each other's eyes. He brought his lips to mine and kissed me. I moved my hips and reached into the water. I wrapped my hand around him to guide him into me. I didn't move right away. I just wanted to be connected to him. He must have understood because he didn't move or say anything. He was letting me take the lead, and that was just what I wanted. I moved my hips while my thighs slid on his. I leaned back, and he brought his right hand to my chest as his left supported my back. He moved his hand between my legs, making me move faster. I sat up and our chests touched. We were wrapped in each other's arms and legs.

"You're so good, Aubrey."

His hands went to my hips, and he took control. He moved me faster, and I could tell that he was getting close as a groan escaped his throat. I grabbed his hair and crashed my lips onto his. Our tongues met, and I lost all control. My legs shook, and I came as he thrust into me. I slowed my pace, and put my head on his shoulder. We sat there for a while, holding each other.

"Babe, the water is cooling down. Let's get out of here."

I hadn't even noticed the change in temperature. I moved to get off him and looked into his eyes. I couldn't help but smile. Alex stood and grabbed a towel and wrapped me up in it before he grabbed one for himself. His body was perfect. The way his muscles moved was enough to send me into orgasmic bliss. I could watch him all day and never tire of it.

Alex glanced at me. “You keep looking at me like that, and we’re going to go right to bed.”

I smiled. “Okay.”

Chapter 16

THE ENGAGEMENT PARTY WAS IN full swing. Alex's father was there, and he was talking with Brian and his wife. I imagined that Brian was pitching him on using Walker-Stone Marketing for Logan Industries. I smiled at that thought. I'd love to work with Jack to prove to him that I'm a hard worker and not relying on Alex to provide for me. Brian glanced up and saw me, so I walked over to them.

"I see you've met my future father-in-law." I smiled at Jack.

"Yes, I have," Brian said. "He's a lucky man to be adding you to his family."

Jack looked at me. "I'm lucky indeed. I knew my son had impeccable taste, but Aubrey is the best." Jack hugged me, and when he released me, he kept his hands on my shoulders. "I want you to know I couldn't be happier for you and my son. You're good for him, and I'm sorry I didn't see that in the beginning."

I nodded and glanced at where Brian had been standing, but he was gone. He must have sensed that Jack wanted to say something private to me. "I know some women were attracted to Alex because of his wealth, but I'm not like that. Material possessions and money aren't important to me, but he is important to me. He's my missing piece, and I'm so glad that you've reconciled." I hugged him.

"Hey, Dad, you know she's spoken for." Alex came up and shook his dad's hand.

"Yes, Aubrey just broke my heart and told me that she's taken."

We all laughed, and I noticed that Alex and Jack had the same laugh. Their eyes lit up in the same way as well. I was happy to see them putting their animosities aside.

"Can I steal you both for a moment?" Jack asked. "I have something for you, and I'd like to give it to you now if that's okay. I promise not to keep you long."

I looked at Alex, and he nodded.

Alex led us to a table in the corner. "Will this do?"

"This is perfect." Jack reached into the inside pocket of his suit jacket and pulled out an envelope. "I was going to wait until the wedding, but I wanted you to have this now." He handed the envelope to Alex.

Alex looked at me and then back at the envelope. He slid his finger underneath the flap and pulled out what appeared to be legal documents. He scanned the documents and then looked at his father. "Am I reading this correctly? Isn't this the house you and mom built on Shelter Island? I thought you sold it years ago."

"I didn't sell it. I couldn't. Your mother and I loved that house and loved watching you and your sister play there. It's yours now. Well, yours and Aubrey's. I had both of your names added to the deed. I hope you and your family will enjoy as many happy times there as we did."

I think my chin hit the table. I looked at Alex. His eyes were glazed with tears, and his dad's were too.

Alex cleared his throat. "I don't know what to say. I'm shocked." He looked at me. "We have a home for our family."

I beamed and looked at Jack. "Thank you really doesn't suffice. This is an extremely generous gift, and I hope you know that our home is yours as well."

Jack stood and blotted his nose with a hanky. "I hope you fill that home with many children. Don't let days pass without appreciating each other. I know I don't have to tell either of you that, but I remind myself every day."

Alex hugged his dad, which brought tears to my eyes.

"Well, what do you say you kids get back to your party? I think I might head home."

I took his hand. "Not until you dance with your favorite future daughter-in-law."

"I'd be a fool to pass up that invitation."

Jack and I walked to the dance floor, and the DJ put on a slow song.

"I'm so happy that you're here," I said. "I know Alex appreciates it as well."

"Young lady, we have you to thank for that. I don't know if another woman would have wanted me here after all I said to you."

I assumed he was talking about Leah and the prenup. "Well, we don't have to worry about that because I want you here and I want you in our lives.

Alex is my world and he's a part of you. That means you're stuck with me."

"I wouldn't want it any other way." Jack kissed my cheek as the song ended. "Thank you for this dance. Please save me one at the wedding."

"I will. Thank you, Jack, for everything." We walked over to Alex, Mark, Val, and Julie. "Jack, I'd like to introduce you to our friends. This is Mark, his girlfriend, Val, and my best friend, Julie."

"It's nice to meet you all. I remember seeing you at the benefit. Son, I'm going to head out. Thank you for inviting me to your wonderful party. Congratulations." He hugged Alex.

I sat with my friends and couldn't wait to tell them the news about Jack's gift.

"That seemed to go well. I'm glad everyone is getting along," Julie said.

"You don't know the half of it. Can I tell them, Alex?"

Alex gave me the go ahead. I told them that Jack had given us Alex's childhood home on Shelter Island as a wedding gift. Everyone just looked at me as if I was speaking a foreign language. They must have been stunned because no one said anything. Alex chuckled.

"Holy shit, Aubrey, he gave you guys a house? How awesome is that? I can picture you as a little homemaker!" Julie was as excited as I was, but the thought of just staying at home and not working wasn't what I had planned. I hoped Alex didn't want me to do that.

"It's pretty incredible, right?"

Alex sidled up to me. "We can all drive out and see

it on Thanksgiving if you'd like. We could have a big dinner for our wedding party."

"I think I'm spending Thanksgiving in the city at my parents' place, but thanks." Julie sipped her drink and gave a half smile.

"Sorry, Julie, I wasn't thinking," Alex said.

"Don't worry about it. Have your friends over and have a great time." Julie walked away.

"Wow, I blew that one," Alex said. "I hate that she isn't with Brett. I know he loves her. He needs to wake the hell up. I'll go check on the caterers. Some of these trays look empty." Alex walked away.

I looked around the club at our guests. From the looks of it, everyone was having a good time. I saw Alex talking to the caterer, and farther down the bar was Brett. He looked horrible. He wore a deep navy suit, but his tie was gone and the top button was undone. He stared at the clear golden liquor in his glass, and he looked deep in thought. I approached him and sat on the stool next to him.

He glanced at me. "Hi, Aubrey, nice party."

"Thank you. Are you okay? No offense, but you don't look great."

He sat up straighter. "I'm sorry, I just have a lot on my mind. Don't be offended, but I can't talk to you about it." He took a sip of his drink and scrunched his brows together.

"It's about Julie, right? Look, Brett, I know she's my—"

"It's not Julie. Well, in a way it is, but not entirely." He took another sip.

It dawned on me. "This is about Nikki, right? You

broke it off with her and she's upset?"

Brett shot me a look. "I really don't want to talk about it."

I was mad. He wasn't that upset when he broke it off with Julie, but he seemed to care about Nikki more. "That's fine, you don't have to tell me. Can I say just one thing?"

Brett looked at me. "Am I going to be able to stop you?"

I shook my head. "No, probably not. I'm a little surprised you're this upset. When you stopped seeing Julie, who you claim to love, you moved on. Are you telling me you're more broken up over Nikki than Julie? Because if that's the case then—"

"She thinks she's pregnant."

My thoughts stopped. I stared at him and then looked at Julie. She was dancing with Mark, and they were laughing. My heart shattered. "Nikki's pregnant?"

"So she thinks." He dropped his head and looked at me out of the corner of his eye. "Ironic, isn't it? Julie left me because I didn't want to get married, and now I may have a kid on the way and I'll probably end up married to someone I don't even love." He looked at Julie. "And the love of my life will hate me forever because of it. I'm stupid. That's all there is to it."

"You said she thinks she's pregnant. She doesn't know for sure? And if she is, how do you know it's yours? She's not really a one-guy type of girl."

"Yeah, I know. That's what I said to her, and she got pissed and said that she's only been with me. We always used protection, but things happen sometimes. She's going to find out in a few weeks if she is, and then we have to wait to find out if I'm going to be a dad." He looked at Julie again. "She's going to hate me, but I need to tell her." He shook his head and tossed his crumpled napkin across the bar. "I'm an asshole. I let her go. What the hell was I thinking?"

Alex came up to us. "Trying to steal the bride-to-be?" He slid his arms around my waist.

Brett threw back his drink. "No, but never let her go. Don't do what I did and totally screw up your life because you got scared. I lost the one person I truly loved, and I'll never get her back."

"You were scared?"

We all turned and saw Julie standing behind Brett. She looked hopeful, and I felt like throwing up.

"Jules, I need to go to the ladies' room. Want to come?" I just wanted to get her out of there. I didn't know what Brett would say.

"No, I want to hear this."

No, you don't. Shit. I looked at Alex, who looked bewildered.

"You look beautiful, Julie." Brett stared at her and had a loving tone.

Julie tilted her head, trying to understand what he had just said. "Thank you. What did you mean when you said you were scared?"

"Babe, let's leave them to talk." Alex started pulling me away.

"No, I think we should hang with our friends."

Alex looked at me and chuckled. "I think they'll be fine. Let's dance." Alex pulled me to the dance floor, but I continually turned around to look at Brett and Julie. Alex held me close. "Want to tell me what that was about?"

I was about to tell him when we both saw Julie slap Brett so hard that his head jolted. He didn't bring his hand up to his cheek. He just looked at her with pleading eyes.

"What the hell was that?" Alex stopped moving.

"That most likely was Brett telling Julie that Nikki might be pregnant with his baby."

Alex looked at me in shock.

I looked into his eyes. "I told you I didn't want to leave them."

We hurried to the bar as Julie rushed toward the ladies' room. I beelined for her, and Alex continued to Brett. I glanced at the other guests. They were oblivious. The new DJ was keeping them on the dance floor and the wine and food kept them preoccupied. I burst into the bathroom to find Julie getting sick in one of the stalls.

"Jules, are you okay?"

The toilet flushed, and she came out wiping her mouth with a piece of toilet paper. "No, I'm not." She burst into tears, and I held her. "Oh my God, Aubrey, she's pregnant? He's going to be a father?"

"Shhh, I know. She might not be, and it might not be his."

"He just told me I'm the one he loves, and he wants to have a family with me. Me! That's what I wanted too, and now . . . now . . . it won't ever happen." She fell into my chest and sobbed.

There was a knock on the door. Alex called, "You two alone in here?"

"Yeah, we are," I said.

Alex walked in and put his hand on her back. "Julie, are you okay?"

She raised her head from my shoulder and wiped her eyes with her fingers. "No, I'm really not. I'm so sorry that I'm a mess at your party. Great friend I am, huh?"

"Everyone is starting to leave. That's what I wanted to tell Aubrey."

Julie waved me off. "Go, go, I'll be okay."

I didn't move. The weight on my chest was horrible. I leaned on the vanity and pressed my hand to my chest. I closed my eyes and took deep breaths.

"Are you okay?"

I looked up and saw Alex's reflection in the mirror. "Yes, thanks. I just needed to catch my breath." I turned to Julie. "Are you going to be okay if I leave?"

"Yeah, I'll be out in a minute. Let me just fix my face." Julie tried to sound upbeat, but between the sniffles, it really wasn't working.

Alex and I walked out, and I stopped when I saw Brett at the bar.

He was facing us and got up to approach us. "Is she okay?"

Alex grabbed my hand. "No, she isn't. You need to give her time. Hang out, and we'll talk after Aubrey and I say some good-byes."

Brett headed back to the bar while Alex and I put on happy faces and said good-bye to our guests. After the last one left, we walked back to the bar. Julie wasn't to be found, but Brett hadn't moved. I wondered where she was until I heard her talking . . . and laughing. I looked around and saw her laughing with the new DJ.

"See that?" Brett used his chin to point at Julie. "I deserve that. I deserve seeing her with someone else because that's what I did to her. I need to get out of here. I'll be back after Thanksgiving, boss."

"Yeah, sure, man. Whatever you need to do. Take as much time as you want."

Brett looked at me. "I'm sorry. I hate that I hurt her, ya know. I love her, and I destroyed us."

I hugged Brett. "It doesn't have to be over. Give her some time. Even if it is yours, that doesn't mean you need to be with Nikki."

Brett kissed my check and left the bar with his head down.

"What a mess. I can't believe this." As soon as those words left my mouth, Julie was next to me.

"I'm going to take off. Thanks, guys." She kissed my cheek and then Alex's.

"Are you going home or would you like to come over?" I asked.

"I think I need to be alone. I need to process all of this."

"I'm so sorry, Jules. I can't believe this is happening."

"Yeah, well, neither can I. But shit happens and there isn't anything I can do about it. He made his choice."

Alex and I watched Julie leave. It was just us and the staff left in the club.

"Please tell me things will get better," I asked Alex. "I want things back the way they were. Brett and Julie were so great together. She's devastated, and I can't help her."

Alex grabbed my hand. "I wish I could tell you what you want to hear, but I can't. I can tell you that I can't wait to get you home. Our place or yours?"

I smacked his arm. "Mine, if that's okay."

"You got it. But we need to start moving your stuff to my apartment. I don't want to be without you."

"I know. I don't want to be without you either."

Back at my apartment, Alex decided to hop in the shower. I opted to wait for him to get out. I had put on a black lace ensemble under my dress, and I knew he'd appreciate it. I took off my dress, but I left on my high heels. I looked around my room and thought about packing up everything. I ran my hand along my dresser and the picture frames that were on top.

Alex was singing in the shower, and I couldn't help but smile. There was something special about being with Alex. It wasn't just his looks or his charm; it was a combination of who he was. I sat on my bed and looked at my nightstand. I opened the drawer and pulled out a pen and a blank piece of paper. I stared at the white page and twirled the pen in my mouth. I pretty much zoned out until I heard his voice.

"That's a lucky pen."

I looked toward the bathroom. Alex stood against the door frame with a towel wrapped around his waist. He was beautiful. "My pen isn't lucky. I am."

He strode toward me and took my hands. He pulled me to my feet and backed up to look at me from head to toe. "You, my love, are stunning."

I felt myself blush, and I closed my eyes. When I

was blind, I had used my other senses. With my eyes closed, I ran my hands up his chest to his shoulders and back down. I felt every ripple, every breath, and every beat of his heart. I opened my eyes and looked at him. My hands went to his towel, and it fell to the floor. I took his hands and pulled him to the bed. He sat on the bed while I stood in front of him. I reached around my back and unhooked my bra. I slowly slid it off. Alex's hands went to my thighs, and he pulled me closer. He kissed my stomach, and my skin prickled. I put my hand under his chin and tilted his head up.

I placed a chaste kiss on his lips. "I'm not done yet."

Alex leaned back with his arms supporting him. I slid off my thong and kicked it aside. Still in my heels, I climbed on his legs. I felt him between my legs, and I didn't need any other foreplay. The look in his eyes as I stripped for him was enough for me. I bent at my waist and kissed him as I slid down on him. His hands went to my hips, which were making slow circles. He flipped me over and stared into my eyes. His hands went into my hair as he kissed me. He moved and my legs wrapped around his. I just stared at him as he moved. He closed his eyes and went faster. I raised my hips, and he slowed and opened his eyes.

"I want you to keep your eyes open for me. I want to look into them," he said.

I felt my eyes fill as I nodded. I always felt so sensitive when we made love. To be connected to him physically and emotionally made my heart swell. I had never been so happy. He increased his pace, and so did the beat of my heart. He reached my g-spot as he thrust. I tried to hang on so we could come together, but I knew I was close and so did he.

"Baby, I feel you, and you're amazing."

His words set me off, and I couldn't stop.

"That's it, baby, let go. You're perfect."

He moved faster. I didn't know how, but I climaxed again.

He brought his hands to my cheeks and swiped away my tear. "I love you."

I threw my arms around him, and our chests were so close that I couldn't have slipped a thread between them. "Just hold me, okay? Stay inside of me."

His lips grazed mine. "I'll hold you forever." He turned us to our sides.

I kicked off my heels and slid my leg between his. I looked up at him. "I can't believe your dad gave us a house. Can you tell me about it?"

He moved some loose strands of my hair and tucked them behind my ear. "That house is where I have some of my happiest memories. I remember playing in the backyard with Ellie and my mom. My dad was around on weekends. Since his office was in the city, the commute was long." Alex looked up as if he was either remembering or looking to heaven. "I haven't been there in over fifteen years. I can't believe my dad never sold it. After we lost them, we moved to an apartment in the city. Maybe we can ride out there this week. We can check it out and maybe we can have our first Thanksgiving there. Can you cook a turkey?" Alex laughed.

I shoved his shoulder. "Yes, I can cook a turkey." I had no idea if I could or not. "Let's put it this way, I'll do my best. I haven't had to cook much lately." I got up to get ready for bed.

I was in the bathroom brushing my teeth when he came up behind me.

"You're so sexy when you're brushing your teeth . . . naked."

I rinsed my mouth and dried it. "Yes, that was very sexy. You're so weird." I reached around him for my pajama top and slipped it over my head.

Alex stood there, in all his naked glory, looking at me. I walked into my room and climbed into bed, and he followed. He lay behind me and spooned with me.

"If you don't like the house, we don't have to live there."

"I'm sure I'll love it. Will we live there or at your apartment?" I turned in his arms and looked at him.

He seemed deep in thought. "I think we should talk about that. I don't want the club hours once we're married. I don't want to be a husband who leaves his wife alone all day if you decide not to continue at Walker-Stone. That's your decision, of course. I'm thinking about being a silent partner and letting Tyler and Brett manage the day-to-day business. We can keep my apartment in the city and go to the house on weekends or live on the island year round. What do you think?"

"What will you do if you don't work?"

Alex laced our fingers. "I think I want to take some time to decide. I've been thinking about my mom a lot and what she'd want for me. Maybe I'll work with my dad. I don't know. I'd love to have something to pass down to our kids other than a nightclub."

I smiled. "Our kids."

"You do want kids, don't you?"

"Of course I do. I just can't believe everything that has happened this year. In a few weeks, we'll be husband and wife. How did this happen to me, a shy, anxiety-ridden certified geek?"

"It happened because we found each other. We don't have to make any decisions tonight. Let's get some sleep, and we can talk about it tomorrow."

He kissed me, and I fell asleep in his arms.

I was so thankful it was a short week. We drove to the house on Thanksgiving like Alex said we would. Shelter Island was different from the city. It was peaceful and smaller than the metropolis I was used to. Alex turned down a long driveway to a sprawling house. Alex parked in the circular drive, and I stared out the window.

"What do you think? Do you like it?" he asked.

The house was gray with white trim. It had a wraparound porch with chairs on it. "It's much larger than I imagined."

"We're not in the city anymore. Come on, let's go in." He opened his door and got out of the car.

I was still in awe when he opened my door. He reached for my hand and helped me out. We walked up the wooden steps to the front door. I stood there taking in my surroundings while Alex unlocked the door. I heard the waves and a few birds. It was so peaceful. We walked in. The interior was impeccably decorated in stripes and nautical prints, which made sense considering the house was on the water. Jack must have had a caretaker for the home, because it was spotless. If I didn't know it had been vacant, I would have assumed a family lived there.

"Looks like my dad took care of everything. This isn't the furniture that was here when I was young. He must have had it decorated for us. If you don't like it, we can change it."

"Are you kidding? It's perfect. I love it."

"Come on, I'll show you around." Alex gave me the grand tour.

The house had five bedrooms, three bathrooms, and a gourmet kitchen with a butler's pantry. It was incredible. He took me to the backyard with a path that led to the beach. One tree had a tire swing hanging from it.

"Was that your swing?"

Alex stood behind me and wrapped his arms around me. "Yeah, I loved that swing. And that dock over there." He pointed to the wooden dock off to the left. "I learned how to dive right there."

I could tell he'd really loved living there. "You know what? I think this is perfect for us. I love it."

"Me too. I always have. I just didn't think this was an option." Alex looked at his wrist. "It's almost noon. I don't think we're cooking a turkey today. Let's go eat, and then we can relax in front of the fire."

We spent the day eating turkey sandwiches Alex picked up at the deli down the street. We laughed, talked, and made love while the fire crackled behind us. It was a perfect day.

Chapter 17

MONDAY CAME QUICKLY, AND I needed to call my parents to tell them everything that had happened over the weekend. My mom would flip out over the house on Shelter Island. I knew she wanted to be kept informed. It was difficult considering she was in Paris.

I was sitting on the couch with a cup of coffee, getting ready to call my mom before I went to work, when Alex walked out of the bedroom in worn-out jeans and a long-sleeved blue Henley. I couldn't stop staring at him.

He looked at me with a shit-eating grin, looked behind him, and then looked at himself. He stretched his arms. "What? Is there something wrong with what I'm wearing?"

Still staring with my mouth open, I wondered how he was all mine. "That depends on where you're going looking like that."

He flashed his brilliant smile. "What do you mean?"

"I mean you look edible. There's no way you don't know how hot you are."

"Edible huh? Well, you do look a little hungry. Do

you want a taste?"

I took a sip of my coffee and almost choked on it. He laughed and sat next to me.

"That's not funny," I said. "You know I need to get to work. I'm not sure if Julie will be in, so Mark and I'll need to pick up the slack."

"I'm going into the club to do some inventory. I texted Brett and Tyler that I need to talk to them. I want to tell them about my plan to let them take the reins at the club. I forgot that Brett said he needed time off." He got up and went into the kitchen for a cup of coffee.

I appreciated the view as he walked away. Damn, my man was fine. I picked up the phone and dialed my parents' number as Alex came back and sat next to me. Just as my mom answered, his hand went to my thigh. I glared at him because I really needed to talk to my mom, and I knew he would be distracting. He chuckled and took a sip of his coffee. I told my mom about the house.

She was beyond excited, as if I had won the lottery. "That is so amazing. I knew Jack Logan had to be a good man. Everything I've heard about him told me so."

"Yes, he's a good man, just like his son." I put her on speaker phone. "Say hi to Alex, he's right here."

Alex cleared his throat. "Hi, Mrs. Ryan."

"Alex, you're going to be my son-in-law. Call me Jill or Mom if you'd like."

I looked at Alex as his face fell. I scrunched my eyes closed. I needed to change the subject. "So, uh, Mom, have you and Dad made your travel arrangements?

"Yes, your father and I will be arriving on the eighteenth so I can help with any last-minute wedding details, and then we'll stay through Christmas. I hope that's okay. I know it'll be your first Christmas as husband and wife."

"That sounds great. Thanks, Mom. I need to get to work. Tell Daddy I said hi and that I love him."

"I will, sweetie. Talk to you soon." She hung up.

Alex hadn't said anything since my mom told him that he could call her Mom. I wasn't sure what to do, so I turned to him and put my hand on his. "Are you okay? You can call my mom Jill. You don't need to call her Mom."

Alex leaned forward and put his cup on the coffee table. His hands were clasped together on his knees. "I never thought about it before she said that." He shrugged.

My heart broke for him. I knew how much he missed his mom and sister. "Well, it's your decision. I just want you to be happy. It really doesn't matter to me what you call her."

"I know, babe. It's just weird for me, that's all." He picked up his coffee.

I watched his muscles flex through his shirt. "So after you go to the club, what are your plans?"

"I was planning on going to my apartment to make space for your things, which we will be moving in this week. It's after Thanksgiving now, and it's time we got moving on this, pun intended."

I felt nervous all of a sudden. "Okay. I guess I'll get boxes and start packing up here."

"What's with that look? You look like your dog

died."

I shook my head. "I just hope you like living with me. What if all my issues drive you crazy? What if you don't like living with me? What if—"

He put two fingers on my lips. "I love you, all of you. I'm not perfect either, no one is, and I'm sure there will be times we'll want to smack each other, but as long as it's on the ass, we should be good." He stood and walked into the kitchen to put his cup in the sink.

I sat there with my mouth open.

He turned. "You just going to sit there, or are you going to bring your cup in here so we can get to work?"

I stood and walked into the kitchen. He was rinsing his cup and reached for mine. He put them in the dishwasher and turned to me.

"See, I'm not messy, so that's a bonus." He laughed.

I smacked his bicep. "Yeah, I see that. What if I am?"

He put his arms around my waist. "Then I'll hire a maid. I don't care if you're messy and leave your cup on the table. I care about you, about us."

My hands went into his hair, and I pulled him toward me. Before our lips met, I said, "I'll do my best to be the best wife you ever dreamed of having." I kissed him with all the passion I had.

He picked me up and set me on the counter. He stood between my legs, put his hands on my face, and looked into my eyes. "You're my forever, and that's more important to me than anything."

I leaned forward and kissed him. "You're my forever too. As much as I'd love to stay here and prove it, I need to get to work. If you keep talking to me and kissing me this way, I'll need to change my clothes."

Smiling, he lifted me off the counter and put me down. "Then we'd better go. You can tell me why you would need to change on the way." He grabbed his keys, and we left.

I made it to work on time, and as soon as I walked through the door, I knew my day would be horrible. "What's going on?"

The look on Mark's face said it all. He walked me to my cubicle. "Brian is on the warpath because we're getting some big client today and Julie is out. What's going on with her? It isn't like her to call in sick. She told Brian she'd be out all week."

I didn't know how much Mark knew. He and Val had left the party early. "I had a feeling this would happen. She has to deal with some news she got over the weekend. I'm sure we'll be fine with the new client. Let's just kick ass and get the job done."

"No way, you're not getting off the hook," he said. "What the hell happened? It's Brett, right? Did he flaunt Nikki in front of her again? Did she show up at your party after we left?"

"No, she wasn't there."

"Come on, Aub, I love Julie too. Do I need to go kick his ass?"

I tilted my head back and forth. "You might want to if I tell you what happened, so no, I don't think I will."

Mark stared at me. "I swear to God, if you don't tell me, I'll go to her apartment and have her tell me. Or better yet, I'll find Brett and beat it out of him." The look on his face said he was serious.

"Okay, I'll tell you, but you have to promise you won't freak out and go beat up anyone."

"Fine, spill it."

I sighed. "Brett thinks Nikki might be pregnant with his baby. Julie found out, and she's devastated."

Mark scowled. "I'll kill him."

"No, you promised. He doesn't even know for sure. He said she'll find out if she's pregnant in a few weeks, and if she is, he'll have a paternity test done. He's pretty upset about it too."

"He should be. What an asshole. I don't get people. First, you have to deal with Leah and Alex, then Jessica shows up, and now this? I get that things happen in threes, but this takes the cake. So Nikki should find out right around Christmas? That'll be great."

I hadn't really thought about it, but he was right. She'd find out around Christmas. "Yeah, I guess so. Maybe she won't be pregnant, or it might not be his."

"Well, if I know Julie, she won't care if it is or isn't. She's got to be a wreck."

"She is, and that's why she's off this week. So let's get to work and make sure everything is fine while she's gone. She doesn't need Brian stressing her out."

Mark kissed my cheek and went to his desk.

I sat at mine. I was so happy with my life, but I felt a little guilty about it. It was hard to be happy when my best friend wasn't.

The next few days at work were the same. Mark and I stayed super busy covering for Julie. Mark's presentations were spot on, and on Friday, Brian offered him a position as a permanent ad executive.

Mark would be in charge of some clients. Brian would hire a new assistant after the holidays, and then Mark could rid himself of those responsibilities.

I hadn't spoken to Julie all week, and according to Alex, Brett had been MIA too. He hadn't returned any of Alex's texts or calls, and Alex was starting to worry.

We were going to meet at the club later that night to celebrate Mark's promotion. I tried calling Julie, but I got her voice mail. I told her where we would be if she wanted to meet us, but she never got back to me.

I walked into the club with Mark, and I was happy to see Julie, Val, and Alex at the bar. Mark and I must have noticed them at the same time because he stopped and smiled. Once we reached the bar, Mark kissed Val on the cheek and pulled Julie off her stool for a hug.

Alex hugged me. "I'm so glad to see you. Julie has been here since three. Thankfully, she's been nursing her drinks, so she isn't wasted."

"Maybe it wouldn't be a bad idea if she was drunk. At least she could forget for a while."

"I don't think she'd forget since Nikki is here." He nodded toward the tables near the dance floor.

"Oh my God, why is she here? Is she drinking? If she's pregnant, she shouldn't be drinking." I tried to see what was in her glass.

"No, she isn't. According to Tyler, she ordered a soda."

"Why is she here?"

Alex looked defeated. "She's waiting for Brett. According to Ty, she hasn't heard from him and wanted to see him. She thought he'd be here, but he isn't. I'm getting worried. I haven't seen him or talked to him in a week."

"I hope he's okay." As I said that, I saw Brett walk in.

He looked terrible. Julie stared at Brett before she turned back to Mark and Val. Nikki didn't take long to notice him either. She ran to him and threw her arms around his neck. He didn't reciprocate. He just removed her arms from his neck.

He walked up to us, leaving Nikki where she was. "Hey, guys. Alex, sorry I didn't return your texts. I thought you might be here. If you want to talk, here I am." He looked at the rest of our friends, especially Julie. "I didn't know everyone would be here. I can come back."

Alex slapped Brett's shoulder. "No, man, you're my best friend and I want you here. Right, Aubrey?"

"Uh, yeah. I mean, yes, of course. Brett, I know things are weird right now, but Alex is right. You guys talk, and we'll be at the bar."

Alex motioned to Tyler, and the three of them went upstairs.

I walked over to my friends. "So what are we drinking?"

Mark looked at his beer. "Mine is obvious. Val is having her usual cosmo. What can I get you?"

"I'll have a club soda with lime please. I'm in the mood for a cocktail tonight, but thanks to my meds, that's out of the question. Julie, do you want one?"

She nodded. "Why not?"

Our drinks came, and Mark and I talked about our week and his promotion. We were laughing and having a good time until Alex, Brett, and Tyler came down the stairs.

Julie stopped laughing. "Maybe I should go." She slid off the stool, taking a final sip of her drink.

"No, don't go. We all need to co-exist, if nothing else. I'm getting married in two weeks, and I won't have my friends at odds over some slut. Oh my God. I'm getting married in two weeks!"

Everyone laughed at my sudden giddiness. Julie, Val, and I jumped around like school girls. Alex and Brett walked up to us.

"What'd I miss?" Alex asked. "Why is my fiancée jumping up and down? I hope you guys haven't been doing shots?"

Julie slapped his arm. "No, we haven't been doing shots. You know Aubrey can't drink. She just realized that you guys are getting married in two weeks. Two weeks!"

We started laughing and jumping again.

Alex rubbed his arm. "Damn, Julie, you didn't have to hit me so hard."

We all looked at him and laughed.

"She has quite the right hook," Brett deadpanned.

We stopped laughing, and Julie said, "You deserved it. You deserve everything you have coming to you."

"Okay, I'm done with this," Brett said. "Let's go, Julie. You want to lay into me? Go ahead. You want to punch, kick, or scream at me? Here I am. Let me have it. Get it all out. Will that make you feel better?" Brett stood with outstretched arms. "Come on, I'm waiting. We're all waiting."

Just like that, the group went silent.

Julie walked up to Brett. She raised her hand as if she was going to slap him, but instead she placed it on his cheek. "I don't want to fight with you or scream at you. What's done is done." She removed her hand from his cheek.

I walked up to her. "Jules, are you okay?"

She looked at me and then back at Brett. "Yes, I'm fine. I can't hide or ignore my friends anymore because my heart was crushed." She looked at Nikki, who was sitting at a table and staring at her. "Brett, I don't forgive you for being with Nikki, but for the sake of our friends, I'll forget it for now. I won't be the dark cloud at their wedding. So . . . yeah, that's it."

Brett just looked at her. He pulled her into his chest and hugged her. My eyes filled with tears as Julie pulled back.

"I love you, Julie," he said softly. Louder, he said, "Did everyone hear that? Did you hear that, Nikki? I love Julie! This woman right here! I will always love Julie!"

Nikki got up and walked toward us, but instead she turned and walked out of the club. Julie didn't say a word.

I put my hand on her back. "Jules?"

She was expressionless. "Yeah, okay. I guess you made your point. We can be friends, Brett, but that's it."

I think the five of us exhaled, and Alex ordered a round of drinks for our friends.

Chapter 18

My parents had arrived two days ago. It was great to see them. I had learned to appreciate my parents after my accident.

I had so much to look forward to. I was getting married tomorrow. My apartment was packed up, but I'd left my furniture there for my parents to use. Alex and I were unpacking my boxes in his apartment. I couldn't believe all the things I'd accumulated. We finally finished the last one, and we had a pile of things to give to charity. We plopped on the couch and looked at each other.

"Well, future Mrs. Logan, do you have your vows written?"

I hadn't believed Alex at first when he said that he wanted us to write our vows. He thought that because I was a writer, I had an advantage, but that wasn't true. "No, I don't. Do you?"

"Yes, as a matter of fact, I do." He smiled and wagged his eyebrows.

"Can I read them?" I batted my eyelashes at him.

"Not a chance. I don't care how cute you are. You can hear them when I say them. You don't have to wait much longer."

"I can't wait to be your wife. So much has happened so quickly, that I can't believe it most of the time."

"Well, you need to believe it," he said. "What do you have left to do? Are the girls all set?"

"Yes, Julie and Val picked out their dresses, so they're all set. What about the guys?"

"They're wearing black suits, and I have a tux, so I'm all set. I ordered the flowers. Val took care of arranging the restaurant with Anthony. I spoke to your mom, and she took care of the wedding cake. I booked a DJ and rented a limo to take all of us from the chapel to Anthony's. We have our marriage license, and the reverend. We really don't need to rehearse, so we're all set."

"Wow, you thought of everything." I was in awe. I had totally forgotten about flowers and the cake, but I wasn't going to tell him that.

"I'm not going to let you worry about any of the details. I just want you to make sure you're there on time."

"You won't have to worry about that. Val and I are staying at Julie's tonight. We're going to have a girls' night. I hope that's okay."

He kissed my nose. "It sounds great. Maybe the guys and I will go out for a bachelor night."

I sat up. "You're going to have a bachelor party?"

He changed his tune quickly. "No. Tyler has to work tonight since he wants the tips. I have Mike working the bar tomorrow, so I won't have to worry about anything but us on our big day. I think I'll call your dad, Mark, and Brett. We can have a drink at the club tonight. I do have a question though."

"What's that?"

"A honeymoon. We never discussed it. Do you have any ideas?"

"I haven't really thought about it. What do you want to do?"

He stroked my hair. "I think I can come up with something. We'll leave after Christmas."

"Okay. I trust you."

A little while later, I grabbed my bag, kissed him good-bye, and headed to Julie's. My mom was going to meet us there for dinner. Julie had called to let me know that Mary had delivered my gown, and I was excited to show it to my mom in person.

I knocked on Julie's door. When she opened it, my eyes went wide. The apartment had been transformed. White tulle was draped on the ceiling and lit up by tiny white lights. White and silver balloons floated in all the corners, and there was a "Congratulations" banner on the far wall.

I looked at Julie and my mom. "Oh my God, I can't believe everything you both did!"

"I wish I could take all the credit," Julie said. "Your fiancé sent some people over, and when they left, this was what my apartment looked like. He's disgustingly perfect." Julie smiled, and my mom agreed with her.

I couldn't believe everything he'd done. There was a knock at the door.

Val had arrived with our dinner. "Holy crap, Julie, you outdid yourself. Your apartment looks amazing."

We all laughed and told her that it was all Alex's doing.

"I can't say that I'm surprised. I went to go pick up dinner, and it had already been paid for."

We all looked at each other. "Alex."

After dinner, I showed my mom my dress again, which she loved. I tried it on, and it was perfect. Mary had told me she would be on call in case I needed her, but thankfully I didn't. We sat on the couch with wine and settled in to watch a chick flick. Julie thought we should watch *Father of the Bride*. We were just about to start the movie when her door buzzer rang. Julie answered it.

The voice over the intercom said, "Delivery for Aubrey Ryan."

Julie buzzed him in and opened the door.

A young guy with a messenger bag held out a wrapped box. "Aubrey Ryan?"

I went to the door. "I'm Aubrey."

"This is for you. Congratulations."

He must have noticed the decorations. I smiled, and Julie tipped him.

She closed the door and turned to me. "Well, open it!"

I sat on the couch between my mom and Val while Julie sat in the chair next to the couch. All eyes were on me. I opened the box. It was a DVD that read, "Play me." I looked for a card but didn't find one.

Julie snatched the DVD and threw it in her player. She sat next to Val and pressed play. We stared at the TV, and Alex appeared. We all gasped, but I think I was the loudest.

He looked gorgeous, and he was wearing the same clothes I had just left him in. "Hi, ladies, please pardon this interruption. Aubrey, I hope your mom is with you because this first message for her. Jill, I want you to know that your daughter means everything to me. I'll take care of her and protect her until the day I die. No one more important to me than she is. I've been thinking about what you said, and I'd be honored to call you Mom."

I looked at my mom, and she had tears in her eyes. I held her hand, and she squeezed mine.

"Julie and Val, I also have a message for you two."

I looked at them. Julie grabbed four tissues from the box and handed one to each of us.

"Val, you're one of my closest and dearest friends. Although your friendship with Aubrey started off on shaky ground, I'm glad you came together and became close friends."

Val and I looked at each other as we each wiped a tear away.

"Julie, I know you're Aubrey's best friend and you will kick my ass if I hurt her. I want to assure you that won't happen. I know you weren't always my biggest fan, and I'll continue to prove that you were wrong about me."

Julie nodded as if he could see her. I wiped another tear and laughed at her. There was a long pause, so I thought he was done. But he wasn't.

"Aubrey."

I looked at the TV, and it was as if he was there. His deep blue eyes penetrated me.

"I thought I knew what I wanted to say to you, but words aren't enough to tell you what you mean to me." He smiled that megawatt smile, and I leaned forward.

"I love you. I think I loved you the first night I laid eyes on you, when you asked me all those ridiculous questions."

I laughed between wiping my tears.

"I never thought I'd need anyone the way I need you. I didn't realize I needed someone until I met you. Going through life pretty much on my own, being sad about my mom and mad at the world, I learned to not rely on anyone. Now that we have each other, I'm not sad about that anymore. I have a feeling my mom sent you to me. You were so unexpected, and I'm so happy I took the chance and sat with you. I promise to make you as happy as you make me."

Julie handed me another tissue as she turned off the video after it ended. "Oh my God, Aubrey, he's so . . . so . . . fucking perfect."

We all laughed, including my mom. I loved Julie. She never held back. There was a knock on the door, and Julie got up. It was weird that the buzzer didn't ring. Julie opened the door, and it was the messenger guy.

"I have a package for Aubrey Ryan."

I got up and went to the door.

He reached in his bag and pulled out another box. "This is for you."

I smiled and took it.

Julie reached in her purse for a tip. Before she gave it to him, she said, "Are you coming back or can I tip you?"

"Sorry, miss, I can't say."

Julie handed him the tip and closed the door. I sat on the couch to open the box. It was heavier than the first gift. I opened the box. There was a velvet box inside. I took it out and lifted the cover. My hand went to my mouth.

"Aubrey, it's stunning." My mom sounded choked up.

I set the box on my lap and looked at the most gorgeous necklace I had ever seen. It matched my bracelet. Three diamond encrusted orchids dangled from a beautiful chain. I noticed a small card inside.

"Aubrey, I'm not sure what your gown looks like, but I hope you'll be able to wear this.

Always yours, Alex."

I was getting ready to call Alex to thank him when we heard another knock on the door.

"Oh my God, Aubrey, now what?" Julie went to the door. She looked at the messenger guy. "Okay, dude, I don't care how many more packages there are. This is the last tip you're getting."

He smiled. "I have a delivery for Aubrey Ryan."

Julie just looked at him. "Yeah, no kidding." She snickered. "I'll take it." She took the box and gave him his tip. She shut the door and brought me the box.

I unwrapped the box and opened it. The gift was a journal and not just any journal. It was a beautiful burgundy leather book with an embossed title, "My Chance." My eyes filled, and I looked at everyone. I didn't want to open it in front of them, and I think they got the hint. Julie suggested they go and have some coffee and dessert. I looked at the journal and opened it.

"I'm not a writer, nor will I pretend to be. I'm giving you this journal so you can write the romance novel you've always dreamt of. Please don't let that dream go. You're an amazingly strong woman who's smart and loving. I didn't know what to expect when we met. I knew that I wanted you, and after I got to know you, I knew I would always love you. I prayed you would always love me. Tomorrow you'll become my wife, and although I can't guarantee what the future will hold, I can guarantee that I'll be by your side through it all. You make me a better man, Aubrey. I look at the world differently because of you. You're my heart, my soul. Thank you for taking a chance on me. Thank you for being my chance."

I put the journal back in the box and closed it. I picked up my phone and dialed Alex.

"Hey, babe. How's girls' night?"

"Alex. I just got your gifts and . . ." I took a moment. "And I want to thank you." I didn't know what else to say.

"I hope you liked everything. I wasn't sure about the journal. I don't want you to feel pressured, but I wanted you to know that I don't think you should give up on your dream. I didn't give up on mine, and now I get you forever."

"Okay, you seriously need to stop talking, or I'm coming over there and we might not make it to the church tomorrow."

"Well, if we weren't getting married tomorrow, I'd say that sounded like a great idea."

"I'll see you tomorrow. I love you, Alex."

"I love you too. See you tomorrow."

I hung up and walked into the kitchen. I poured myself a cup of coffee.

"So the journal . . . Are you okay?" Julie asked.

"Yes, I'm fine. I just can't believe he's going to be my husband tomorrow."

We spent the rest of the night watching movies and laughing. It was really a perfect evening.

I woke to the smell of coffee and the sound of chatter in the kitchen. I hopped out of bed. It was ten in the morning. I couldn't believe I'd slept that long. I was getting married in four hours! I hustled into the kitchen where Julie was getting her hair done by a woman I'd never met. I looked at my mom. She was perfectly styled, as was Val.

"What's going on?" I asked.

"Your fiancé arranged for a hair stylist to come over and do our hair," my mom said. "He told me about it yesterday. I figured you knew too."

"No, I didn't, but I'm thankful, considering you all let me sleep until ten!"

Julie hugged me. "My best friend is getting married today. I'm so happy for you. Grab a cup of coffee and take a shower. Then Natasha will do your hair. You won't be late, I promise. You'll be right on time."

"Aubrey, I bought this for you as your something

new." My mom handed me a pink box.

I lifted the cover to find a beautiful peignoir set. I pulled the silky white material out of the box and held it against me. "I love it! Thanks, Mom." I hugged her and placed it back in the box.

I drank my coffee while I waited for the shower to heat up. I was dying to know what Alex was doing, but I refused to call him. I was in a daydream when I noticed steam pouring out of the shower. I set my coffee on the vanity and got under the hot water. *This is my last shower as a single woman.*

I thought about what I'd say for my vows. I didn't want them to be normal "until death do us part" vows. I needed to come up with something great. I turned off the water and toweled dry. I grabbed my robe and went into the bedroom. My gown was hanging on the closet door, and I stared at it. I smiled and headed into the kitchen to have my hair and makeup done.

I told Natasha I didn't want to look too made up. I wanted to look like myself. When I was done getting primped, I joined Val, Julie, and my mom in Julie's room. They'd just finished getting dressed. Julie and Val wore beautiful black cocktail dresses that looked amazing on their killer figures, while my mom looked stunning in an emerald green dress.

"Wow, you're all gorgeous! The guys are going to freak when they see you—even Daddy, Mom!" I said with a wink.

Val laughed, and Julie looked as if I'd just killed her dog.

"I'm sorry, Jules. I just meant that they're going to love the way you look." That comment didn't help either. "Can you help me get my gown on? It's almost time to go."

Julie smiled a little. "I can't wait to see this on you. You're going to be the most beautiful bride."

We carefully slipped the gown over my head. Val buttoned me up in the back while Julie brought me my Jimmy Choo pumps. I'd splurge on them because they were too stunning to pass up, as Julie put it. My mom helped me put on my orchid bracelet and my new necklace. I was looking in the mirror, not believing what I was seeing, when Julie's buzzer rang. I didn't know who it could be since everyone should be heading to the church.

Val went to the door and pushed the intercom button. "Yes?"

"It's Jack Logan. Can I come in please?"

Val looked at me and Julie. I nodded, and Val pushed the button to release the outside door. I couldn't imagine what he wanted. He knocked on the door, and Val opened it. Jack walked in, looking handsome in his black three-piece suit.

"Hi, Jack. Is everything okay?" I asked.

"Wow, Aubrey, you look beautiful. Alex told me where I could find you. I'm sorry to intrude, but I have something for you, and I wanted you to have it before you went to the church." He had a small white box in his hand. He stretched his arm out. "This is for you."

I took the box. "Thank you." I opened it and found a delicate cotton and lace cloth with a blue ribbon running through it. I set the box down and took out the cloth. It looked like a small bonnet.

"Alex wore that at his baptism," Jack said. "Angela saved it. She always said that his bride could carry it with her flowers. I forgot about it until I looked for the deed to the house. It opens up and becomes a handkerchief. Angela said it could be his bride's old and blue. I'm not sure what that means, but I'm hoping you do."

I hugged him. "Thank you so much. Yes, a bride is to have something old, new, borrowed, and blue. I forgot about that. Other than the borrowed, I'm all set."

"Well, I have something else for you. I was going to give them to you, but if you'd rather borrow them for today, I'll let you keep them at a later date." He reached into his jacket pocket and pulled out a small velvet box. "Angela wore these on our wedding day." He opened the box. The most beautiful diamond stud earrings were inside. "Please go ahead."

I swallowed hard, took off the earrings I was wearing, and put on the ones Jack brought me. "What do you think?" I turned to Julie and Val.

"I think you're very lucky. They are really beautiful, Jack," Val said. She kissed him on the cheek, and Julie did the same.

"Well, I'd better go," he said. "I need to get to the church too. I saw a limo pull up. I'm assuming that's your ride. If you're ready, I'll walk you down."

Val, Julie, and my mom grabbed their purses and headed out the door.

I picked up mine from the table and looked at Jack. "Thank you very much. You have no idea how happy I am to have you as a father-in-law." I kissed his cheek, and we left.

We pulled up to the church, and I couldn't wait to get inside and see Alex. Julie and Val helped me out of the limo. I saw my dad waiting by the church door. He looked dapper in his tux.

I walked up the steps to greet him. "Hi, Daddy."

"Look at my baby girl. You look stunning." He kissed my mom on the cheek. "You look as beautiful as the day I married you." My mom blushed. He turned his attention back to me. "Are you ready to do this? Your fiancé looks like he's about ready to burst."

I laughed. Mary was there to fluff my gown, and she took my purse. Julie and Val came around the corner with bouquets of white orchids. They were simple but elegant. The stems were wrapped in pale blue organza. I held them in my left hand along with the gift from Jack.

Mary opened the double church doors, and the music started. I peeked inside and saw Mark, Brett, and Tyler. They looked beyond handsome. I looked at my girls. They were all smiles. I prayed that Julie would be okay. Val went first, and Julie followed her.

My dad placed my right hand on his arm. "Ready?"

"I am."

The guests stood, and we walked down the aisle. I looked straight ahead. There he was. I almost had to stop and stare at him. He smiled at me, and I relaxed. My dad stopped, and I turned to look at him. He kissed my cheek and shook Alex's hand. Alex put his hand out, and I placed mine in it. I felt his touch down to my toes, just like the first night we met.

The reverend started the ceremony, and soon it was time for the vows. Alex and I faced each other.

"Aubrey, I had a whole speech prepared, but after seeing you—by the way, you look gorgeous—I don't think it's good enough. So I'm going to speak from my heart." He cleared his throat. "I knew I had to have you the first night I saw you. You were the most beautiful woman I had ever seen. When I sat with you, I felt something I'd never felt before. I wasn't sure what it was, but now I know that it was love. I loved you from the moment I saw you." Alex looked down and then back at me. "When I lost you, I thought I was going to die. I can't live without you, and I'm so thankful you're going to be my wife. I promise to show you the world, to lift you up when you're having a bad day, and to celebrate with you when you're having a good one. I promise to support you mentally, emotionally, and physically." He winked. "I promise I'll be the best husband and father that I can be. You're my missing piece, Aubrey. With you by my side, I know I'll be whole. So will you . . . be my wife?"

"Yes, I will." I wiped a tear away with the handkerchief Jack had given me. I saw a tear leave Alex's eye, and I wiped his away. Then the reverend told me it was my turn.

I put my hands back in Alex's and noticed him look at the cloth in my left hand. I whispered, "Your dad gave it to me."

Alex grinned and nodded.

"I didn't really prepare anything. Well, I tried, but I knew I'd forget it all." Our friends laughed which made me smile and relax. "Alex, you said that you fell for me the first night you saw me, and I feel the same way. Being with you makes me a better person. You give me confidence and make me feel like I can take on the world. With you at my side, I believe that I can. I took a chance the night I met you. I didn't know what to expect, but I certainly didn't expect you. You were my unexpected chance. I want to give you everything I have and everything I am. I'm not perfect, and I'll make mistakes, but I'll be the best wife and hopefully mother that I can be. I love you, Alex Logan, and I want you to be my husband. Will you marry me and make me the happiest woman?"

Alex kissed my hand. "I will."

We exchanged rings, and before I knew it, the reverend pronounced us husband and wife. We smiled at each other until we heard, "You may kiss the bride."

Alex put his hands on my cheeks and kissed me. My hands ran up his back as I held him. Our tongues danced, and he dipped me. Our friends applauded. We walked down the aisle and out of the church hand in hand. We stopped at the bottom of the steps and waited for our bridal party. Brett came out first, then Julie walked out with Tyler while Val was on Mark's arm. We all piled into the limo to head to our reception.

"So, Mrs. Logan, are you ready to start the rest of your life?" Alex beamed.

"I've never been more ready, Mr. Logan."

Chapter 19

Valentine's Day

I COULD THINK OF NOTHING better than waking up next to the most gorgeous man in our home. Alex was still sleeping, and I couldn't help staring at his strong jaw line and perfectly messed up hair. Since the sheet was below his waist, I appreciated his fine body. My hands were tucked under my cheek, and I let out a quiet sigh of appreciation. He smiled and opened one eye to look at me.

"Have you been awake this entire time?" I asked.

"You mean the entire time you've been staring at me? No."

I grabbed my pillow and smacked him with it.

He rolled on top of me and kissed me. His lips were soft and strong. He broke the kiss and looked into my eyes. "Happy Valentine's Day."

I smiled at him. "Happy Valentine's Day. I can't believe I finally have a Valentine."

He rolled to the side and propped his head up with his left hand while his right rested on my stomach. "You've never had a Valentine?"

"Pathetic, right?" I laughed. "Nope, I never have. The only Valentine's Day cards I got were when I was young and the entire class had to bring in cards. But the girls who got flowers and real cards . . ." I shrugged. "I was never one of them. So you're my first and last Valentine."

He looked at me as though he couldn't believe what I was saying. "The boys in your school must have been idiots."

"Yeah, that's what the problem was." I sat up and looked at him. "I never in my wildest imagination thought my one and only Valentine would be a drop dead gorgeous reformed player and former member of the most wanted bachelor list." I wrapped my arms around my knees.

He shrugged it off. "Whatever." He got out of bed and walked into our bathroom.

I heard the shower running, so I threw on my robe and made a dash to the kitchen to make our first Valentine's breakfast. I decided on French toast and bacon. I made a pot of coffee and whipped the eggs. I felt him looking at me. I turned. He had on a pair of loose-fitting running pants and no shirt. My eyes grazed his impeccable body. His hands were behind his back, which made his chest look even broader.

"I wanted to surprise you with breakfast. That was a really quick shower," I said.

He moved toward me, and the look in his eyes said he wanted something other than food. "Breakfast can wait. I have something for you."

"Are we exchanging presents now? I have something for you too. I'll go get it." I went into the spare bedroom for the present I'd hid there. I carried it into the family room where he stood holding a white orchid. "Where did you get that? I swear, do you have them just growing around here?" I asked.

He chuckled. "I'm not giving away my secrets." He winked, and I melted. He brought me to the couch and pulled out a small square box. "Go ahead, open it."

I unwrapped it and lifted the cover to find a beautiful diamond ring that matched my bracelet and necklace. It was a single orchid, and it was stunning.

"That's the last piece to the set. I hope you like it," he said.

I slid it on my finger. "I love it. Thank you." I leaned over and kissed him. "Okay, your turn." I was beyond nervous as I gave him his gift.

He unwrapped the box, lifted the cover, looked inside, and then at me. "It's the journal I gave you."

"I added to it, and I wanted you to read it."

"I'm glad you're writing again. Can I read it now?" He beamed and opened the book. He turned the pages past the ones he'd written on to find my words.

Entry 1—Alex—My husband and chance at love

When I first met you, I didn't know what to think other than "Why is this man talking to me?" As time passed, I fell in love with you. I knew that I wanted to be in your life forever. Then I had my accident and things changed, but my love for you didn't. You proved to me, beyond a shadow of a doubt, that you loved me and we were meant to be together.

When I started writing, I was looking for romance. What I didn't expect was to find you, my romantic hero. You're more than that to me. You are my best friend, my lover, my husband, and in October, you will be the father to our child.

I love you, Alex, more than you will ever know.

He looked at me with tear-filled eyes. "I'm going to be a father?"

I nodded.

"We're going to be a family?"

I nodded. He wrapped his arms around me.

"Happy Valentine's Day, Alex."

"Happy Valentine's Day, Aubrey."

The End

Ryker
A Standalone Novel

Chapter 1
Faith

The day I had been waiting for was finally here. My reflection in my full-length mirror winked at me as I ran my hands down my denim-clad hips. I turned left, right, and back to center to take in how I looked. Did I look different? I shook my head and laughed at myself. Nothing on the outside had changed, but I felt different inside.

Twenty-one, the age I had vowed to make changes in my life. Everything else had fallen into place: I was graduating college a year early and in the top ten percent of my class; I was starting a new job soon; and I was finally going to tell Ryker Jeffries how I felt about him. When he spoke, I melted like ice on a hot day. Thinking about finally running my fingers through his long blond tresses and my hands down his taut abs made me shiver. I could feel his muscular arms wrapped around me, and see that tattoo move as he flexed his arm. I needed to clear my head and focus on the task at hand: getting Ryker Jeffries. Thinking about telling him made my insides twist and turn like a rollercoaster, but I was looking forward to the ride. The anticipation of the climb, without knowing how steep the drop on the other side would be, was terrifying and exciting. The only problem was Ryker's attitude toward me. No matter how hard I tried, he didn't want to get close to me. It was as if he purposely tried to push me away.

I looked at the picture stuck in the frame of my mirror, and I couldn't help but smile at the cute boy with a hula hoop hanging off his waist. My best friend and next-door neighbor, Max Morrison, was my rock. He was also the lead singer of the band Raging Urge. Ryker was the drummer and Max's other best friend. I had asked Max about Ryker's attitude once, and he didn't have an answer for me. All Max had said was he didn't want to get in the middle of us, but he'd be cool with it if we got together. I knew Max would never say anything to hurt my feelings, but he wouldn't let my heart get crushed either. I took his words as a green light to move forward with my plan.

In a few hours, Raging Urge was playing at a club in town called The Ruins, and I'd told Max I would come out to be their number-one fan. They had enough groupies who thought they were Raging Urge's top fan, but I'd been listening to these guys for years, so I called dibs on that title. My plan was to go to the club with Paige, a former classmate I'd tutored. We weren't close, but she'd offered to take me out for my first "legal" drink. Paige wasn't in on my plan to tell Ryker I had feelings for him because I knew that if I told her, she'd screw something up for me. Paige and I had hung out at a party once, and when I told her I thought a guy was hot, she devoted her attention to him for the rest of the night and probably into the next morning.

I sat at my makeup table and applied finishing touches to my eyes and lips. Once my baby blues were lined in black and my lips were shiny, I was ready to go. My phone chimed with a message from Paige that she was outside. With my purse in hand and my confidence coated with a bit of nerves, I headed out, determined to make it a night I wouldn't forget.

She waved at me through the window, and I prayed the night went off without a hitch. The weather was perfect for a May night in Rochester. It wasn't too cold, and the gentle breeze was calming. I took in a deep breath before I got in her car. *Here we go.*

Paige was wearing a black mini-skirt, high-heeled pumps, and a white top that left little to the imagination. She beamed at me. "Happy birthday! Are you ready to have fun and have your first legal drink?"

"Thank you. Yeah, let's get the show on the road."

Her zippy little red car careened through the neighborhood, turning the street lights into a blur. She pressed a button on her steering wheel and cranked the music. The band booming through her speakers was Blanco Diablo, the guys' favorite group. Raging Urge aspired to be like them one day.

"I didn't know you liked BD," I said.

Her thumb pressed the button to lower the sound. "I remembered you telling me that your friend and the other guys in the band liked them, so I figured I should listen. You know, so I had something to talk about with them. Not that I plan on doing much talking tonight." She winked, and my nerves spiked.

Even though we were zipping by other cars, I felt as if we were moving in slow motion as my heart sank into my stomach. "What do you mean?"

"Are you kidding?" She glanced at me before putting her eyes back on the road. "You have to realize how hot these guys are. We are going to have a blast tonight. I call dibs on the drummer. Who do you want?"

Did she just say her plan was to go after Ryker? *No way, this isn't happening to me. Shit, what do I do?* I took a deep breath and twisted my hands in my lap. "Paige, I need to tell you something."

"Yeah, okay, what?" She turned the car into the club's parking lot.

I needed to make it fast. "Please don't go after the drummer."

She tossed the gear shift into park and pushed a button that turned off her car. "Why?"

"Because, I . . . um . . . I . . ." My voice hitched, and my breaths were short.

Her eyes widened. "Oh! I get it. You like him. Does he know? He doesn't seem like your type, and you definitely don't seem like his. What about your friend? Why don't you go for him?"

"Max? He's like a brother to me! No, I like Ryker, and I have for years. Just leave him alone for me. Consider it a birthday present."

"Fine, but if he comes on to me, all bets are off." She opened her door and got out.

If he came on to her, she could bet her ass all bets were off; why would I want him if he wanted her? My hand was on the handle of my door, and after taking three deep breaths, I opened it and followed Paige inside.

I was ready to pull out my license, but the bouncer just took one look at Paige and waved us in. Paige walked straight to the bar, passing some guys at a table lined with pitchers of beer.

One of the frat boys called, "Hey, ginger!"

Paige turned around and threw her hand on her now cocked hip. "Yes?" She really was stunning, and she had confidence in spades. Her five foot eight body sauntered up to their table.

Some guy with a backward baseball hat stood and flashed an award-winning smile. "Why don't you and your friend join us?"

Paige looked at me with a pleading expression, but I just shook my head.

She strode back to me. "Come on, these guys are hot! It's free drinks, and it's your birthday! Come on!" She looked back at the guys and put up her index finger. "Live a little, let your hair down, and have fun. Your friends aren't even here yet."

Maybe drinking with them wasn't a bad idea. If she liked those guys, then I would have the chance I needed with Ryker. "Okay, fine." I gave her my best smile and started walking with her toward the table of frat boys.

She stopped in her tracks and whispered to me, "Once the band gets here, we'll ditch these guys. If I wanted to sleep with a college man, I would go to parties on campus." She giggled and continued on.

She was using me to get to Max and the guys. Great. I was an idiot for thinking she wouldn't go after Ryker.

I sat down at the table next to Paige.

Mr. Backward Baseball Cap introduced us to everyone. I didn't really pay attention because I couldn't care less what their names were. One guy poured us each a glass of beer and handed us shots. The beer I was fine with, the shots not so much.

As the small glass of foggy liquid was passed to me, I held up my hand. "No, thanks."

Paige slammed hers back and batted her eyes. "Yum! I love lemon drops!"

It didn't take them long to offer her another and then another. She was getting giddy, and I was getting nervous. I lifted my glass and took a sip of my beer; actually, it was more of a guzzle. As soon as I placed the half-full glass on the table, it was filled again. Paige was laughing, and the guys were all over her. She thrived on the attention. When some guy—I think his name was Mike—sat next to me, I felt as though I needed air, so I excused myself to go to the ladies' room.

I spun around and smacked right into a hard mass of muscle. "Excuse me." With my head still lowered, I tried to walk around the man.

"No worries, Dude."

I stopped moving. I'd dreamt about that voice. I looked up to see the hazel eyes that haunted my dreams. "Oh, it's you. Sorry, and don't call me dude."

"Whatever. Where's the fire?" Ryker asked.

My eyes went to the table of guys. Paige was sitting on one of their laps. I felt alone. "I . . . um . . . I'm just going to the ladies' room." Should I tell him now? The clicks of the chains pulling the rollercoaster up the hill sounded in my head. I swallowed hard. "Ryker?"

He looked at me, over my shoulder at the table I'd just left, and back at me. I thought I saw something in his eyes, something different. His eyes were soft, almost kind. Did he care about me? A smile grew on my face as he looked at me.

"Yeah, what's up?" He motioned his chin toward Paige. "She a friend of yours?"

"Yeah, I went to school with her." My body relaxed until I noticed his lip curl up as he looked at her. Like a dope, I turned and saw her crook her finger for him to come to her.

I shook my head, took a deep breath, and walked away. Apparently I hadn't seen softness in Ryker's eyes. What I had seen was Paige running her hands down Ryker's torso as I left. How I longed to do that. But she'd never stop until she had exactly what she wanted from him, and he definitely wouldn't say no.

Rather than going to the bathroom, I sat at the bar. I ordered another beer and reached into my purse for money. My stool swiveled just in time to see Paige and Ryker getting cozy. She whispered in his ear and then looked over his shoulder to shrug and smirk at me. It was my twenty-first birthday; I should have been the one getting cozy with him. I'd had such high hopes for the night, and as usual, it wasn't going as planned. My roller-coaster ride had ended before I'd made it to the top of the hill. Hell, I hadn't even buckled in for the ride.

The bartender placed what I had learned was a lemon drop shot in front of me.

"I didn't order this," I said.

A gruff voice caught me off guard. "I did."

Mike from the frat boy's table sat next to me. "Your friend said it was your birthday. I thought we'd do a shot together since you left us."

I smiled. "Thank you."

He picked his up and raised it. "To you. May your birthday be everything you hoped it would be, and may all your wishes come true."

All I could do was say, "Cheers." I tossed the liquid back, and it actually tasted really good.

"So what's your name?"

"I'm Faith." Did I want to get to know the guy? I watched Paige sitting on Ryker's lap as they drank beer together. Unbelievable. "You're Mike, right?"

He grinned. "You got it, babe."

"Well, Mike, I appreciate the shot, but I'm going to be heading out. I was just stopping in tonight. I didn't intend on staying." I'd just lied through my teeth to what could be a fun guy.

He made some idle conversation, but I wasn't paying attention. I'd just wasted time on this guy, and I wasn't going to get it back. I picked up my purse and slid off the stool, but not before draining my beer.

Mike looked shocked. "Are you seriously leaving?"

"Yup. Thanks again, and it was good meeting you." I gave him a flippant wave and walked to the back of the club, where I knew the band would be. My head spun a little, but not enough to deter me from seeing Max; I needed him.

The bar was getting crowded, but I finally got to the back hallway to find my rock. Instead, I found Paige pinned against the wall. Her leg was around Ryker's waist. Her skirt rode high, and it looked as though his finger was in her thong. My eyes filled, and I couldn't move as Paige's lips covered his. I wished I was near a ladies' room, because I thought I was going to throw up.

Max walked out of the back and witnessed the scene. He shook his head and looked at me. With one look at my face, his fell. Max nudged Ryker as he walked by. Paige didn't notice, but Ryker turned and looked right at me. Our eyes locked, and I thought I saw regret, but for what: the interruption or me? I couldn't stop staring as he went back to work on Paige's lips. Must have been for the interruption.

Max took my arm and led me away. "What are you doing back here? Is that your friend with Ryker? I thought I saw you come in with her."

"Yeah, I guess she is. I was coming to find you to tell you that I'm going home." Just then it dawned on me that Paige had driven me. I didn't have a ride home.

Max sighed. "Are you okay? Why are you leaving?"

My eyes closed, and my lip trembled. I willed tears not to come. "I just can't be here. I tried, I really did. Tonight was going to be my night, and now all of my plans are ruined. I just want to go home." The throbbing in my eyes verged on painful, and I chastised myself for being so upset. I willed the tears to stay at bay.

He put his hand on the small of my back and walked me into what must have been a break room. There were lockers in it, and some guy in an apron was on the phone speaking in Spanish. That was good. At least he couldn't understand us. Or maybe he would. I didn't know, and I really didn't care.

Max leaned up against a metal door. "Talk to me. What's wrong?"

"I was going to tell him tonight." My voice cracked, but I had managed to get it out.

"Tell who what?"

"Ryker. I was going to tell him how I felt about him, but then Paige happened. Now I can't, and I won't. Why, Max? What's wrong with me?" A tear escaped, and I wiped it away.

"Faith, nothing is wrong with you. You know how he is. I tell you all the time, and you've seen it with your own eyes. Ryker doesn't do relationships. He just does . . . women."

"Yeah, I know. I just wanted to be that woman."

Max hugged me. "I know you do, but you aren't like that—unless something happened that I don't know about."

I shook my head. "No, I want him to be my first. That's stupid, right?"

His arms loosened, and he rubbed my arms. "You like him that much? I mean, I knew you liked him, but all women like him."

My voice was lost. I couldn't tell him anymore. I loved Max, but I didn't know if he would understand.

"Are you going to be okay?" he asked. "Want to hang with me until we go on? We aren't playing long sets tonight, and I can cut them back."

It sucked. All I wanted to do was hang out, listen to Raging Urge, and talk to Ryker. I should have known that bringing another woman was a bad idea. Not many women shy away from Ryker. The man made me crazy. "No, I'd rather go. I'm really sorry, but I had big hopes for tonight. I've been planning it for a while. I'm just tired now. Is your car here? Can I borrow it?" I thought about it and decided I probably shouldn't drive. "Or do you have time to give me a ride?"

"I didn't drive. Ryker picked me up. I assume your friend drove?"

I nodded as we walked back into the hallway of doom. Ryker and Paige were gone. I wished it had all been a bad dream, but it had been just my one of many "Ryker reality checks."

Max said, "Why don't you just stay and watch the set? We'll take you home. It's your birthday. I want to buy you a drink. Please?" Max broke out his puppy dog eyes, which would normally get me to do just about anything. Max offered me his hand, but I remained stock still.

"No way am I getting in a car with him. I'll call a cab. I'm sorry, Max." I kissed his cheek and grabbed my cell phone out of my purse. I googled Yellow Cab and called for a ride. Rochester, NY, wasn't like NYC. Cabs didn't just wait outside clubs for a fare.

"I wish you wouldn't leave, but I understand." Max kissed my forehead. "Call me tomorrow, okay?"

"Okay." The look of disappointment on my friend's face made me feel like shit. I'd let a non-friend ruin my night. Trying to assuage his feelings and my guilt, I agreed to watch them the next night instead.

As I crossed the planked floor toward my refuge, which was anywhere outside of that bar, I noticed couples everywhere. Paige and some other girls were at the frat table, and Mike seemed content with the blonde on his lap. Paige didn't even notice me exit the bar. The bouncer opened the door, and I was finally out of that godforsaken place. I took a breath of relief until I saw Ryker alone on the sidewalk, smoking a cigarette. As soon as I saw him, I turned away but didn't get too far.

"Where ya going, Dude?"

I glared daggers at him. "I'm leaving. Where's your flavor of the night? Get tired of her already?" I knew where she was, but did he? Did he even care?

Ryker snickered. "Something like that. She really isn't my type."

Yeah, not his type, my ass! "Oh? You could have fooled me." I turned and stared at the parking lot, willing my cab to appear.

"If you're leaving, why are you just standing here?"

"I'm waiting for a cab."

His voice became full of concern. "You called a cab? Are you drunk?"

"No, I'm not, although it would have been a nice way to celebrate tonight." *Yes, it's my birthday, asshole.* "Not that it's any business of yours, but my ride was busy, so I called for a cab."

"Shit, I forgot today's your birthday." He flicked his cigarette into the parking lot and turned toward me.

I averted my eyes and stared straight ahead.

His lips landed on my cheek. "Happy birthday."

With wide eyes, I turned toward him and tried to contain my smile.

"Don't get excited, Dude. It was just a birthday kiss."

I faced forward again. "Of course. Why would you want to kiss me? I mean, I'm not your type. I'm just the girl who tags along with Max, right? Oh, and I'm a 'dude.' What if I told you I like you and I want to be with you?" *Holy shit! Did I just say that?*

"You're not just a girl who . . . I just . . . wait, you want me?" Ryker's eyes became blank and devoid of any emotion.

"You just what? Don't want me *that* way? I'm not hot like Paige or your other women? I'm just the woman who pals around with guys? Maybe you're the one with the problem. Maybe you're not as 'good' as you think you are, and that's why Paige is off giving someone else a lap dance. Your little guy not satisfying enough?"

His eyebrows creased as Ryker took my chin between his thumb and forefinger and tilted my face up toward him. "I don't want you. Is that clear enough?"

I felt my face heat up. Willing my tears to stay away, I just looked at him. My heart pounded before it shattered and splintered.

He pushed further. "And as far as my 'little guy,' it satisfies just fine. Don't you worry about me. If you doubt that, you can ask Paige. She danced on my 'not-so-little guy' like she was on a stripper pole."

Again I was struck with nausea. Our eyes locked until I lowered mine to the ground. I was devastated. A car horn broke the agonizing silence. My head turned, pulling my chin out of his grasp, before I walked to the cab. I tried to hold my head high until the door closed and I told the driver to go. When we were out of sight, I gave the driver my address and tried not to sob.

I looked out the window and wondered what I'd done to him to deserve being treated like shit. Was I that horrible? My mind was playing back the evening like a re-run when we arrived at my parents' house. I paid my fare and walked in the house.

As I made my way into my room, I felt alone. Not in the physical sense, but emotionally. Good ol' Faith, always the one to give people a chance. I thought I'd seen something in his eyes when he looked at me, but I realized I'd been wrong. For someone so smart, I sure was stupid.

Acknowledgments

When I think about writing acknowledgements, it really isn't easy. There are so many people in my life that have supported me, encouraged me and quite frankly put up with me while writing My Chance, that I hope I don't forget to mention anyone, but if I do, I apologize up front and tell you that you really weren't forgotten; and I thank you.

I couldn't have done this without the support of my entire family. Especially my husband Dave and my sons Nick and Zack, thank you for everything. For understanding why dinner is late, why the laundry isn't quite done and why I am constantly glued to my computer. I am very blessed to have all of you by my side on this crazy ride!

A very special thank you to my beta readers. Thank you for taking the time out of your busy schedules to read for me. Your feedback and comments were incredibly helpful. Thank you for putting up with my numerous IMs. Hopefully, I didn't drive you too crazy!

My friends that always have my back, thank you for supporting me!

I'd like to thank Madeline Sheehan for always being there for me; to answer questions, give advice or for that occasional virtual slap. You are a fabulous person and I am so happy that I've met you.

To all the bloggers, thank you for everything that you do. Your support and kindness means the world to me. I wish I could list all of you, but that would add several more pages! Thank you for all the time you spend pimping authors out. You take time out of your personal lives, and I appreciate it more than you know!

Thank you to Otilia Baker for taking a stunning cover photo. I love it!

I've been very fortunate to have Erik Fellows' handsome face on my covers. Erik, you are a wonderful person with a heart of gold and I can't tell you how happy I was to be able to work with you on Unexpected Chance and My Chance. You know you are more to me than just a cover model; you are my friend, teammate and "second cousin twice removed" ha-ha. I think the world of you and I hope to work with you again.

Thank you Tami Norman from Integrity Formatting for formatting My Chance. You are awesome, and I look forward to working with you in the future.

Special thanks to my editor, Cassie Cox. I absolutely loved working with you. Your skills are amazing. I look forward to working with you in the future. I'd also like to thank Elizabeth Himes who proofread My Chance.

Thank you to Sommer Stein for creating my cover. Your vision and creativity are unsurpassed.

Thank you all for encouraging me to take this chance; it means the world to me.

About the Author

Originally from Rochester, New York, Joanne Schwehm now lives in Northern Virginia with her husband, Dave, her two teenage boys, Nick and Zack, and her cute Bichon, Torre, who is aptly nicknamed "Mommy's White Shadow." It's a good thing Torre only barks or she could give away many secrets!

Joanne loves spending time with her family and friends. She enjoys meeting new people, traveling, relaxing on a beach, and shopping . . . especially for shoes. She has a bit of a fetish.

She is an avid sports fan and loves the New York Yankees and the Dallas Cowboys. She also enjoys playing and watching golf.

Thank you for reading *My Chance*

If you enjoyed this book, please consider supporting this author by leaving a review. Reviews are a valuable resource in helping readers find other books they may enjoy.

Stay In Touch

Facebook:

www.facebook.com/joanneschwehm

Twitter:

twitter.com/JSchwehmBooks

Goodreads Group Page:

www.goodreads.com/group/show/156533-joanne-schwehm-s-romantic-reading-friends

Facebook Reader's Group:

www.facebook.com/groups/joanneschwehmsreaders/

Subscribe to Joanne's **Newsletter**:
http://eepurl.com/bAKaDf

Books by

Joanne Schwehm

The Chance Series:

Unexpected Chance

My Chance

A Heart's Forgiveness—A Chance Novel *(Brett and Julie's Story)*

Standalone Novels:

Ryker

The Critic

The Prescott Series:

Incumbent

Gripped

CPSIA information can be obtained
at www.ICGtesting.com
Printed in the USA
FSOW03n0204190217
30875FS

9 781682 307847